Rest for the Wicked

ALSO BY ELLEN HART

The Lost Women of Lost Lake
The Cruel Ever After
The Mirror and the Mask
Sweet Poison
The Mortal Groove
Night Vision
The Iron Girl
An Intimate Ghost
Immaculate Midnight
No Reservations Required
Death on a Silver Platter
The Merchant of Venus
Slice and Dice
Hunting the Witch
Wicked Games
Murder in the Air
Robber's Wine
The Oldest Sin
Faint Praise
A Small Sacrifice
For Every Evil
This Little Piggy Went to Murder
A Killing Cure
Stage Fright
Vital Lies
Hallowed Murder

Rest for the Wicked

ELLEN HART

MINOTAUR BOOKS ✖ NEW YORK

This is a work of fiction. All of the characters, organizations, and events portrayed in this novel are either products of the author's imagination or are used fictitiously.

REST FOR THE WICKED. Copyright © 2012 by Ellen Hart. All rights reserved. Printed in the United States of America. For information, address St. Martin's Press, 175 Fifth Avenue, New York, N.Y. 10010.

www.minotaurbooks.com
www.stmartins.com

Library of Congress Cataloging-in-Publication Data

Hart, Ellen.
    Rest for the wicked / Ellen Hart.—1st ed.
        p. cm.
    ISBN 978-1-250-00186-3 (hardcover)
    ISBN 978-1-250-01807-6 (e-book)
    1. Lawless, Jane (Fictitious character)—Fiction.   2. Women private investigators—Fiction.   3. Murder—Investigation—Fiction. 4. Minneapolis (Minn.)—Fiction.   I. Title.
    PS3558.A6775R47 2012
    813'.54—dc23

                                                                    2012026736

First Edition: October 2012

10 9 8 7 6 5 4 3 2 1

For Pat Frovarp and Gary Shulze,
owners of Once Upon a Crime Mystery Bookstore in
Minneapolis.
My bookstore heros.

And for Christopher.

Cast of Characters

Jane Lawless: Owner of the Lyme House Restaurant and the Xanadu Club in Minneapolis. Private investigator.

Cordelia Thorn: Artistic director at the Allen Grimby Repertory Theater in St. Paul. Jane's best friend.

DeAndre Moore: A. J. Nolan's nephew.

A. J. Nolan: Retired homicide investigator. Jane's partner at Nolan & Lawless Investigations.

Vince Bessetti: Owner of GaudyLights in downtown Minneapolis.

Emmett Washington: Pilot for AirNorth. Roddy's father. Member of the Gillford Wildcats.

Roddy Washington: High school student. Emmett's son.

Royal Rudmann: Member of the Gillford Wildcats.

Avi Greenberg: Bartender at GaudyLights.

Shanice Williams: Executive chef at GaudyLights / Café Bacchus.

Diamond Brown: Manager at GaudyLights.

Georgia Dietrich: Exotic dancer. Law school student.

Elvio Ramos: Dishwasher at GaudyLights.

Luis Ramos: Elvio's brother. Dishwasher at the Xanadu Club.

Jason Dorsey: Bartender at GaudyLights.

Octavia Thorn Lester: Cordelia's sister. Hattie's mother.

Bolger Aspenwall III: Hattie's nanny.

Burt Tatum: Schoolteacher in St. Louis. Member of the Gillford Wildcats.

Ken Crowder: Businessman in Utah. Member of the Gillford Wildcats.

The end is where we start from.

—T. S. Eliot

Rest for the Wicked

1

After tossing back one last vodka shooter, DeAndre Moore tore through the crowded strip club, certain that the knee breaker who was hot on his heels would send him to the hospital if he didn't get lost—and fast. He'd come early to have himself a couple of drinks and try to calm down. Tonight was the night. Either she would leave with him or . . . or what? Would he really turn her over to the cops? Did he have that right?

As soon as Sabrina stepped onto the nightclub floor and saw him, she walked straight to one of the goons stationed at the front door, pointed back at DeAndre, and said a few quick words. Time to bounce, he thought. He'd catch up with her later.

He took off running, dodging this way and that around the tables, thinking that if he could just put some distance between himself and the hired muscle he could make it to the kitchen, where he knew there was an exit out to the alley. Making a mad dash for a pair of swinging doors, he pushed inside. One of the line cooks thrust a knife at him and shouted, "Get the hell out of here."

DeAndre plunged out the back door into the frigid night air, hearing a click as the door shut and locked behind him. That would be enough for the knee breaker. He merely wanted him out, with as little fuss as possible. The front door, his only way back in, would be barred for the rest of the night.

Standing in the dank, narrow alley, trying to catch his breath, he cursed himself for ever coming to Minneapolis. He should have stayed in St. Louis, minded his own business, let her sink or swim on her own. Yet when it became clear what she'd done, he couldn't let it drop. He loved her. She'd always looked out for him, and now it was time he returned the favor. Even more, Sabrina held the key to his past. She'd been dangling it over his head for years, and he was sick of it. He'd come for an answer. One way or the other, he intended to get it.

Passing several Dumpsters, he moved to the edge of the sidewalk. The snow was coming down so hard that he could barely make out the buildings across the street. For the last four nights, he'd been staying in a downtown hotel, an outlay of money he could ill afford. It had taken him months to track Sabrina to Minneapolis. Checking out the local strip bars had been the next logical step. He'd found her at GaudyLights, persuaded her to meet up for lunch the next day. Though they talked easily, just like old times, she refused to open up. He came back to the club that night, and the next, and the one after that. He'd smiled a lot, tried to talk to her when she was not busy. Drinks flowed freely.

Just before closing last night, she'd whispered in his ear. "You want to know what happened? Why I left St. Louis in such a big hurry? Here it is. I did it. He deserved it. And I'm not done." She walked away from him and left him sitting there, stunned. He'd been so sure she would offer an explanation that would somehow make it all right. Instead, she'd admitted to a cold-blooded murder.

Now he was here, standing at the edge of a dark alley, unsure what to do. Removing his cell from his jacket, he fished inside his shirt pocket for the business card his uncle had given him. He held it up, tipped it this way and that until he could read the number at the bottom. Punching it in, he waited, hoping the call would be answered by a real live human. Instead, he was put through to voice mail.

Fixing his eyes on the driving snow, he said, "This message is for Jane Lawless. You don't know me. My name is DeAndre Moore. I need to talk to you. I can meet you anywhere you want, just name it. So you know, my uncle is Alf Nolan, your partner. He told me that if I ever needed any help and he wasn't around, that I should call you. Since this is a . . . a private matter, and he's family, I need you to keep this quiet." Here, he paused. "I'm desperate, Ms. Lawless. There's someone I know . . . someone I love . . . who's in bad trouble. I'm trusting you, okay? I need you to help me figure out what's going on before someone else gets killed. Anyway, that's enough over the phone. Hey . . . what—"

DeAndre felt a sudden fierce sting in his shoulder. Dropping the cell to the concrete, he whirled around, only to feel a second sharp thrust enter his gut. He doubled over, pitching backward against the bricks. A warm, sticky liquid oozed into his hand. In the darkness, he could barely make out the face of the person standing over him. "You're— "

"Shut up."

His thoughts began to scramble. "Why?" he whispered.

"You stick your nose in where it don't belong."

"No," he repeated, feeling suddenly weak.

"At least you die like a man. That's more than you would give me."

2

Jane Lawless felt like a waitress who knew she wasn't going to get a good tip. Carrying as much as she could manage on the only small tray she could find in Nolan's somewhat less than state-of-the-art kitchen, she entered the living room and began to hand out food.

Cordelia sat cross-legged on the couch, staring at Nolan's new forty-six-inch flat-screen TV, bought especially for this year's Super Bowl. During the past year, Nolan and Cordelia had bonded over the TV show *Friday Night Lights*, which had sparked an interest—for Cordelia—in all things football. Since Jane had no interest in the sport, and tonight was the big night, she was happy for something productive to do—if you could call making a rather boring array of snacks for the game productive. She handed Cordelia her bowl of popcorn.

"Extra butter?" Cordelia asked, never taking her eyes off the screen.

"I sprayed it with rat poison," said Jane with a smile.

"Perfect," muttered Cordelia. "Thanks."

Moving on to Nolan, who sat riveted in his leather La-Z-Boy, Jane set a beer next to him on a small end table and then handed

4

him a bowl of Totino's Pizza Rolls. She'd offered to make them all something from scratch. Nothing too gourmet. Buffalo wings. Barbecued riblets. A baked brie covered in brown sugar and cranberries. But no, they all wanted what they wanted. Nolan said that pizza rolls were his Super Bowl tradition. Far be it from Jane to get in the way of a long-standing gridiron ritual.

On her way back to the kitchen, she handed Hattie, Cordelia's seven-year-old niece, a pint-sized carton of Nestlé's Quik. Mouse, Jane's brown Lab, had curled up on the carpet next to the little girl. Jane was able to satisfy him with a quick scratch behind his ears. The girl lifted her eyes to Jane, offered a coy smile, then stuck her nose back into her book. She was precocious for her age, reading at a fourth-grade level, according to her proud auntie. At the moment, she was deep into *The Dangerous Book for Boys*. She'd already finished *The Daring Book for Girls*. At least she wasn't into any adventures with kid wizards yet. That would be a particularly difficult phase for Jane.

Returning to the kitchen, Jane sat on a stool next to the breakfast bar and watched the snow fall outside the back window. It had been a hectic seventeen months. Jane owned two restaurants in the Twin Cities, which were more than enough to keep her occupied 24/7. Yet this had been a time of radical change in her life. She'd finally succumbed to Nolan's pressure to join his PI agency and work on a Minnesota state license of her own. She'd been granted that license two weeks ago.

In truth, it wasn't Nolan's pressure but her own personal needs and desires that had driven her to make the decision. Her two restaurants were both going strong. Seven months ago, her original partner at the Xanadu Club in Uptown had sold his share of the business—with Jane's approval—to a local restaurateur, Barry Tune. Jane liked Barry, trusted his judgment because of his success with other venues in his thirty-plus years in the business,

5

and was pleasantly surprised when he offered to take over the everyday management of the club. She felt she was in a great place in her life—confident about how her restaurants were doing and deeply absorbed by her new role as a licensed PI. Life was indeed good. Crazy busy, but good.

Nibbling absently on one of the pizza rolls, she wandered back into the living room, thinking about taking a walk. This was her day off. She hadn't had one in . . . well, she couldn't remember when. She loved windy, snowy nights. Nolan lived close to Minnehaha Creek, one of Jane's favorite parts of the city.

As Cordelia and Nolan jeered in unison at one apparently sightless referee, she could tell her presence would not be missed. She'd retrieved her coat from the front closet and was about to put it on when the doorbell rang.

"I'll get it," she called, smiling at her dog, the only other soul in the room who'd heard it.

Melanie Gunderson, Cordelia's main squeeze, stood outside on the porch.

"Come in before you get buried in white," said Jane, helping Mel brush herself off. For some reason, the usually chipper Mel looked less than happy. "Something wrong?" asked Jane.

"Cordelia," said Mel, stepping over to block her view of the TV.

"Hey," said Cordelia.

"We need to talk."

"Can't it wait? It's third and twelve."

Nodding at Jane, Mel issued an order. "Get her up and tell her I'll be in the kitchen."

"I hear you," said Cordelia with a groan. "Your timing is lousy."

"No worse than yours."

Jane watched Cordelia's face turn as grim as Mel's.

Giving Jane a look that said, "Geezsh, girlfriends," Cordelia stomped past her into the kitchen. Since there was no door to close, Jane assumed they knew their conversation couldn't be completely private unless they whispered. She stood in the archway between the dining room and the living room and had no trouble hearing everything they said.

"So," said Mel. "Have you decided? Did you go see the place?"

"It's exactly what I've been looking for," said Cordelia.

"You're leaving."

"That's the plan."

"Even if I'm against it."

"Why would you be? Don't you want me to be happy?"

"This won't make you happy. You're Cordelia Thorn. You have a reputation to uphold. I mean, why not simply jump off a building. It would be quicker."

"You're *such* a drama queen."

"*I'm* a drama queen? Do you even hear yourself anymore?"

"Are you going to throw that pan at me?"

Jane moved closer to the door. Cordelia and Mel's fights were legendary, often involving pots and pans. Their romantic makeups were equally legendary, but at the moment, they were in full battle mode. What upset Jane most, if she cared to admit it, was that she had no idea what they were talking about.

"Put the pan down," said Cordelia.

"You're telling me there's no way to make you change your mind?"

"This is my destiny."

Melanie hooted. "Well, it's not mine." A moment later, she flew out of the kitchen, past Jane, and slammed out the front door.

"That was charming," said Jane as Cordelia emerged, a stony look on her face. "What's going on?"

"Personal stuff."

"Are you two——"

"We'll work it out." She pointed at the TV and said, "Now, where was I?"

No sooner had Cordelia resumed her Buddha-like position on the couch than Jane's cell phone began to vibrate inside the pocket of her coat. She pulled it free and said hello.

"Who's this?" came a deep voice.

"Excuse me?"

"Who am I talking to?"

"You called me and you don't know who I am? I'm hanging up now."

"Wait, wait. This is Sergeant Kevante Taylor, Minneapolis PD."

Jane eased down on the arm of a chair. As it happened, she knew Sergeant Taylor. "This is Jane Lawless."

He didn't respond for several seconds. "Ms. Lawless." He sounded annoyed. "Do you know a man named DeAndre Moore?"

"No. Why?"

"He was knifed less than an hour ago in an alley outside Gaudy-Lights. I'm at the crime scene right now."

She'd heard of the downtown Minneapolis strip club—or gentleman's club, as it was advertised—although she'd never had any desire to go inside. "Is he okay?"

"He's dead. Thing is, looks like he was talking to you on his cell when he died."

"Talking to *me*?"

"Either that or leaving you a message."

"You say this guy's name was DeAndre Moore?" she asked. Nolan swiveled around to look at her. "Honestly, I've never heard of him."

"Then why would he be calling you?"

"Can't answer that."

Standing up, Nolan said, "What about DeAndre?"

"Hang on a minute," said Jane. Drawing the phone away from her ear, she said, "You know him?"

"My nephew's name is DeAndre Moore."

Jane returned to Taylor. "Can you tell me anything about this guy?"

"He's black. Late twenties. Driver's license says he's from St. Louis. One of my men just handed me a business card. Found it in the snow a few feet from the body. Nolan & Lawless Investigations."

"That's me."

"I thought you owned a restaurant."

"I do, but I'm also working as a part-time PI."

"You're licensed?"

"That's what I'm told."

"Hell." He shouted for someone to watch where he was walking. "Look, I need you to check your cell phone messages and get back to me ASAP. I'll be busy here for the next couple of hours. I need that information. Don't erase it." With that, he hung up.

Nolan stood over her, his eyes demanding an explanation. "What's going on?"

Jane repeated what she'd learned, ending with "The man was in his late twenties. From St. Louis."

Nolan sank back down in his chair. "My nephew is from St. Louis—but he wouldn't come to town without calling me."

"So maybe it's not him."

"What are you two talking about?" asked Cordelia, tossing a popcorn kernel into the air and catching it in her mouth.

While Jane explained, in couched terms because of Hattie's presence, she tapped her phone and brought up her missed calls, finding only one. She played back the message, then handed the phone to Nolan.

After listening, Nolan said, "I'm going down there." He was already on his way to the closet to get his coat.

He seemed so shaken that Jane said, "I'll drive." To Cordelia, she added, "Will you let Mouse out before you leave? He can stay here until I get back."

"Not a problem," said Cordelia. "I'll lock up the house when I go." Looking up at Nolan with concerned eyes, she said, "I'm sorry."

"Yeah." Opening the front door, he motioned for Jane to precede him. "Let's go."

Nolan spoke little on the way downtown. Under the best of circumstances, he wasn't a man given to easy conversation. Jane had a ton of questions but kept them to herself—for the moment—allowing Nolan the space he so clearly needed.

Turning onto Washington Avenue, Jane saw the throbbing lights of several police cruisers toward the end of the block. Since parking was problematic on any wintry night, and Nolan was itching to get to the alley, she stopped as close as she could to the nightclub, telling him that she'd be along as soon as she found a place to stick her car. If she'd been driving her Mini Cooper, she might have been able to fit into a smaller space. Nolan had advised a more "generic" kind of vehicle for investigative work; thus she'd purchased a second car, a 2004 Honda CR-V. She had to drive several blocks until she found a spot big enough to accommodate even such a modest-sized SUV.

Flipping her collar up and digging her hands into the pockets of her peacoat, she jumped over a mound of snow left by a city snowplow and headed through the deepening drifts toward the club. The alley in question was in the middle of the block and ran from the sidewalk to the rear of the building. The entrance was approximately a hundred feet from the front door, which sat at an angle to Washington and Second Street.

Nolan stood at the edge of the alley, inside the police tape, talking to Kevante Taylor. Three uniformed officers were doing their best to keep gawkers at bay. If it hadn't been for the wind gusts and the swiftly falling snow, more people would likely have gathered.

Slowing her pace, Jane edged her way through the crowd and waved to Nolan. Taylor, a black man wearing a heavy wool topcoat, motioned for an officer to let her through.

"Ms. Lawless," said Taylor, nodding slightly as she moved under the tape. "Nice to see you again."

Based on their last encounter, she doubted his sincerity. "Is it your nephew?" she asked Nolan.

He gave a curt nod. "There's a wound just below his left shoulder and one in the stomach. If someone had found him sooner—" He choked on the words and couldn't finish the sentence.

Forensic workers had set up lights and were diligently taking photographs and documenting the scene. Jane guessed, by the looks of all the Dumpsters lined up against one wall, that the battered door toward the back probably led to a kitchen. With the temperature in the high thirties for most of the week, and only a few degrees cooler now, the alley stank of garbage. Nolan's nephew had sunk down against a brick wall. His leather jacket was open, the dress shirt underneath soaked with blood. Bloody footprints led away from the body and disappeared into the snow at the edge of the sidewalk.

"Those prints look like they came from an athletic shoe," said Jane.

"This guy," said Taylor, rubbing the back of his neck in contemplation, "made a mess of it. Makes me think it wasn't premeditated, that it was a spur-of-the-moment decision. The way I see it, Moore probably came out that door to make that call to you. That's when he was attacked."

"By someone who saw him leave?" asked Jane.

"Would be my guess. I need to hear that cell phone message."

She took her phone out of her back pocket and set it up. The sergeant listened to the message twice before handing it back.

"You have no idea what he was calling about? This *private* matter he referred to?"

"None," said Jane.

"Have you found the murder weapon?" asked Nolan.

"I've got men canvassing the area, and I'm about to head inside and start the interrogations. Far as I know, nobody saw it happen. We'll apply some pressure, see what we can shake loose."

"Would you call me when you find the guy?" asked Nolan.

"Of course. My sincere condolences. Will you call his family, or would you like me—"

"I'll take care of it," said Nolan, his eyes fixed on his nephew.

On the way to back to the truck, Jane asked Nolan if they should spend some time looking into DeAndre's death themselves.

"No reason," he said, his voice heavy with resignation. "The police are good at what they do. They'll get to the bottom of it."

Nolan urged Jane to leave as soon as they got back to his house. She followed him into the kitchen, where he dumped some ice in a glass and poured himself several inches of bourbon. When he sat down in the living room, he continued to urge her to go home, and yet little by little, he began to open up and talk about his nephew, about the phone call he dreaded making to his sister in the morning.

DeAndre Moore was twenty-nine years old, unmarried, and living in St. Louis, where he worked as a security guard at an office complex near the airport. He'd been the foster child of Nolan's younger sister, Fannie Lou Moore. When DeAndre was thirteen, Fannie Lou and her husband, Henry, had adopted him. Nolan said the boy was as close to a musical prodigy as anyone he'd ever known. He'd been focused on jazz since he was in his teens and had worked hard to become a jazz pianist. He was beginning to make a name for himself at jazz clubs in and around St. Louis. Nolan said he'd talked to him over Christmas and he was in great spirits.

DeAndre's early childhood had been troubled. His biological mother had been an alcoholic and addicted to OxyContin, which meant he'd been subjected to some pretty intense abuse, both from his mom and from a series of vicious boyfriends. The abuse was the main reason he'd been taken away and put in foster care. Nolan said that DeAndre had never known his father and that his mother had died several years after he'd been removed from her custody. His world had changed for the better when, at age eleven, he'd first come to live with Fannie Lou and Henry. Nolan underscored the fact that DeAndre was a survivor, that he wasn't interested in looking back, only in moving forward. He claimed that DeAndre took virtually no time at all to fit himself into his new family and that he had thrived under Fannie Lou and Henry's loving care. He'd grown up to be a good, clean kid. He had a bumpy relationship with his girlfriend, but even so, he'd confided to Nolan that he hoped to marry her one day. His life was on track, going well. That's why what had happened was so inexplicable.

Nolan eventually tired of the conversation and told Jane he had to go to bed. She made him promise to call her if he needed anything, and then, with a heavy heart, she left, driving home through a midnight blizzard, thankful for the four-wheel drive. Glancing around at Mouse in the backseat, she said what she hadn't said to Nolan. "I think that's a wonderful story. But that's all it is. A story." It may have taken on the status of family dogma, something they all believed in, but the truth about DeAndre's life after he was adopted had to be more complex.

Pulling into the driveway next to her house, Jane cut the motor and sat for a few minutes listening to the whirlwind beat against the windows. It felt like sitting inside a snow globe.

Turning back to Mouse, she said, "It's not every day you get a call from a dead man, you know?"

Mouse thumped his tail against the backseat, his dark brown eyes fixed soulfully on hers.

"Come on, boy," she said, holding up his leash. "Let's get out of here while we can still find the front door."

3

The next morning, Jane stood at her dining room window, drinking from a mug of coffee and thinking how truly Currier and Ives the world looked after a blizzard. It was a pleasant thought, followed by a less appealing image of herself spending the next few hours, if not days, digging out.

"Ah, Minnesota" was all she could dredge up, smiling over her shoulder at her dog, who was chewing on his favorite green tennis ball under the arch that led from the dining room into the front foyer. It had taken her a good ten minutes to get the screen door on the back porch open so she could shovel a patch for Mouse to do his morning ablutions. He came back inside with a fat clump of snow perched on top of his muzzle, about as frisky as she'd ever seen him.

The day had dawned with a brilliant blue sky and sunlight glinting off a world covered in billions of glittering diamonds. Those glittering diamonds had buried her CR-V up to the wheel wells in the front and nearly erased the rear under a four-foot drift. Her one-stall garage was already filled with her Mini, so the SUV, of necessity, had to be parked outside. After a good old-fashioned Minnesota blizzard blew through, the wind generally died down and the temperatures plummeted. The weather woman on the morning news had urged everyone to get their snow removal done early because the high for the day would be a balmy twelve degrees. By nightfall, the temperature would be in the minus fifteen range, with wind chills close to thirty below.

Jane didn't want to repeat herself, but she couldn't help it. "What a wicked glorious place to live," she said, this time with a little more sarcasm than vigor. "All I can say is, I'm glad it's Monday." Both her restaurants were closed on Mondays, which made it easier for the snowplow service she used to do a decent job of cleaning out the parking lots. Squinting at the road that ran in front of her house, she was pretty sure one of the city plows had already come through. Minneapolis had snow removal down to as much of a science as was humanly possible.

"You know, Mouse, I should teach you how to use the snowblower."

He looked up from his tennis ball long enough to yawn.

"I'll take that as a 'no thanks.' "

On her way to the kitchen, her landline rang. The answering machine said, "Call from Abilene Mar." It repeated the message one more time, cutting off the last part of Abilene's last name, which was Martell. Jane leaned her hip against the kitchen counter and picked up the receiver. "Guess we won't be doing dinner tonight."

"Umm, no," said Abilene, "guess not. Actually, there's another reason we won't be having dinner."

"And that is?"

"I'm in Aspen. I flew out yesterday, right before the storm hit. I need some downtime in my life, Jane. Okay, so you told me you were a workaholic before we started dating. I've dated workaholics before. I figured, hell, not only have I dated workaholics, I am one. But you . . . you're world class."

Jane was sick of hearing the criticism. If Abilene wanted to date someone with a lot of free time, she should have found herself a nice dental hygienist.

"I didn't come here alone, Jane. Carrie's with me."

"Carrie? Your new *producer*, Carrie?"

Abilene hosted a local radio show on KBLW, an unfortunate series of call letters, known more crudely around town as K-Blow by those who didn't like her liberal politics.

"Yes, my producer."

"Are you two——"

"We are. As for you and me, we're over."

Jane wasn't sure they'd ever really "begun." To be honest, she was more surprised than hurt——and when she thought about it, not all that surprised. Always the matchmaker, Cordelia had introduced the two of them at a theater party and then pushed Jane to call for a date, saying that Abilene was smart, attractive, and available, the dating trifecta in Cordelia's humble opinion.

"Good wishes to you and Carrie," said Jane, pouring herself more coffee.

"I thought you'd be more upset."

"Well, I mean . . . I am."

"Really."

"But if you're in love with Carrie——"

"I didn't say that."

Jane was handling this all wrong, and she knew it. She considered herself highly competent in most areas of her life, but when it came to women, she felt as if, somewhere along the line, she'd lost the knack for commitment. She also regarded with more than a little suspicion people who tried to make her feel guilty for the way she lived her life. "I only want what's best for you."

"Right. So, I guess this is good-bye, then."

"I guess."

"Maybe I'll call when I get back. No reason we can't be friends."

"None at all," said Jane.

"Okay, then. Don't get stuck in any snowdrifts."

"Don't worry about me."

"Oh, I don't. You're about as self-sufficient as they come."

After hanging up, Jane sank down on one of the kitchen chairs. She knew that was exactly how people saw her, especially those who didn't get the emotional rise out of her that they wanted. It wasn't that she didn't care about Abilene; she simply wasn't in love with her. She was beginning to wonder if she'd been burned so many times that she wasn't capable of falling in love anymore.

"Wouldn't be the end of the world," she murmured.

What she was beginning to understand—to *admit* to herself— was that that special something, a frisson, a deep connection, had been absent from all of her recent relationships. She hadn't felt that special rush of emotion for so long that she was beginning to think it was a chimera. In many ways she'd been playing at being in love. She knew how it was supposed to feel, so she tried to convince herself that, with whomever she was involved with at the time, it wasn't just physical attraction but something deeper. She'd over-looked the lack in herself, tried to ignore it, or attempted to convince herself that she loved the people who said they loved her. It hadn't worked, no matter how much she cared about these women, no matter how much she wanted the feelings to be more serious.

Perhaps, in the end, the hand she'd been dealt in life didn't include more than one passionate love. Her first partner, Christine Kane, had died ten years into their relationship. Jane still thought of her as her one true love. Add to that the fact that she was middle-aged, possibly too set in her ways, too used to her solitary life to let anyone in, and her inability to form a lasting connection made more sense. Still, the entire subject made her squirm like nothing else. In a world that seemed to be delimited by couples, her single status suggested inadequacy, selfishness, or worse. So she did what she usually did these days when her self-reflection took her into this personal bog. She changed the subject.

"Mouse, time to brave the elements." A little physical exertion always put her in a better mood.

Rubbing away the cocaine from under his nose, Vince Bessetti strode down the back hall from his office to a rear door that opened onto the nightclub floor. He'd spent the night on his office couch, preferring it to the chaos at home. His wife, Shelly, had recently admitted to an affair. She'd picked, of all nights, Christmas Eve to drop the bomb and plead for forgiveness. By Christmas morning, her tone had changed and the recriminations had begun.

This was a delicate situation. Shelly's father, Klaus Rappenborg, owner and CEO of DTL Industries, was the man who had made Vince's dream come true. He was the main money guy, the one who'd underwritten the biggest part of the expense of getting GaudyLights up and running. Although unstated, Shelly had been an integral part of the deal.

Klaus's only daughter, the jewel in his crooked crown, was a successful businesswoman in her own right. She was smart and intense but had an unfortunate tendency to make even the simplest of decisions overly complex. Thanks to that, and a mulish, uncompromising stubbornness, she was, at the ripe old age of forty-one, wholly unsuccessful in the husband department. Vince was seventeen years her senior, a confirmed bachelor, although he was also a pragmatist. He knew a good deal when he saw one. He understood her desperation and self-loathing from the inside out. Together, they were a perfect mix of Calvinist pessimism and modern acid cynicism. If putting an MRS in front of her name meant that much, he figured they could work the other angles and both get something they wanted.

Vince and Shelly had been married in a Presbyterian church in Wayzata. When one of her self-help books fell out of her flight bag on their honeymoon in Santorini, Vince was beginning to see that he'd made a deal with the devil. Shelly was gunning to change him into the man of her dreams. He would be the clay and she would be the sculptor. Until the honeymoon, he hadn't fully appreciated the zeal with which she approached this new task.

He'd first met Shelly Rappenborg when he was working at Baylor Hotels International, a hotel chain headquartered in the Twin Cities. As the senior vacation planner, he could stay for free at any of the properties all over the world. Shelly was attractive in a youngish Kathy Bates sort of way, a good conversationalist and obviously sexually desperate, so on a whim, Vince offered to take her to Edinburgh for a weekend. When they came back, she invited him to her home for dinner. He wasn't all that interested in seeing her again but decided to go anyway, more out of boredom than anything else. Little did he know that this date would open the door to his future.

Shelly lived with her father in a palatial home on Lake Minnetonka. Daddy was thrice divorced and liked cigars, single malt Scotch, Swedish cars, and, by the looks of the pictures on the wall of his den, loose blondes. The two of them struck up a conversation about an idea that Vince had been toying with—a new gentleman's club in downtown Minneapolis. One thing led to another. Within the month, Vince found himself engaged to be married and signing on the dotted line for a property on Washington Avenue. The building was an old DeSoto dealership. That had been five years ago. Last year, the business had turned a significant profit. This year, however, with a second recession in full bloom, or perhaps the first one had never really gone away, receipts had been down. He needed another infusion of capital but knew that this time around he couldn't go to Shelly's dad for it.

Walking through the cavernous main floor, chairs upended on the tabletops, Vince bent down to pick one of the girls' garter belts. Seeing the slipshod way the floor had been cleaned, he kicked a pink Day-Glo bikini bottom halfway to the catwalk. He had to constantly be on top of these things or the club would disintegrate to the level of the tacky corporate-owned cat clubs. GaudyLights customers weren't supposed to feel as if they'd walked into some sleazebag's creepy basement.

Vince's entertainers were mostly young and good-looking, and they knew—or were taught—how to squeeze every possible dime out of the customers. The vibe was part hard rock urban sheik, part neon and glitter, but the hustle was and would always be hard-core. The lack of cleaning last night was probably due to the cops closing down the place early. The head cop, a man named Taylor, had paid special attention to Vince, suggesting several times that he must know more about the murdered man than he was willing to let on. Although cops were some of his best customers, he loathed their swagger and general sense of entitlement. Taylor, with his curled lip and self-righteous manner, was worse than most. When he spent nearly half an hour talking privately to one of the black strippers, a few of the other girls started giving each other knowing glances. The guy had to be negotiating the price of a bed dance.

Climbing the wide, open factory stairs to the second floor, Vince ducked into several of the private VIP rooms and found that each one needed work. In the VIP lounge, also known, in keeping with the car motif, as the Service Bay, the bar was covered with used napkins and dirty plates and glasses. His frustration ratcheting into high gear, Vince began collecting all the dishes and dumping them into a bus pan. On his way downstairs carrying the filled pan, he was startled by a scraping sound. He'd been positive he was the only one in the building. Thinking that the noise had come from the kitchen, he pushed through the swinging doors and set his load down on one of the stainless steel tables, glad to see that at least the kitchen was clean.

"Shanice," he called, thinking Shanice Williams, his head chef, might have come in the back door while he was upstairs. "You here? Diamond?" Diamond Brown was his general manager. When he received no response, he walked down the line, checking the knobs on the gas ranges and listening. He wasn't sure why, but he had a weird feeling that he was being watched. He opened the door to the cooler and stepped halfway inside. "Anybody in here?" He flipped open a plastic container of lychee nuts and snatched a couple, popping them into his mouth. Maybe he should cut back on the blow.

Returning to the show floor, he switched on the track lights over the main bar. It was going on ten, which meant he'd better get busy if he intended to rouse his employees and get them moving. Lunch was an obvious no go. Some of the girls probably assumed that they were looking at a day off because of the snow. No such luck. He didn't care if they had to rent dogsleds or buy cross-country skis, the club, a clean one, would be humming by happy hour.

Grabbing his clipboard from under the counter, Vince found himself a can of Red Bull and sat down on one of the bar stools to make the calls. He figured he'd contact Diamond and a few of the alpha strippers. They could form a phone tree.

Four cigarettes and seven arguments later, he was done. Being a hard-ass came easily to him, although it wasn't his preferred management style. He liked to wind people up, give them a pep talk, then let them go do their jobs. If they proved unable to work without constant supervision, he fired them, clean and simple.

As Vince glanced one more time at his notes on the clipboard, his cell phone rang. Checking the number, he groaned. "Hey," he said, firing up another cigarette.

"I need money," came Royal Rudmann's soft, almost sweet voice. "Five thousand should do."

"Five thousand dollars? Are you kidding me?" Rudmann was a friend of sorts—a dangerous old friend. "Where are you?"

"A motel. How soon can you get me the cash?"

"I'm strapped," said Vince. "Which you already know."

"Yeah, yeah, but you got assets and I don't."

Tapping ash onto a plate, Vince said, "Look, if I give you the money, I want you to leave the state." And *never come back*.

"I'll think about it."

"Are you working?"

"Met a guy in a bar. He owns a janitorial service. I'm helping clean a couple offices, a couple of day care centers."

Rudmann was a festering problem. Three months ago, he'd been granted a provisional release from St. Peter, Minnesota's first psychiatric prison facility, where he'd been held on a locked ward for two years. He was allowed to leave after a special review board recommended his release, and true to form, he'd violated the conditions of that release almost immediately, failing to attend his mandated AA meetings or report in to his case manager. He needed to stay under the radar or he ran the risk of being sent back.

Vince had read an article in the local paper a few weeks ago about the number of violent, mentally ill offenders who had been let out of St. Peter, only to violate the terms of their release. Some of them, like Rudmann, were still at large, and nobody seemed to be looking for them. An official police spokesman was quoted as saying the problem had been fixed, although the author of the article seemed skeptical, saying it continued to be a glaring breakdown in state and local law enforcement. Obviously, it wasn't information Vince had passed on to Rudmann. He figured if his old buddy got scared enough, he'd take off.

23

"I could come by the club tonight and pick it up," offered Rudmann.

"No," said Vince, taking a deep drag and then blowing the smoke over his shoulder. "You know what happened the last time you were here."

"Man, I don't hold that against you. I got drunk. Sloppy. Still, that guy had it coming."

"You don't start a fight in my club and think you're going to waltz right back in."

"Yeah, yeah. So how you gonna get me the money?"

Why the hell was Rudmann's insolvency *his* problem? He knew the answer, and yet it rankled. Every time Rudmann needed something it came with an unspoken threat: Do what I tell you or live with the consequences. The fact that Rudmann was as guilty as Vince didn't seem to penetrate. Maybe he figured he would likely be spending a good part of the rest of his life in prison anyway, so why not take Vince down with him, *if* Vince didn't cooperate. "Give me the address of the motel. I'll see what I can do. Might not be the full five thousand." He wrote it down, then repeated it to make sure he had it right.

"Call when you have it. Be sweet, man. Peace."

"Peace," repeated Vince, smashing the end of his cigarette against a dirty plate, wishing it was Rudmann's face.

After Jane finished digging her truck out, she ran across the street to help her neighbor Evelyn Bratrude, whose car had become stuck as she tried to back it out of her driveway. With Evelyn behind the wheel, Jane and another neighbor pushed from the front. After a lot of huffing and puffing—and slipping and skidding— the car rolled backward onto the street.

This was one of the things Jane liked most about winter snowstorms. It brought out the best in neighbors. She stayed around long enough to make sure that the car didn't get stuck again as Evelyn made her way to the end of the block. When she turned the corner, Jane waved and returned to her house.

As she was digging through her garage a few minutes later, looking for the snow rake, she heard a horn honk. Stepping back outside into the hard white glare, she saw that Nolan's silver Ford Five Hundred had stopped at the end of the drive.

"Hey," she said, trudging around to the driver's side window. She'd been planning to go in and call him when she was done putting the rake together. "You braved the snow. How are the roads?"

"Miserable. The morning news said the snowplows were out all night. Most of the main streets are generally passable. The side streets are a mess."

Jane rested a gloved hand against the roof. "Did you call your sister in St. Louis?"

He looked straight ahead, adjusted his sunglasses. "That was a hard one."

"You okay?"

"Taylor and his crew found the murder weapon. Tossing it in a Dumpster less than a block away from the nightclub wasn't exactly the act of a homicidal Einstein."

"Did they find any prints?"

"Two perfect specimens. They're running them now to see if they get any hits."

"Fingers crossed," said Jane.

"This investigation is moving fast," said Nolan, flipping open a container of orange Tic Tacs. "When I worked homicide and we got breaks like this early in the game, more often than not we solved the case. I could be wrong, but I think we'll have answers soon."

"You want to come in? I could put on a pot of coffee. Make us some lunch."

"Nah. I hurt my back. Slipped on some ice. Think I'll go home and lie down on the heating pad."

"You need anything, you call."

"Will I see you tomorrow at the office?"

The office he referred to was a local bar—the Rat, his current favorite. He particularly liked their "unhappy hour," when the beers were cheap and the TVs were all tuned to sports channels. Nolan liked to mix the concept of relaxation with low overhead.

"Maybe I can stop by later in the day. You take care, okay? If you want some company—"

"I'm fine," he said. "It's just going to take some time to wrap my head around the fact that I'm never going to see my nephew again." He took a breath, closed his eyes for a second, then put the engine in gear.

Jane tapped the roof and stood back, wishing there was more she could do to help him through this rough time. In the coming weeks, she'd find a way. For now, all she could do was stand in the street, shading her eyes from the sun, and watch his car rumble away.

4

He had to be alert for the descent. Pull it together, he ordered himself, refusing to look at his first officer. The Boeing 767 was traveling at nearly five hundred miles per hour. This was no time for reflection, not the place to parse out what had happened.

Emmett Washington had been awake for eighteen hours, nine of them since reporting to the airport. Long waits, even for pilots, had become far more frequent in the last five years. As always, before the plane could land in the Twin Cities, he had to play runway roulette with the air traffic controllers. He'd done it so many times before that the normalcy felt soothing. Still, every flight he piloted from here on out would come with a threat. A fine or a license action would be the result of any deviation from the prescribed altitude, course, speed, and heading. Since he'd already blown that, he needed to get it right, even though sweat was dripping off his forehead into his eyes and his body was shaking so hard he wasn't sure his hands were steady enough to use the controls.

With the low ceiling and the darkness, there wasn't all that much to claim his attention except for the runway lights. Down to 160 mph. Line it up. Lower the gear.

"Thank God," whispered Ted Kulakov, the first officer, when the wheels finally bumped against solid concrete.

Emmett felt the welcome g-force press against his body.

The flight had been lucky to hit a window in the departure traffic. The taxi to the gate took just a few minutes. As passengers began to head up the jet bridge, Emmett finally worked up the nerve to look at his FO.

"How you going to handle it?" asked Ted.

Emmett removed his glasses, ran a hand over his eyes, and then pinched the bridge of his nose. "Jesus. I feel like I've been through a war." He looked straight ahead as the ground crew began to swarm the plane. "At least no passengers were hurt. This time."

"We were never in any real danger."

"That right? You willing to bet money?"

"Don't file your report until we've talked," said Ted. "As far as I'm concerned, it never happened."

"But it did."

"Okay, okay. But . . . hell, maybe we could get away with calling it a mechanical malfunction. There's no way to prove it wasn't."

If only it could be that easy. Ted was young. He'd been working for AirNorth less than five years. His entire career was ahead of him, and he didn't want anything messing it up. Emmett, on the other hand, would be retiring soon. He had less to lose.

"I'll think about it," said Emmett.

"Let's get together for a drink, talk it over. I'll buy."

Emmett waited until the plane had cleared and then strode alone up the gold concourse on his way back to his car, dragging his black overnight bag behind him.

Shortly before eight, he pulled into the parking lot of Angela's Liquors, half a mile from his house. He examined a few of the bottles, finally deciding on the Johnnie Walker Black Label. He paid the cashier and watched as she slipped a narrow sack out from under the counter and stuffed the bottle inside.

"You in the military?" She nodded to the epaulets on the shoulders of his blue uniform. Four white bars bordered by four blue bars.

"An airline pilot."

"Wow. Cool."

The truth was, unless you were a senior widebody captain at one of the majors, the job was anything but cool. The only part he still loved was the actual flying, which, in truth, was less than half of the time he spent on duty. He did have seniority. AirNorth generally gave him the prime times and destinations. He missed the long-haul flights he'd done in his forties, though at fifty-nine, he didn't have the stamina for them anymore. His hair had turned gray in his early fifties. He was a man with an impossibly young face and a body wracked by arthritis.

When he finally turned into his drive and opened his garage door with the remote, he saw that his son's car was gone. Monday night was a school night. It might not be football season anymore, but his star athlete kid still had a ten o'clock curfew. Football was everything to this boy. Rodger—called Roddy by almost everyone—was a senior in high school, the best running back in the state. This wasn't merely Emmett's fatherly opinion. He was proud of his son, not just for his athletic achievement, but for the kind of young man he'd grown to be. His grades were good. He was on the student council and had joined the Black Achievement Club. Emmett always felt a twinge of guilt when he thought about his work schedule, how often he had to leave Roddy on his own. Then again, maybe the added responsibility had helped the boy mature. His son wasn't perfect. They butted heads like any father and son, but they loved and respected each other, which was more than Emmett could say about his relationship with his own dad.

Emmett had flown out yesterday morning, before the big snowstorm was scheduled to hit. Since the snow removal company he employed never did a particularly good job after a big snow, he'd asked Roddy to do the final cleaning up. As always, the work was done, the salt thrown in all the places likely to form ice. "Great kid," whispered Emmett on his way up the back steps.

After entering the kitchen and setting the brown-paper-wrapped bottle on the counter, he felt a wave of nausea wash through him. What had happened on the plane wasn't going to leave him alone. He removed the wrapper and held the bottle up for a few seconds, knowing the Scotch was a bad idea. He'd had some trouble with alcohol in the past, which was why he'd quit drinking. It had been fifteen years since he'd touched a drop. He didn't think he was an alcoholic, just abusive. It was probably okay—just this once.

Shutting the cupboard, he set the glass and the bottle on the kitchen table, then pulled out a chair and sat down. An unread newspaper lay next to a familiar yellow legal pad, the first page listing the names of various colleges. These were the institutions that had offered Roddy a football scholarship. Two of the names had stars next to them—the top two. He would go with LSU if he could keep his grades up. Generally, just thinking about his son's athletic career could pump Emmett up for hours. Not tonight. Holding out his hands and watching them tremble convinced him that a drink was definitely the right move. He poured himself an inch of Scotch and tossed it back. "Better," he whispered, feeling the slow burn, remembering how much he'd loved that first sip.

How was he ever going to explain to his superiors what had happened? He might be close to retirement, but that didn't mean he wanted to lose his job. He'd made a few investments over the years, none of which had ever earned him much. When he'd lost half his money in the stock market crash in '08, he'd pulled out. His banker's advice was to never invest in anything that would interfere with his sleep. Now that a second recession was in full swing, with the rest of the world teetering on a financial precipice, he wasn't sure where he was supposed to invest what little money he'd managed to hang on to, someplace where the speculators and thieves on Wall Street, or the political gangsters fighting their perpetual wars in Washington, couldn't get their hands on it.

Emmett was standing at the kitchen counter pouring himself a second drink when his son walked in.

"Hey, you're home," said Roddy, grinning.

Emmett stood, and they both half hugged, half slapped each other on the back.

"How was the flight?"

"Okay."

Roddy was a good looking kid with his mother's eager eyes, his dad's square chin, and a muscular body that was 10 percent heredity and 90 percent sweat and hard work.

"Everything okay while I was gone?" asked Emmett.

"Sure. Why wouldn't it be?"

Emmett caught a whiff of defensiveness.

"Everything's fine, Dad. Chill." His eyes dropped to the bottle of Scotch.

"Long day," said Emmett. "I needed something to help settle me down."

"Problems on the plane?"

"Something like that."

"I don't think I've ever seen you take a drink before," said Roddy.

"When you were a little kid, I used to. Not really my style anymore."

Roddy moved over to the refrigerator and opened the door. "We need food. You wanna go to the store tomorrow or should I?"

"I'll go," said Emmett. "You make a list." An image from the flight floated in front of Emmett's eyes, catching him off guard. He wobbled, grabbed the back of a chair to steady himself.

"You okay?" asked Roddy.

"I need to eat," said Emmett. "Why don't I order us a pizza?"

"Great. Extra cheese, okay? Let me know when it's here."

After his son had headed off to his room, Emmett sank onto the chair. He downed the drink, stared at the bottle for a few seconds, then hunched over the table and put his head in his hands.

Drenched in sweat, Emmett awoke a few minutes after midnight to the sound of a ringing phone. Switching on his bedside lamp, he fumbled for the cordless. He couldn't imagine who'd call him at this time of night. "Hello," he managed, noticing that he hadn't bothered to take off his clothes before he got under the covers. Not a good sign.

"We need to talk."

Amazed that he could recognize a voice he hadn't heard in more than ten years, Emmett said, "Vince? Is that you?"

"We've got to do something about Rudmann. He called me from a motel up in Brooklyn Center. He wants money. Again. He must think I'm a bank."

"What's he doing at a motel? Last I heard he was in jail."

"They let him out."

"You've been in contact with him? Lord, I would think you'd want to stay away from a guy like that."

"He contacted *me*. What was I supposed to do? I gave him money once before. Now he wants more. That man has no self-control. He doesn't think logically. I tell you, he's a disaster waiting to happen. A disaster for *us*."

"Meaning what?"

"Do I need to spell it out for you?"

Emmett pulled off his tie and tossed it aside. "Once upon a time we may have been on the same team, but I wasn't any part of that."

"Sure, buddy. It was simple guilt by association."

"Exactly."

"Look, I'm in my car, about ten minutes from your place. Since we have this window of opportunity, I suggest we use it."

"To do what?"

"I can handle it alone if I need to, but it seems only fair that you come with me. We need to take him out. We all talked about it once before."

"That was years ago."

"And now it's time."

Emmett's thoughts all tumbled together. He felt dizzy, unfocused. "I don't know. What if . . . I mean, maybe we could find someone to do it for us."

Vince's laugh was mirthless. "Like how? Someone from your church? I assume you're still a churchgoing guy."

"Now and then," he offered weakly.

"Face it, Emmett, you're not exactly a badass. I'm more connected than you are, and I have no idea how to go about finding someone like that. We have to do it ourselves. Now. Be ready when I get there."

5

The navigation system in Vince's new Infiniti G37X wasn't working, so he'd MapQuested the address before he left the club. With Emmett sitting next to him smelling like a distillery, the hope he'd entertained—that Emmett would actually be of some help—was fading.

"Thought you'd stopped drinking years ago."

"No lectures," said Emmett, drawing a pack of cigarettes out of the pocket of his parka. "I know what I can handle and what I can't."

"You can't handle booze. You were the worst of all of us."

"Look, this has been one of the most god-awful twenty-four hours of my life, so just shove a sock in it. I'm not interested."

"By the way, no smoking."

Emmett glared at him. "Since when?"

"Since I bought the new car."

"You care more about your *stuff* than any guy I ever met."

"I don't want to mess up the new-car smell with your stink. You smell bad enough as it is."

Emmett shifted his gaze to the side window and remained silent for the next few minutes. When a plane, lights flashing, passed overhead, he quickly looked down at his hands.

"You still flying?" asked Vince.

"Yeah."

"Did you have a bad flight or something?"

"You could say that."

"I don't know how anyone can fly day in and day out. I hate it. Hate airports. Hate airport security. And then when I get on the goddamn plane, I feel like I'm packed into a tuna can. The air inside those planes is shit. The food is shit."

"It's a living." Emmett pulled a pack of gum out of his pocket.

"Hey, there it is." Vince pointed to a low building almost completely obscured by the mounds of snow left by the snowplows. If it hadn't been for the J&L Value Inn sign, half-lit by one of two floodlights, he might have missed it. "Thar she blows," he said, turning off the highway into a plowed drive. "We got lucky."

"How on earth could anything about this be lucky?"

"Only one other car in the lot, and it's all the way on the other end, near the office." Lights were on in the unit near the car. The rest of the rooms were dark—except for number 14. Rudmann's room. "I don't see my Nissan."

"Your what?"

"I lent Rudmann an old junker car when he got out of St. Peter."

"Why would you do that?"

"He kept calling, demanding I take him places. Everything that guy ever says comes out like a threat."

"Lord."

"The Lord gave up on us a long time ago."

"Maybe Rudmann's not here."

"Or he parked the car somewhere else."

One of the reasons Vince had wanted Emmett to come along was so he could drive the Nissan home. He wasn't slurring his words, so maybe it was still possible. Vince cut the lights before he eased into the spot in front of number 17, three doors down from Rudmann's room.

"What do we do now?" asked Emmett.

Vince had it all worked out. "You knock on the door, call his name. I'll stand behind you with the gun."

"You brought a gun?"

"You planning to knock him over with your breath?"

"Funny."

"When he answers, you tell him there's been a change of plans. You've got the money, but before you give it to him, tell him the three of us need to talk. That will get us inside. I'll take it from there."

"What if someone hears the gunshot?"

"That's what silencers are for." He leaned over and removed a Walther from the glove compartment.

As they crunched through the snow up to the door, Vince's breath came in nervous puffs. "Just play it cool," he said, hoping he hadn't made a mistake bringing Emmett along. He removed the silencer from the pocket of his jacket, attached it, and then held the gun behind his back.

"I can't do this," said Emmett, bending over as if he were in pain.

"Pussy," muttered Vince. "Get out of my way." He edged him aside and knocked on the door. "Rudmann? Open up. It's me." Glancing over his shoulder, he hissed, "Straighten up. We only get one chance at this." He knocked again.

Coughing against his fist, Emmett whispered, "Maybe he's not in there. We should go."

Feeling more frustrated by the second, Vince tried the handle. To his surprise, the knob turned easily in his hand.

"I'll stay out here," said Emmett, wiping beads of sweat off his forehead.

"What's wrong with you?"

"For God's sake, just do it."

Fine, thought Vince. Rot in hell. How had he ever gotten mixed up with these losers? "Royal? I'm coming in, okay?" He couldn't imagine why the door had been left unlocked.

A lamp attached to the wall next to the bed cast a weak greenish light on the rumpled sheets. Pillows had been stacked against the headboard, and a newspaper and a few sports magazines were piled on the nightstand. The room smelled like dirty socks. Across from the bed, a thirteen-inch TV was tuned to an old *3rd Rock from the Sun* episode.

"Royal? You in the bathroom? Hey, man, I've got your money." He edged forward, the gun held firmly in both hand. "You okay, man?" Glancing over at an empty bottle of Svedka on the nightstand, he began to get the picture. "You been drinking, huh? Guess maybe you passed out. What a shame."

He eased up to the partially closed bathroom door. Kicking it open, he smiled, then froze at the sight that greeted him. Rudmann lay under the sink, half on his back, half on his side, arms and legs spread wide, a look of astonishment on his unshaven face, as if the blast that had carved the crater in his chest had come out of nowhere. Dark blood soaked his shirt and pooled on the cracked tile underneath his lifeless body.

"Shit, shit, shit," hissed Vince, lowering the pistol and stifling an urge to vomit. The last thing he needed was to leave his DNA in the room. Pressing a hand over his mouth, he rushed back through the door, past Emmett and his questioning stare. He ran in a circle around the parking lot, hoping the nausea would pass. When it didn't, not knowing what else to do, he opened up the back of his shiny new car and hurled all over the empty trunk.

37

"Gee, that sucks," offered Emmett.

Vince wiped the back of his hand across his mouth.

"What did he say?"

"Jack shit," said Vince, ordering Emmett to get in.

Skidding out of the lot, the car fishtailed through the snow toward the highway.

"He's dead," said Vince, forcing his eyes to stay on the road.

"That silencer was amazing," said Emmett. "I never heard a thing."

"You are one useless son of a bitch, you know that? He was already dead. I never touched him."

Vince took one last look around for his car. If it wasn't in the lot, maybe the cops wouldn't go looking for it. He prayed like hell that nobody at the motel had seen them arrive or leave. Somebody had done the job Vince thought would fall to him. Maybe it would all work out for the best.

Or maybe it wouldn't.

6

Just before lunch on Tuesday, Jane was in the downstairs pub at the Lyme House replacing an ink cartridge on the printer attached to the POS computer when she spied Nolan walk in. He moved so slowly and looked so flushed that she immediately came out to see what was wrong.

"Everything okay?" she asked, concerned that something had happened with the police investigation.

Nolan motioned her to a booth. As he eased onto the bench, he grimaced.

"Is it your back?"

"Yeah," he said, trying but obviously failing to find a comfortable position.

"You must have really hurt it," she said, sliding in across from him.

"Afraid so. I hit the ground pretty hard."

Nolan had to be extra careful about jarring his back because of a bullet he'd taken to the stomach some eighteen months ago—an injury he'd sustained while saving Jane's life. At the time, his doctors had considered an operation to remove the fragment, but in the end had decided to leave it where it was. If it had shifted because of the fall, it could be a big problem for him. Jane searched his face, trying to determine how worried she should be.

"I've got some news," he said. "Taylor called me a few minutes ago. Seems a dishwasher at GaudyLights walked into the homicide division this morning and admitted to killing my nephew. His name is Elvio Ramos. Twenty-six years old. Married with three kids."

"I don't understand. Why give himself up?"

"Apparently he figured it was only a matter of time before they caught him. He'd heard that they'd found the knife. He'd been arrested once before, so his prints were on file and he assumed there had to be prints on the knife."

"But . . . why admit to it? A lawyer might have been able to work some sort of plea deal."

"It's a good question."

"For which Taylor had no answer?"

"Ramos admitted to the crime. Didn't ask for a lawyer. Gave up a DNA sample without a fight. He told Taylor how it happened, that he bolted from the alley and got rid of the knife, then returned to the kitchen to finish out his shift. He didn't think anyone had missed him. Get this. The athletic shoes he was wearing when he walked into city hall were covered in my nephew's blood." Nolan paused, pressed his lips together, and cleared his throat. "He didn't own another pair of shoes. When it came to the why, he just stopped talking. He said something like 'I'm here to tell you I did it. You can lock me up and throw away the key. God forgive me, I deserve it.' He had a cross in his hand and kept fingering it throughout the interview. For him, apparently, that was the end of it. Taylor tried to get him to open up and state a reason, but he refused to say another word."

"Makes no sense."

"It does if he's hiding something."

"Like what?"

Nolan shook his head.

"Are the police going to leave it at that?"

"Taylor said he'd give it a couple of days. There's always the chance that Ramos may change his mind when he talks to his court-appointed lawyer."

"And if he doesn't? If he stays silent about his reasons?"

Nolan pulled the salt shaker in front of him, began to spin it. "I can't leave it like that. If he won't talk, then I'd say it's up to us to figure it out. When I spoke to my sister yesterday morning, she had no idea that DeAndre had left St. Louis. He was here for a reason, Jane. He was murdered for a reason. I need to know what it was."

"Where do we start?" This would be her first official case as a licensed PI. She was, of course, sorry that it had come as the result of such a personal tragedy for Nolan and his family, and yet she was eager to dig in and get to work.

"I've been making some notes," said Nolan. "I've got several appointments this afternoon on another matter. Maybe we could meet at the Rat later. I'll call and we can work out a time."

"Are you hungry? Can I get you something to eat before you leave?"

"Wouldn't turn down a pub burger."

She smiled as she slipped out of the booth, knowing it was one of his favorites. "Raw onions, extra mayo." Turning back to him to ask what he'd like to drink, she saw that he'd eased out of the booth, too. As he stood, one of his legs buckled and he fell hard. In an instant, people were rushing toward him. Jane bent down and gripped his shoulder. "Are you okay?"

The look on his face was a mixture of embarrassment and pain.

The pain won out. "My left leg," he said, his face twisting in agony. "It's like it isn't there. And my back hurts like hell." He closed his eyes, gritted his teeth.

"Call 911," Jane shouted to one of the bartenders. "Get an EMT here *now*."

"I'll be okay," said Nolan, trying to sit up. "Just give me a minute."

"You're going to the emergency room," said Jane, moving behind him so he could lean against her. "No arguing."

"I'm fine."

"Of course you are. But I won't be until a doctor checks you out."

Cordelia appeared in the emergency waiting room door dressed head to toe in leather. She whipped off her sunglasses and swept the room with a hawklike stare.

From the corner, Jane wiggled a couple of fingers.

"There you are," she said, marching through the crowd of waiting patients, some on crutches, some sneezing or coughing, others talking on cell phones or trying to quiet children. Squeezing into a chair next to Jane, she said, "I got here as soon as I could. What do we know?"

"The doctor ordered X-rays. That was three hours ago."

"Typical. How's he doing?"

"He was in a lot of pain when we arrived. A nurse got him settled in one of those curtained-off rooms, and then she whisked him away. I was asked to wait out here."

"You told the doctor about the bullet in his back?"

"They know. They're sending for his medical records." Jane was far more worried than Nolan seemed to be. "He wanted them to give him some pain pills and send him home."

"But you said his leg had gone numb."

"He's not thinking clearly."

"He's scared."

Jane glanced over at Cordelia and saw her own worry reflected in her friend's face, which didn't do much for her general sense of well-being. "What if they want to operate? I read a ton of articles on that when he was in the hospital last time. It's never an easy decision, and the outcome is always uncertain."

"Don't catastrophize. Let's take this one step at a time."

"You're telling *me* not to catastrophize? *You?* The queen of daytime drama?"

"Think soothing thoughts, dearheart. Deep breaths."

"This can't be happening." She'd been so sure that, after a year and a half of good health, Nolan was out of the woods.

"I can see into that motley soul of yours, Janey."

"Motley?"

"I use the word in the pure Shakespearean sense, not the more recent rock group diminution. You blame yourself for Nolan getting shot."

"He wouldn't have been in the woods if it hadn't been for me."

"But *you* didn't shoot him."

At the moment, it seemed like a fine point.

Cordelia patted Jane's knee. "Not to worry. When I get home tonight, I'll dig out my tarot cards. Do a reading for him and one for you. That should put your mind at rest."

Oh goody, thought Jane. Haul out the tarot cards for true peace of mind. "Let's change the subject. Want to tell me about your heated conversation with Mel the other night?"

"Not really."

"You're keeping something from me. Something big."

"And you know this how?"

"I couldn't help but overhear some of what you two said."

"You were eavesdropping."

"Maybe a little. Then again, unless I employed earplugs, it would have been hard to miss what you were saying. You weren't exactly whispering."

"I'll tell you all about it when the time is right."

"And when will that be?"

Cordelia wiggled her eyebrows.

"Are you moving out of state? Taking a position somewhere else?"

"Heavens, no."

"Because I always thought you'd end up in New York one day, directing at a major theater."

"This is my home. I find it invigorating living amongst the corn rows."

"You're such a snob."

"I know, but you love me anyway."

With little else to occupy her besides her own anxiety, Jane spent the next few minutes bringing Cordelia up to speed on Elvio Ramos and his confession.

"Can't they shine a bright light in his eyes and *make* him talk?"

"I think torture went out with the Bush administration." At least, she hoped it had.

Jane eyed the fish tank, watching one of the bigger fish chase a smaller fish around. "What a world we live in." As she was about to move to deeper philosophical ground, she caught sight of the doctor who had ordered the X-rays. The woman had on a white coat over blue scrubs and stood in the doorway, scanning the crowd.

Jane stood as the woman made her way toward her. Cordelia rose, too, dwarfing the doctor with her height and size.

"How's he doing?" asked Jane.

"I'm calling in another doctor—Robert Schulman. He's a specialist. It looks to me like the bullet has migrated. I started him on antibiotics and Vicodin. He's resting fairly comfortably. Dr.

Schulman will take a look at the X-rays and the myelogram and perhaps order more imaging studies, and then he'll talk to you and your uncle about what he thinks should be done."

"Uncle?" said Cordelia, raising an eyebrow.

"Do you think he'll want to operate?" asked Jane.

"If it were up to me, I'd do it immediately. Regardless of the level of injury, this kind of deterioration is an indication for urgent decompression, at least in my opinion. On the other hand, optimal surgical timing is only one of the issues that need to be addressed. Dr. Schulman will do the studies needed to develop the best treatment options. Your uncle is in excellent hands."

"Thanks," said Jane, feeling overwhelmed by the seriousness of the situation. "One more question. Will he be able to walk when all is said and done?"

"I wish I had more firm answers for you."

Jane was hoping for a simple yes.

"Dr. Schulman is the one to ask about your uncle's prognosis."

"When can we see Uncle Nolan?" asked Cordelia.

"He's being transferred to a room on Five West. That may take some time. I'm sure he'd like company while he waits. Why don't you follow me back?"

Jane felt Cordelia's hand slip around hers, grateful for her best friend's steadying presence.

7

Avi Greenberg was an emotional mess. One minute she might be depressed, sitting in the bathtub watching the faucet drip; the next she might be pissed as hell and ready to throw the nearest heavy object through a window. At the moment, she was propped up in bed, hands poised above her laptop, urging the words to come. She'd written through depression before, but this was more like writing her way out of a block of cement. She had money in the bank, a cool car parked out on the street, a reasonable job, a decent apartment in which to hide—on those days when she felt like disappearing—and yet if she had to say how she felt at this moment, at this juncture in her train wreck of a life, only one word came to mind.

Terrified.

Always the optimist—believing in hope over reality—she'd begun a new novel. This would undoubtedly become her seventh *unpublished* book. The first six had been pure dreck. She suspected that "dreck" would be the perfect label for this one, too. So why did she keep the dream of becoming a writer alive? Simple. It was all she had.

Writing, even under the best circumstances, had never been

an easy road. She remembered a quote she'd heard when she first entered an MFA program in creative writing. "There's nothing to writing," Red Smith had once said. "All you do is sit down at a typewriter and open a vein." She figured that, since she was already bleeding, maybe this book would have a better chance.

Avi was a bartender, a job that suited her needs. After moving to Minneapolis, she'd been lucky enough to find an opening at a strip club downtown. It was a scene she knew well, a place where, for better or worse, she felt comfortable.

Bartending, especially for a woman, was a sexually charged profession. Not that she minded. The money was good, and the people were, if nothing else, entertaining. Bar customers ran on a continuum from fascinating to dreadfully boring, from slightly tipsy to totally hammered. Avi enjoyed the up-close-and-personal, liked digging out people's stories. Preparing drinks, especially when the bar was buzzing, felt like an alternate state of reality. It was actually kind of peaceful. Her hands and feet moved, her brain calculated, all without much conscious thought. She had a few flashy moves and she was a good listener, both of which helped with the tips. She wasn't one of those "cooler than thou" types. Her bar persona was more wised-up good girl. She still played it that way—decent, friendly, occasionally even salty—though underneath, the innocence it took to stay that good girl had long ago melted away.

After another few fatalistic minutes of staring at the empty page on the computer screen, she finally gave up, stripped off her clothes, and went to take a shower. It was getting late. Once she was dressed—all in black, her usual bartending drag—she grabbed her coat and purse, wrapped a scarf around her neck, and headed to the front door. A framed photograph on the end table next to the couch stopped her. Picking it up, touching the glass, she gazed at the child's face, the sweet, impish, gentle expression.

For just an instant, Avi had the sense that she was going to lose it. She placed the frame carefully back on the table, took a deep breath, mentally stuffing her feelings back behind the protective wall she'd erected inside her mind, then headed down the hall to Dorsey's apartment.

Dorsey had been working as a bartender at the club a couple of months longer than she had. He usually took the bus to and from work, but one sweltering, stormy summer night, she'd been moved to pity and offered him a ride. When she dropped him off at his apartment she noticed a FOR RENT sign in the front yard. She asked him what his place was like. By then, she'd pretty much had it with the cheap motel thing. He'd said his apartment was okay. Not exactly high praise, but she decided to check it out.

Right off, Avi had pegged Dorsey as a loner, though over the course of the next few months she'd come to see that it was more than that. He might have a yen for engaging in the odd bit of idle gossip, the sleazier the better, but at other times he seemed more like a covert CIA operative—secretive to the core. She was certain that he didn't want her to move into the building, although he couldn't seem to work up the guts to come right out and tell her to find another place to live. The strange thing was, they'd become friends. Weird friends. She knew nothing about his personal life, his history, which was dandy with her. She wasn't big on telling tales of yore either. They never got together outside the club, but little by little, they had started to connect at work—not over trivia, like she did with the other employees, but honestly. Every now and then they would tell each other the truth. It felt like touching a light socket. It would happen and then they'd both back away.

After knocking on his door, number 203, Avi slipped into her fleece-lined leather gloves. A moment later the door opened a crack and Dorsey edged out. Maybe he wasn't CIA after all. If he

48

was, he needed to be terminated immediately. He sucked at spy-craft.

Jason Dorsey was extremely skinny, with a trendy scruff, light brown razor-cut hair, and narrow, dark-rimmed glasses. His clothes were always fashionable, worn in layers, tended to baggy, and were pressed and creased to within an inch of perfection. She figured he was gay, although she'd never heard him say it out loud.

"Thanks for giving me a lift me tonight," he mumbled, following her down the stairs. "I wasn't supposed to work, but Erin wanted the night off and I can use the extra money."

They stepped into the frigid night air, making quickly for her car.

"Man, you must have been rich in an earlier life," he said, climbing over a mound of snow to get to the street.

"Just because I drive a Porsche doesn't mean I'm rich."

"It does in my book. I looked this thing up online. You know the base cost?"

"It was a gift."

"Right."

After glancing in the rearview, Avi looked over her shoulder and then pulled out onto Colfax Avenue. She drove along for some minutes, lost in her own thoughts, before realizing that Dorsey hadn't said another word. Although never exactly loquacious, he did know how to make small talk. "You're kind of quiet tonight."

"Am I?" He tugged at the front of his leather jacket.

She gave a shrug and switched on the radio. A while later, after taking a right onto Hennepin Avenue, Dorsey reached over and turned down the sound. "That guy who got knifed outside the club on Sunday night. I saw you talking to him."

"A few times."

"He say anything that, you know . . . made you think he might get killed?"

"We just talked ordinary stuff," said Avi.

"I can't get his face out of my mind. Never been around shit like that before. I mean, why would someone want to murder a guy like him? I hope they find the douche and put him away forever."

"You haven't heard?"

He turned to face her. "Heard what?"

"Georgia texted me this afternoon. She said one of the kitchen staff had turned himself in to the police."

"Kitchen staff?"

"Elvio Ramos."

A stunned expression froze on his face.

"You were friends with Elvio, right?"

"Yeah. No. Sort of."

Occasionally, after the kitchen closed, Avi would notice Elvio wander out to the bar to have a beer before he went home. He usually sat down wherever Dorsey was pouring.

"Hey? Are you crying?" she asked, watching him scrape a hand across his face.

"Of course not." He shifted in his seat and turned an impassive gaze toward the street.

When he offered nothing more, Avi decided it was best to let the subject drop. They rode the rest of the way listening to KFAI-FM.

Jane paced outside Nolan's hospital room door. She'd been banished by a nurse who had closed the curtain and was going about doing whatever nurses did. Cordelia had left around six, saying she needed to get back to work. She'd been the artistic director at the Allen Grimby Repertory Theater in St. Paul, one of the most prestigious regional theaters in the country, for the past ten years. She could take time off when she needed to, but some evenings were a command performance. She made Jane promise to call if she learned anything new.

"You can go back in now," said the nurse, stepping out of the room studying a clipboard.

"Do you have any idea when the doctor might be coming?" asked Jane.

"Sorry. But your uncle is resting comfortably. I'll have someone stop by to pick up his dinner tray."

Dinner, such as it was, had been a rather watery affair. Coffee. Jell-O. Broth. She assumed it might be in preparation for his possible surgery tomorrow. No solid food need apply. People in hospitals were kept alive on nasty, bland bilge, as far as she was concerned. It was obvious why a person had to go home to get well.

Standing at the edge of the bed, Jane held a cup of water steady while Nolan sipped from a straw. Her state of nervous frustration had morphed into something more akin to nervous boredom. She'd been watching TV for the past couple of hours while Nolan slept. "How's your blood pressure?" she asked. "Your temperature?"

"I didn't ask."

"On a scale of one to ten, what's the pain like?"

"That kind of question has never made sense to me. My back hurts, although the painkillers help. It's worse when I move. I wonder when that doctor plans to show up?"

Sitting down on a blue plastic chair, Jane felt like a deflating balloon. Before she could offer another nonanswer, a gray-haired man in an equally gray three-piece suit with a metal folder tucked under his arm swept into the room. He stuck out his hand to Jane, then to Nolan. "Robert Schulman."

Jane introduced herself and thanked him for coming.

"I've looked at the X-rays," he said, adjusting his glasses and opening the folder. "I'm afraid it's not good news. Gunshot wounds to the spine are often stable and don't require surgery. That was Dr. Padderson's diagnosis eighteen months ago. Unfortunately, in the interim, you've developed neurologic deterioration and inflammation due to migration. The serial neuroimaging showed that the fragment has lodged itself between two vertebrae. In my opinion, it needs to come out."

"When?" asked Nolan.

"I'd like to do it tomorrow. The decision to remove a bullet is a tricky one. If I schedule you for a surgery tomorrow morning, there are some further tests I would need to do tonight. Also, I'd need to start you on methylprednisolone."

"Talk about the risks and benefits," said Jane. It wasn't a question Nolan was likely to ask. She needed answers.

Schulman slipped a hand into the pocket of his jacket. "I won't lie to you. Results are often mixed. We could remove it and you might regain full use of your left leg and be pain free."

"Or?" said Nolan.

"Or you might have some degree of residual pain and numbness."

Some degree, thought Jane. In other words, the surgery was a gamble.

"If we don't remove the bullet," continued the doctor, "the prognosis is unquestionably bad. In my opinion. You do have a number of things going for you. You're not a young man, but you're in generally good health. I would recommend that you quit smoking."

"Yeah, yeah."

"Again, if you'd like to get another opinion, I'd be happy to suggest another doctor. Or you can always contact your health provider directly for a referral. However, I would suggest that you don't wait too long to make a decision."

"I want the operation," said Nolan flatly. "Set up the tests."

"Are you sure?" asked Jane. She'd assumed she would get to talk to him about it before a final decision was made.

"I know what I want. I've never felt comfortable with that bullet in my body. It needs to come out."

So that was it. Jane understood Nolan well enough to know that she couldn't change his mind. It was his decision to make. His body. His future.

"All right," said Dr. Schulman. "I'll set everything up. We'll give you something to help you sleep tonight. I want you rested. I'll stop in to talk to you before the surgery. Any questions?"

"How long will the surgery take?" asked Jane.

"A few hours. I can't be more specific until I get in there and see what's going on. Are you planning to be at the hospital?"

"Absolutely. I'd like to talk to you when it's over."

"Give your name to the receptionist in the waiting room. I'll call for you when I'm finished. Surgery will be scheduled for 9:00 A.M." He handed her a card, then nodded to both of them and left.

Jane stepped to the edge of the bed.

"Time for you to head home," said Nolan. "It's been a long day."

"I'll stay and keep you company."

He patted her fingers. "I need some time alone. By the way, don't feel you have to be here for the surgery tomorrow. I'll be fine."

"That one's my call. I'll be here." They talked for a few more minutes. Before she left, she he kissed him good night on his forehead, hiding her worry behind an encouraging smile.

8

"What are you reading?" asked Vince, drying his hair with a towel as he walked into the bedroom wearing nothing but a T-shirt and boxer shorts. His wife lay on the bed on her stomach, a book propped up against a pillow. Her Pekingese, Emperor Po, lay next to her, half chewing, half slobbering on a rubber chew toy.

"You'll just make fun of me."

"No, I'm interested," he said, sitting down next to her. He rubbed her back.

The furry Emperor gave a soft growl, picking up his toy and plopping down closer to Shelly's hip.

Vince had to give his wife credit. During dinner, she'd tried to make nice. She'd prepared his favorite deep dish pizza. Opened a good bottle of Pinot Noir. He felt he owed her for that, and for not starting another argument. On the other hand, it cheered him that he had his own chip to play if she went running to Daddy, blabbing about what a miserable husband he was. Daddy might have had plenty of affairs himself during his multiple marriages, but the women in his life, and that included his daughter, weren't allowed the same latitude. Shelly had no idea how often Vince strayed, nor was he about to enlighten her. "Where's my shirt?" he asked. "Dark blue with gray pinstripes? I laid it on the bed before I went down to take my workout."

"I assumed it was dirty," she said, turning a page, "so I tossed it in the hamper."

"Perfect."

"I thought I saw you wearing it yesterday."

"Must have been one of your boyfriends."

"For God's sake. Give it a rest."

He couldn't help himself. Torturing her was so easy.

"Why is everything such a big deal?" she asked. "It's just a shirt. You've been in a total funk ever since you came home last night."

He could hardly give her details about Rudmann's murder. He rose and ducked into the walk-in closet. "I'm just worried about money."

"And I'm worried about *us*. What's more important than that? As far as I can see, you have no respect for me at all."

"I never said that."

"I work sixty hours a week running my company, and when I come home, I try to make a beautiful, comfortable home for you. I try to better myself constantly. I do yoga. Meditate. Journal. While you're at the club every night, I work on learning about stress management and relaxation. I've been spending a ton of time lately trying to understand how to communicate with you better. You know—*Men Are from Mars, Women Are from Venus*? And I just signed up for a class on Mindfulness."

"Good for you." Eyeing his shirts, all hanging neatly on wooden hangers, he chose black silk. His ran his hand down a row of suits, finally settling on a Hickey Freeman cashmere. He always dressed up for the club. As he tucked the shirt into his pants, he caught sight of himself in the long mirror. Leaning closer, he noticed that his eyes were bloodshot. "Have we got any Visine?" he called.

55

"You've haven't heard a word I've said."

"I told you. I think what you're doing is admirable." Emerging from the closet, he repeated, "The Visine?"

"In the medicine chest."

At fifty-nine, Vince admitted to a certain vanity about his looks. He'd been a rough-and-tumble kid, growing up dirt poor. A baseball scholarship had been his entrée into college. Sure, he coveted what money could buy, although, over the years, he'd figured out that it couldn't buy him peace of mind or a young man's body. Grabbing a pair of socks and shoes, he forced a smile as he sat back down on the bed. "Truce."

"Whatever."

He tried to snatch the book playfully out of her hands, but she wouldn't let go.

"What I'm reading is my own business."

Probably something like *Self-Empowerment Through Origami*. Squinting over her shoulder, he read the actual title at the top of the page. *Sexual Self-Esteem in Marriage*. "I'm all for that."

"You've got a one-track mind." She turned and pitched the book at him. Emperor Po started yapping and yipping, leaping up and down. "I'm trying to make our marriage a success, even if you don't care."

"I do care." He did, too, in his own way.

"You work with those whores all day long. You've probably slept with all of them at least a dozen times."

"That would be sexual harassment. Not only could I get sued, but I could go to jail. Give me some credit." Sometimes he lied so easily it worried him.

Shelly dragged the dog into her arms. "I married you because I love you."

Maybe she did believe that. Maybe he loved her a little, too, in his own way. Before he figured out how to respond, the doorbell rang.

"Let's talk about this later, okay?" he asked, shrugging into his suit coat.

Shelly scraped tears away from her face. "One of these days I'm going to stop crying and buy myself a gun."

"It's a thought," he called over his shoulder. "We could duel at sunrise."

"You're never up until noon. I'd have to shoot you in bed."

"Cute." How was he supposed to take a woman hiding behind a Pekingese seriously? He trotted down the stairs to the front door. Switching on the porch light, he found a tough-looking Hispanic man and a middle-aged woman standing outside.

"Mr. Bessetti?" asked the woman, flashing him a badge.

His stomach tightened. "Yes?"

"I'm Sergeant Classen, MPD homicide. This is Sergeant Muñoz. We'd like to talk to you."

"About what?"

"Can we come in?"

His mouth opened and closed twice before anything came out. "Sure," he said, glancing up the stairs, hoping his wife would stay put in the bedroom.

The cops entered the living room and took chairs on either side of the carved wood fireplace. Vince turned on a few lamps before sitting down on the antique Chesterfield couch opposite them. The grandfather clock in the corner ticked, but otherwise, the house was quiet.

The woman removed a pad from the pocket of her coat. "Do you know a man named Royal Rudmann?"

"Yes," he said, trying to keep his voice even.

"When was the last time you heard from him?"

"Well now, let's see. A few months ago, I suppose. No, I take that back. He came to my club before Christmas. I own Gaudy-Lights in downtown Minneapolis. We had a drink, talked for a few minutes. He stuck around for a while, got drunk, and then started mixing it up with one of the other patrons. I had to ask one of the doormen to eject him."

"Have you talked to him recently?"

He shook his head, wondering if someone had reported seeing his car last night outside Rudmann's motel room. "We weren't exactly pals."

The cop glanced back down at her notes. "Good enough friends, though, to lend him one of your cars."

Busted. "The Nissan. I can explain that." He pulled absently at his goatee, remembering, even at a time like this, not to press the hair back and reveal his ridiculously weak chin. "First off, it was a major beater. When Rudmann was let out of St. Peter, he asked for my help. I felt sorry for the guy. You know how it is."

"Any idea why he was in St. Peter?"

"The mental problems? Sure, I knew. He always seemed normal to me, but yeah, he wasn't a nice guy."

"Go on," prodded the male cop.

"Well, I mean, I never used the car, so it was no sweat to lend it to him." He twisted the wedding ring on his finger. "Why all the questions about Rudmann? Did he do something bad? Is he okay?"

"He's dead," said the female cop. "He was murdered yesterday afternoon at a motel up in Brooklyn Center."

"Murdered," said Vince. "How? Who?"

"He filled out a card at the motel that gave his address as 10927 Fairlawn Avenue in St. Paul. We checked. The house belongs to a man named Emmett Washington. You happen to know Mr. Washington?"

"Oh, man, that goes way back. I knew him when I lived in St.

Louis. Him and Rudmann and me, and a bunch of other guys, were all on this community baseball team together. I knew he'd moved up here. We haven't stayed friends."

The female cop scratched some notes on her pad.

"You have any idea what Mr. Rudmann might have been doing at a motel up in Brooklyn Center?" asked the male cop.

"None."

"He called your cell phone on Monday morning. You spoke for seven minutes."

"Oh . . . yeah, right. I forgot about that." He could feel sweat forming under his shirt.

"You forgot?" asked the female cop.

"It's been a rough couple of days. We had a murder outside my club on Sunday night."

The two police officers exchanged glances.

"DeAndre Moore," said the male cop to the woman. "Black guy. Late twenties. Seems to me he was from St. Louis."

"Has to be a coincidence," said Vince. "I'd never met him, never even seen him before. But, so, I mean, that's why I forgot. I've had a lot on my mind." A muscle twitched in his cheek. "Anyway, I guess you could say Rudmann was just checking in. He mentioned that he'd met some guy in a bar who offered him a job as a janitor. He thought he'd take it."

"You know anybody who might have had a grudge against Mr. Rudmann?" asked the woman.

Vince squeezed the back of his neck. "I'm sure he had plenty of enemies."

"But no one person in particular comes to mind."

"Sorry."

Removing a piece of paper from the pocket of her coat, the woman opened it and handed it to Vince. "You recognize that?"

Vince took the paper, aware that he was being scrutinized.

Staring down at a weird-looking word, "ἀκαθαρσία," he asked, "What is that? It's definitely not English."

"It's Greek."

"I don't speak Greek. Is it supposed to mean something to me?"

"You tell us."

He looked from face to face, still struggling to figure out how to play this.

"Ever heard of the word *akatharsia*?"

He shook his head.

"It's used in the New Testament. It means physical uncleanness."

"Okay. And? What's it got to do with Rudmann's murder?"

"We thought you could tell us."

"Hell," he said. "I don't know what you're after here, but I can't help you."

"You own any guns?" asked the woman.

"I keep one at the club locked in a safe. It's a Walther P99. I have a license."

"That's it?" asked the female cop. "Just the one gun."

He nodded.

"You know if Mr. Rudmann owned any guns?"

"I have no idea."

"Mr. Washington?"

"You'd have to ask him." Hearing the stairs creak, Vince was sure that his wife must be listening. He hoped like hell that she'd stay where she was and not try to insert herself into the conversation.

"If you think of anything that might help us find Mr. Rudmann's murderer," said the woman, "give us a call." As she stood, she handed him a card.

Vince walked them back into the front hall. "I have to say, I'm not entirely surprised his life ended violently."

"Still," said the male cop, looking at him with frank, probing eyes, "he didn't deserve what happened."

The direct nature of the gesture unnerved Vince.

"Have a good evening," said the woman.

After closing the door and locking it, Vince shoved his trembling hands into the pockets of his slacks and looked up, watching his wife come down the stairs.

"That man, Royal, is dead?" she asked.

Vince returned to the living room to turn off all but one of the lamps.

"I never did understand why you two were friends."

"We weren't."

"I thought you said he was in jail for beating up on his girlfriend and his girlfriend's daughter?"

She didn't know the half of it. Rudmann had raped the daughter, beaten the mother with a garden hoe, then tied them both up and locked them in a bathroom. He came back the next day with a picnic basket full of food, untied them, and drove them to a park so they could have some "family time" together. Thankfully, the daughter was able to sneak away and call the police.

"What's that?" asked Shelly, pointing to the piece of paper the police had brought with them.

Before he could stop her, she picked it up off the coffee table. "Looks Greek. Did the police bring it?"

Grabbing the page out of her hand, he stuffed it in his pocket and then went to the front closet to get his coat.

"Vince? What's going on?"

"Nothing. Not one damn thing." He dug in his pocket for his car keys and billfold. "For once in your life, Shelly, just leave it alone."

9

Bundled in her heavy wool peacoat, Jane trudged the block and a half to Cordelia's loft, marveling at how busy the streets were these days in the old warehouse district. Gentrification had taken hold in a big way. Cordelia had moved into Linden Lofts, an old livery and rug warehouse, early in the process, when the neighborhood had been rougher and far less trendy.

Jane was too keyed up by Nolan's sudden medical problems to simply go home or go back to work. It was early. Not quite nine. She'd called her neighbor Evelyn from the hospital and asked if she would mind going over to her house to let Mouse out. Not only did Evelyn say she'd do it, but she offered to bring Mouse over to her place and play with him while she watched the latest episode of her current favorite TV show, *Hawaii Five-O*. She said she'd give him a treat and a good brush and then bring him home before she turned in. Jane was glad she had a neighbor who loved Mouse almost as much as she did.

Standing at the corner, waiting for the light to turn green, she was surprised to see Melanie, Cordelia's girlfriend, emerge from her condo across the street from Linden Lofts. Melanie and Cordelia had moved in together for a time, but both came to the conclusion that their often stormy relationship was better served by living apart—if only across the street. Jane waved, trying to get Melanie's attention, but she was in the process of hailing a cab. She was all dressed up—for Melanie. Tan wool coat over jeans and high, slouchy suede boots. A Yellow Cab maneuvered to the curb, and Melanie hopped in. Jane watched the red taillights disappear up the street, still wondering what she and Cordelia had been fighting about on Sunday night.

Entering the Linden building, Jane was hit by the smell of roasted garlic, fresh rosemary, and lemon that drifted tantalizingly toward her from the restaurant on the first floor. As she made her way to the old freight elevator in the back, her stomach began to growl. Earlier in the day, trapped in that culinary wasteland otherwise known as the modern American hospital, she'd bought herself a roast beef sandwich and a cup of coffee. It was all she'd had to eat all day, so the idea of a decent meal definitely appealed. She'd been hoping she could interest Cordelia in some kind of takeout, perhaps from Brasa Rotisserie. Her stomach growled even more loudly when she thought of their pulled chicken smothered in cream and pepper gravy, or the slow-roasted pulled pork seasoned with fresh garlic and lime. It was usually easy to talk Cordelia into a late dinner after she returned from the theater. The fact that they both loved food, almost as much as they cared for each other, was one of life's lucky constants.

During the last year, the building's ancient elevator had been fitted with a new security system. No longer did Jane have to call up to Cordelia's loft to be buzzed in. Cordelia had issued her a series of numbers that allowed her access to the upper regions of Linden Lofts. After pulling the heavy doors shut, she tapped in the security code. The elevator rumbled slowly to life, finally disgorging her on the fifth floor.

Standing before Cordelia's door, Jane knocked softly, not

wanting to wake Hattie. Instead of Cordelia, Bolger Aspenwall III, Hattie's new nannie, appeared. He looked exhausted, his curly brown hair wreathed in a cardboard crown, a frilly white apron tied around his chest, red lipstick smeared on his lips, and brown greasepaint whiskers adorning his cheeks. Black tights and bright green elf shoes completed the ensemble.

"Epic outfit," said Jane.

"It's the true me, don't you think?"

"Especially the shoes. Is the little one asleep?"

He offered her a wan look. "From your lips to God's ears. She's in bed. Her eyes are shut. All good signs."

"Hard evening?"

"You could say that. Come in." He held the door for her. "Can I interest you in a slightly used peanut butter sandwich?"

"Think I'll pass."

"Wise choice."

Bolger was finishing up his BFA in acting at the University of Minnesota. Next year, he would start on his master's in directing. He'd been dithering about moving to California to go to film school in Los Angeles but had changed his mind when he found someone in town with whom he wanted to study, all of which worked out wonderfully well for Cordelia.

Bolger was a natural with kids, adored Hattie, and was generally awed by Cordelia's status in the theater community. His trust fund wouldn't kick in until he turned thirty. Until then, he needed a steady paycheck and a place to live. Because his hours were flexible, he made a perfect nanny. He was gay, from a wealthy family who insisted that he work hard to make his own way in life. At the same time, his parents agreed to finance any education he might deem necessary for his future success, with the one proviso that he live frugally, pay for his own living expenses, and not ask for more than his standard allowance, which was substantial by ordinary standards but not enough to cover all his needs. He also liked challenges; thus his desire to take on Hattie Thorn Lester, the daughter of two icons—Roland Lester, the famous Golden Age Hollywood film director, and Octavia Thorn, the stage and international movie star, who also happened to be Cordelia's dirtbag sister.

"Is Cordelia back from the theater?"

"I expect her any minute."

"Wicked cool apron."

"Think of me as Mother Hubbard with closeted elf tendencies. Help yourself to a drink. I'm going to change into something less comfortable." He winked.

Eyeing the general disarray in the living room, Jane was drifting toward the floor-to-ceiling, small-pained windows that covered one entire wall when Cordelia burst in.

"Someone chasing you?" asked Jane.

Shivering, Cordelia replied, "My plan is to get into a hot bath and never get out." Doing a double take, she added. "What are you doing here?"

"I just left the hospital."

"How's our uncle?"

Jane gave her the quick down and dirty.

"Not good news."

"No."

"Want a drink? Something to eat?"

"You know," said Jane, having come up with a great idea in the last few seconds, "what I'd really like is to take a stroll over to GaudyLights. It's only a short walk."

"How did I know you were going to ask me that?" She tugged her coat more snuggly around her body. "I knew you'd drag me there one of these nights. It's *four* blocks, Janey. Four *long* blocks. If we walk, we'll freeze to death."

"What's four blocks?" asked Bolger, coming out from the back of the loft wearing a Burberry check bathrobe and gray silk lounge pants.

"GaudyLights," said Cordelia, giving him a pained look.

"Seriously? Had no idea you two were so hardcore."

"It's part of Jane's newest sleuthing case," said Cordelia.

"Don't call it a sleuthing case," said Jane. "Makes me sound like Miss Marple."

"What's wrong with that?" asked Bolger.

"My *man*," said Cordelia. They touched fists.

"You should get Melissa to go with you," said Bolger, disappearing into the kitchen. He reappeared a moment later nibbling on a ratty-looking half-eaten sandwich.

"Can't," said Cordelia.

"Because of that fight you had the other night?" asked Jane.

"If you must know——" She hesitated, then blurted, "Our relationship is kaput."

Both Jane and Bolger started talking at the same moment.

"Why didn't you tell me?" asked Jane. "I'm your best friend."

"I wondered why she was never here anymore," said Bolger.

"Are you okay?" asked Jane.

"You can count on Brother Bolger to help you through this terrible time."

Cordelia's arms shot up, demanding silence. "Look," she said, eyeing them sharply, "I was the one who called it off. I still love Mel. We just couldn't agree on some very important issues."

"What issues?" asked Bolger.

"You two are way the hell too nosy." Her eyes scanning the room, she dropped her voice. "If you must know, I made a momentous decision a few weeks ago. Melanie tried to argue me out of it. I mean, all I could say was . . . 'Excuse me? Have we met? How could you understand me so poorly?' And then, well, things got ugly."

"Decision?" asked Bolger, pointing the sandwich at her.

"Full disclosure will come in time. But not tonight, so don't push Mother Nature."

Bolger hooted. "Mother Nature. That's good."

"You think of me as anything less than an elemental life force?"

"No. Of course not. Never."

"So," said Jane. "If you're okay—"

"I'm fine. Never better."

"Will you come to GaudyLights with me?"

"Only if you find someone to carry me on a litter."

"Umm—"

"Oh, all right," sighed Cordelia. "If I must go and look at scantily clad women, I must."

"When you put it that way," said Jane.

"Have either of you ever been to a strip club?" asked Bolger, sauntering into the living room and making himself comfortable on the couch across from the TV.

Cordelia rolled her eyes. "What do you think?"

Jane turned to her. "Have you?"

"I'm not a Puritan."

"How come you never said anything to me about it?"

"Janey, just think about it. Would you have come along if we'd invited you?"

"We?"

"I have a bunch of friends who occasionally like to take in a show."

"So you've been to GaudyLights?"

"Sure."

Switching her eyes to Bolger, Jane said, "It's not a strip club precisely. They call it a gentleman's club."

He shot her a wry smile. "If you think there's a difference, you really are naive. Did you know that you can't serve liquor in a

67

strip bar in Minnesota if the women are fully nude? The Lutherans won't allow it. For example, the Vu doesn't serve any booze."

"He means Déjà Vu," said Cordelia. "It's just down the street from GaudyLights. Definitely not one of my faves."

"I've been to GaudyLights a couple of times," said Bolger. Taking a bite of his sandwich, he added, "Let's debrief when you get back. I'll be interested to hear what you have to report." He winked. "Get along now, little dogies. Me and my foursquare family values will stay home and take care of the kid."

10

Oh, the agony," bleated Cordelia, slogging along a badly shoveled sidewalk next to Jane. "My feet stopped tingling a block ago, and now I can't feel them at all—if that's of any interest to you."

"We're almost there."

"My fingers are totally frostbitten. What kind of morons would choose to live in a godforsaken place like this?"

Jane glanced at her, thinking an answer was unnecessary.

Stepping up to the front door, they gazed up at the neon sign. Tiny lights in every color of the rainbow spelled out the name. Under it, in a lurid, Day-Glo red, were the words DANCING GIRLS!

"Used to be an old car dealership," said Cordelia, stomping her feet to get some feeling back into them.

"It was a restaurant back in the early nineties," said Jane. "Sat empty for a while. I heard the city wanted to tear it down to build a parking lot."

"Now it's a flesh palace. Gotta love those city fathers."

The building was a two-story rectangle. The original oversized picture windows had been darkened, revealing nothing about what was going on inside. From the outside, Jane couldn't tell if the windows had been painted over or if they'd been replaced with heavily smoked glass. The architectural details were 1930s modern. The building was covered in what looked like beige plaster, with three dark green accent lines that ran the length of the upper story. These were broken up by four round porthole windows facing Washington Avenue, also edged in dark green.

Inside, they paid the cover charge and left their coats at the coat check, then entered the main floor near a catwalk that extended out from the main stage.

Jane nodded to a sign that said CAFÉ BACCHUS, with an arrow pointing toward a back hallway.

"I heard he was in town," said Cordelia, raising her voice because of the loud music.

Jane wasn't at all sure what she was getting herself into. "I think our eyes will adjust to the light."

"Said the spider to the fly."

The owner had spent a ton of money on mirrors. From virtually every angle in the room, patrons could watch the dancers' reflections. Some of the women were working the poles, others doing freeform routines. The interior was lit like a jazz club, sultry and low, although the bar that ran along the back wall had a smaller version of the neon GaudyLights sign hanging above it, along with hundreds of tiny colored lights that draped behind the bar. Multicolored neon was a motif that ran throughout, with the words WILD, SEXY, HOT, BABE, LUSCIOUS, NAUGHTY, RED HOT, and HELL CAT, affixed to the walls.

At the opposite end of the room was the main stage, where a lone woman in a G-string and pasties gyrated to AC/DC's "Back in Black." The song faded before it was finished, replaced by Ted Nugent's "Cat Scratch Fever." The dancer edged up to a pole and began another sort of dance. The look on her face was pure punk hostility.

"Golden oldies," shouted Cordelia. "Good for pole moves."

"You know a lot about pole moves?"

70

"Takes skill and great muscle tone to do it right."

Men lined up by the catwalk gestured for the dancers to come closer to the rail. They waved money and shouted. Some tossed bills onto the stage floor for the featured dancer. A maze of tables and padded chairs stretched from back to front, probably seventy-five feet or more. Jane did a quick count. Tuesday nights must be slow. There weren't more than twenty-five guys sitting at the tables. The room could easily have accommodated five times that number. Some of the dancers sat with the men. A few were giving table dances, while others clustered together at tables by themselves, looking bored.

"Let's get a drink," said Cordelia, leading Jane back to the bar.

The stools might look like expensive chrome ladder backs, but Jane had scoped out the same chairs when she was outfitting the Xanadu Club and knew they were cheap aluminum, bargain basement stuff.

Two bartenders were on duty. The one farther away was a skinny guy with a dark scruff and glasses, who appeared to be in a heated discussion with a black woman. Jane pegged her as a manager. The other bartender was an attractive thirty-something woman, above average height, with dark brown hair, parted on one side and swept back over her ears, and large, dark eyes.

"What can I get you?" she asked, her gaze lingering on Jane.

"A Negroni. Don't use the rail gin. I'd like Beefeater if you've got it."

"I want full-court Blitzkrieg," said Cordelia, leaning her elbows on the bar and grinning.

While the woman set up the shots and prepped the drink, Jane asked her what felt like an important question. "Do you get many women in here?"

"Sure," she said. "Believe it or not, some men bring their wives. College coeds drop in occasionally."

"Any lesbians?"

Looking up, the bartender scrutinized Jane more openly. "Now and then." She placed a white cocktail napkin in front of Jane and three in front of Cordelia.

"Do they ever get table dances?" asked Jane, drawing a bowl of pub mix toward her.

"Anything they want."

"What's the difference between a table dance and a lap dance?"

The bartender gave Jane an amused smile. "The price."

Jane returned the smile. "That's all?"

"Table dances are more, just, you know, sensual. The dancer usually stands between the person's feet. No body contact, but she's allowed to put her hands on the customer's shoulders or knees for balance." The bartender set the first of three shots in front of Cordelia. "We have couch dances upstairs. They're done on the love seats in the VIP lounge. The girls still have to keep their feet on the floor, but it's more intimate. A lap dance is also done on the love seats upstairs. There's more actual, you know . . . contact up there. The dancers are supposed to stay six inches away at all times, but in reality, if they want a good tip, they get closer. If you're after a bed dance, you have to use one of the private suites."

"That's a new one," said Cordelia. "What's a bed dance?"

Hoisting the last two shots up in front of her, the bartender said, "Use your imagination." She pointed to each in turn and said, "That's the Rumple Minze, that's the Jager, and that's the cinnamon schnapps."

"Excellent," said Cordelia, rubbing her hands together.

"And one Beefeater Negroni." She placed the drink in front of Jane.

Again, the song cut out before it was over. A voice came through the speakers. "Say good-bye to the beautiful Gypsy!" Some of the men clapped. Some just sat staring at the stage.

"Not a very good vibe in here tonight," said Cordelia.

"Tell me about it."

Jane turned to watch the strippers cruising the room as the DJ's voice called, "Put your hands together for the lovely Sharona!" A few waitresses moved between the tables, taking orders and delivering small plates of food and drinks. They were all dressed in purple leather tank tops and matching miniskirts, with purple fishnet stockings and spike heels.

A gorgeous African American woman in a tight red spandex dress and red platform heels stepped out onto the stage to the pounding beat of "My Sharona." She seemed far more into the music than the first dancer.

"Can I get you anything else?" asked the bartender, glancing briefly at Cordelia but once again lingering on Jane. "I'd be happy to show you a menu. Or if you're interested in something more substantial, you might want to try our new restaurant. Café Bacchus. It opened a few months ago. The food is excellent."

Jane had heard of it, although she'd had no idea it was part of a strip club. "You've got a full kitchen?" she asked.

"With an award-winning chef."

"What's the chef's name?"

"Shanice Williams."

Jane did a double take. "Award-winning?"

"That's what I'm told. You know her?"

"She worked for me last fall."

"Worked for you?"

"I own a couple of restaurants in town."

She seemed even more intrigued. "Which ones?"

"The Lyme House and the Xanadu Club."

"Oh, sure. I've heard of those. Never visited."

Shanice Williams was a mistake from day one. She'd been a sous chef at the Xanadu, hired by Jane's new partner, Barry Tune.

Jane had fired her when she didn't show up for work two days in a row and failed to call and let someone know she wasn't coming. If she'd ever won an award, it was no doubt for throwing plates at kitchen staff.

Using a polishing cloth on the bar, the bartender continued, "I haven't seen you two in here before."

"I've been in," said Cordelia, tugging on her over-one-shoulder snake print dress, "but I sat at one of the tables."

"You two just out for a little adventure tonight?"

"That's us. The adventure sisters," said Cordelia.

As they talked, one of the topless waitresses came by, leaned partway over the bar, and said—using her best Minnesota nasal— "Thanks bunches, Avi. You saved my ass."

"That's what I'm here for."

"Not many regulars tonight," the waitress continued, "and the guys who are here aren't buying jack shit. Tips are lousy. If this keeps up, I might have to look somewhere else for a job." She glanced down the bar to the skinny male bartender. "Dorsey having a problem with Diamond?"

"So it would seem."

"Tell him from me to chill." She winked and hustled away.

"This is bullshit," said one of the dancers, strutting up to the bar, hands on her hips. Perfume hovered around her like a fog. "I really banked on Friday and Saturday night, but tonight . . . what a waste of time. That dude's murder is going to sink this place, mark my words. We're on the way out."

The dancer was Hollywood beautiful—full lips, curvaceous hips, shoulder-length honey blond hair, and deeply tanned, flawless skin.

Gazing into Cordelia's eyes, the dancer said, "I'm Georgia."

Matching her phony breathy tone, Cordelia said, "I'm Cordelia." She tossed back one of the shots. "I like your dress."

74

"This old rag?" Her ultrawhite teeth gleamed. Running her hands suggestively down the front of her shiny turquoise full-length gown, she pulled back a deep slit, revealing a silver garter stuffed with cash. "You like?"

"I'd like to know where you bought the bustier," said Cordelia, hoisting another shot.

"Not interested in the fairer sex, are we? Bet I could change your mind."

"Oh, I'm interested," said Cordelia. "I simply don't like to pay to be seduced."

"Hell, you pay all the time. Books. Movies. TV shows. Magazines. Taking that 'special someone' out to dinner. With me, you get a simple transaction."

"Thanks, but not right now."

"Your loss," said Georgia, the sparkle draining from her eyes. She sat down, letting her shoulders droop. "My feet are killing me."

"It's not that I don't find you attractive," said Cordelia.

"Save it. I've heard every incarnation of that line a thousand times."

"Have you been stripping long?" asked Jane.

The woman looked over, checking Jane out. "FYI, I'm not a deeply disturbed slutty sleazoid. I am an exotic dancer."

"I'm not judging you," said Jane.

"Some people get it, some don't. Thought I'd head your attitude off at the pass."

"I don't think Georgia would mind my telling you that she's working on a law degree at William Mitchell," said the bartender, wiping down the surface of the counter.

"You are?" asked Cordelia.

"It's not polite to act so surprised. Yes, I have a brain as well as a body. I have a BA in criminal justice, with a minor in organizational psychology."

"I'm impressed."

"Then buy me a drink."

"Whatever she wants," said Cordelia, fingering the edge of Georgia's gown. "I like this. Must have rayon in it."

"Nope. Pure polyester. Make it a dirty martini."

"One dirty martini coming right up," said Avi.

"Hey, wait," said Georgia, holding up her hand.

The front door had just opened, and at least a dozen preppy young men in suits and ties elbowed their way inside. They were loud and laughing, already well oiled.

"Ah," she said, readjusting her bustier. "Looks like a stag party." She waited until the men were seated, then rose. "Later, comrades." Moving past Jane, she stopped for a moment to look her up and down, from her boots to her jeans to her blue cotton shirt and short leather vest. "Nice," she whispered in Jane's ear, running a hand down her arm. "I'll see *you* later."

Jane watched her walk all loosey-goosey up to the tables. The other dancers who'd been cruising the room also descended like vultures to fresh carrion, but Georgia seemed to cause the greatest stir.

"She's good," said Avi. "She'll bleed them for every dime they've got, and they'll love every minute of it."

Jane watched a minute more, then turned back to the bartender. "You have an unusual name."

"Avi? It's short for Avigale. My father's Jewish. Mother's Hispanic, born in Guatemala."

"Not a natural-born white-bread Minnesotan," said Cordelia. "You don't make hotdish or say ufda?"

"Say what?"

Onstage, a new dancer appeared. "Let's hear it for the enchanting Burgundy," came the DJ's voice. Pink's "Raise Your Glass" boomed over the loudspeakers. When Jane turned to take a look, she noticed a man in a tan suit and a dark shirt open at the collar step out onto the floor from a side door. He had a square, boxy build, not exactly fat but moving in that direction. With his silver hair combed straight back from a high forehead and thick black eyebrows and goatee, he had a certain gravitas about him. "Who's he?" asked Jane.

Avi removed the two empty shot glasses from the counter in front of Cordelia. "That's Vince Bessetti, the owner."

Bessetti inspected the room, paying particular attention to the knot of dancers surrounding the four tables newly claimed by the stag party, then headed up an industrial-looking staircase to the second floor.

"You know," said Avi, pointing at the last shot glass in front of Cordelia, "you're supposed to drink those fast, in order, one after the other."

"If I did, I'd be on the floor."

"She's the artistic director of the AGRT in St. Paul," said Jane. "She has an image to protect."

"That repertory theater? Wow, I've got some high rollers in here tonight."

"Let me ask you something," said Jane, taking another sip of her drink. "The dishwasher who supposedly murdered the man outside the club, did you know him?"

"Elvio? I knew who he was. I don't think I'd ever talked to him."

"Is there anyone here he did talk to regularly?"

She glanced at the other bartender. "Dorsey. I think he knew him pretty well."

"Have you heard any scuttlebutt about why he might have done it?"

"No."

"No opinions at all?"

"Sorry. None."

Two waitresses descended on the bar with drink orders from the stag party. Avi and Dorsey immediately went to work.

Jane was frustrated by the interruption. Someone around this place had to have an opinion on the subject of Elvio Ramos. Turning to Cordelia, she said, "Let's order something." She opened the menu and placed it flat on the counter between them. "Will you look at that," said Jane, disgusted. "Shanice stole some of the recipes from the Xanadu. Why doesn't that surprise me?"

Finishing her last shot, Cordelia said, "Yup. The Prawn cigars. And the shrimp-stuffed deep-fried wontons. You serve them with that Bloody Mary cocktail sauce, heavy on the horseradish."

"I suppose we could order a plate of each. See if she's done any damage to our recipe."

Cordelia pointed to the hot roast beef sliders. "Let's get those, too."

"Can you eat that much?"

"Is rain wet? Do vacuum cleaners suck? Do cheerleaders, like . . . you know . . . whatever."

Avi sailed by, reaching for one of the beverage guns. "You two planning on sticking around?"

"I guess we're going to try some appetizers."

"Good choice," she said, a smile spreading across her face when she looked at Jane.

While they waited for their food, Jane excused herself and moved down the bar, where she sat by the male bartender.

"People call me Dorsey," he said after Jane had introduced herself.

"I was hoping to ask you a few questions about Elvio Ramos."

"You a cop?"

"No. I'm a friend of the dead man's uncle."

He digested that. Resting his elbows on the bar, he said, "Shoot."

"Did you ever see Elvio and DeAndre Moore talking?"

"Nope."

"What kind of man is Elvio?"

"Hard worker. Religious. Got a wife and kids. I liked him."

For a bartender, Dorsey wasn't much of a talker. Maybe Jane was reading him wrong, but she had the sense that he was almost angry with her for bothering him.

"Did you ever spend any time with Elvio outside work?"

"You sure you're not a cop?"

"Positive."

Dorsey grabbed a rag and wiped up a spill. "I have no idea why Elvio knifed him. Far as I'm concerned, it was totally out of character."

"You ever talk to Moore?"

"A few times."

"He say anything about Elvio—something that might shed light on why he died?"

"Look, lady, all I know is he started coming in last week. Spent every night in here drinking and watching the dancers. That's it. We talked about the weather once. We talked about the upcoming Super Bowl while I pulled him a beer. I don't spend my time keeping track of customers."

"You never noticed if he paid particular attention to any of the dancers?"

"No. Now, if you'll excuse me?" He began to kick a double-wide Stolichnaya box to the end of the counter, where he picked it up and stuffed it next to a side door. Jane figured it was all she was going to get.

11

One A.M. An hour before closing. Vince sat behind the computer in his office thinking that his desktop was as chaotic as his life. It had taken him almost an hour to find the article he'd been searching for, something he'd saved out of a sense of human solidarity, a connection that had been buried out of necessity long ago, though one that still tugged at him.

There he was on the screen. Burt Tatum. The long, narrow, austere face. With looks like that, he should have been a monk—or a paid assassin. Of all the guys on the team, Vince had been closest to Burt. They'd been best buddies ever since grade school, gone out for the same sports in high school, double-dated in college. When their friendship ended, as they both knew it had to, a large chunk of what had made Vince feel good about life had gone with it.

Scrolling past the photo, he read the details of his friend's death. Tatum had been a science teacher at a middle school in suburban St. Louis. Fourteen months ago, he'd been gunned down in the basement of his home. According to the article in the *St. Louis Post-Dispatch,* the police had developed a couple of promising leads. Vince followed the story closely and was sickened to learn that, in a matter of weeks, all the leads had dried up. Here it was more than a year later and nobody had been arrested for the murder.

At the time, Vince considered it a strictly St. Louis matter, a simple equation: Burt must have stepped into some deep personal shit and someone had come after him. Two recent events, however, had changed his mind.

First had been the death of the African American man in the alley outside GaudyLights. Initially, Vince's only concern had to do with the effect the man's murder might have on business. Learning that the guy was from St. Louis had not set well, though he'd brushed it off as mere coincidence. Then, after discovering Rudmann's body last night at the motel—like Burt, shot in the chest at close range—his belief in simple coincidence had been shaken. He'd spent the rest of the night sitting on his living room couch, drink in hand, trying to work it out. Were the deaths connected? Was he in any danger? If the deaths *were* part of some payback scheme, who was behind it? Two members of the team were gone, murdered in the same way. The odds that he was going to live to see a ripe old age had been cut significantly. Still, he couldn't quite bring himself to hit the panic button. Not yet.

Vince hadn't heard from the fifth member of the team, Ken Crowder, in well over a year. He'd kept in touch with Crowder mainly because of his business success. In the back of his mind, Crowder was a card Vince hoped he might be able to play one day when he needed it. In his last e-mail, Crowder had mentioned that he'd bought himself a cabin in the mountains above Park City, Utah. He'd bragged about the great views from the front deck, how he could see all the way down the valley to a reservoir. Of all the Wildcats, Ken had been the most successful. He'd retired a rich man after selling his software company for $8.5 million at the age of forty-eight. Vince and Crowder occasionally shared a piece of Internet hilarity via e-mail and always sent cards at Christmas. This past year there had been no e-mails from Crowder and no Christmas card.

Scrolling through his address book, Vince found Crowder's and shot him a quick note:

Hey, man, what's up? I've got bad news. Rudmann's dead. Murdered. With Tatum murdered last year, I can't help but wonder what's going on. *Write when you get this.* We need to talk. Let me know a good time to call—give me a phone number. Or e-mail me. ASAP. I need to know you're okay.

Vince

For now, it was all he could do. That and transfer his Walther from the safe to the bottom drawer of his desk.

After getting up to lock his office door, he set up a line of coke, spreading the last of it across his teeth. Good thing he had an in-house dealer. Thus fortified, he locked the door to his office and went out to the main pit to see if business had picked up. He stood along the wall and watched a couple of stage rotations, depressed by the lack of the usual psychosexual drama. Heading upstairs, he found four of the nine suites empty. Even with the loud music pulsing, the place felt like a tomb.

After he got himself a double bourbon on the rocks from the bar, Diamond Brown, his assistant manager, caught his eye and walked him back down the hallway to his office.

"We got a problem with one of the bartenders," she said.

Vince liked Diamond. She was somebody he didn't need to micromanage. Saucy, wily, and beautiful enough to be one of the dancers herself—if she'd been twenty years younger—she knew how to get what she wanted from the staff. Vince had tried his best to seduce her on more than one occasion. So far, she'd managed to elude him, though always with the unspoken promise that it was only a matter of time before she succumbed. That was Diamond. She knew how to play the game.

"Jason Dorsey," she said. "You know him?"

"The skinny kid?"

"He accused me of stealing from his tip glass."

"Did you?"

She grinned. "Of course not, sugar."

Her Southern accent drove him wild.

"But he may come talk to you about it. Just wanted to give you a heads-up."

He moved in close, so tantalizingly near that he could almost taste her chocolate brown skin. "We may need to talk about this in more detail."

"I'll be around," she said, drawing a finger across his chest as she walked away.

"Woof," he whispered, carrying the bourbon into his office. As he closed the door and sat back down behind his desk, he felt suddenly depressed and jittery. For the next few hours he tried to get some work done, checking his e-mail every fifteen minutes to see if Crowder had written back. A knock at the door finally interrupted him. "It's open," he called.

Diamond stuck her head inside. "We're done with the payout. Everyone's leaving."

"How'd we do?"

"You don't wanna know. We've got some definite grumbling in the ranks. I'm taking off."

"You could always stay, you know."

"Not tonight, baby." She winked. "See you tomorrow."

Switching off the desk lamp, Vince leaned back in his chair, propping his feet up on the edge of a file cabinet, the darkness wrapping itself around him like a comfortable old sweater. When it came down to it, he was a simple man with simple needs. He wanted his business to thrive, a good sex life with an occasional pop of Viagra to invigorate the plumbing, enough money to live a comfortable life without financial worries, and for the world—and his past—to leave him the hell alone. Was that so much to ask? He sipped his bourbon, pissed, even a little bitter, that everything was always such a goddamn struggle.

When he heard the floorboards creak outside his office door, he dropped his feet to the floor and sat bolt upright. It wasn't the first time the old wood floors had warned him someone was headed his way. Glancing at the time on the computer, he saw that it was a quarter of three. Surely everyone had gone by now.

Removing his pistol from the bottom drawer, he switched the light back on and moved carefully over to the door. He hid the pistol behind his back as he stepped out into the hall.

Ten feet away a man stopped dead in his tracks, his face hidden in shadows.

"Who's there?" demanded Vince.

The man didn't answer.

His voice rising, he shouted, "I asked you a question."

"What are you hiding behind your back?"

"Tell me who you are and what you want."

Moving under the light of a wall sconce, the weedy-looking guy said, "I'm Jason Dorsey. One of your bartenders. We need to talk."

Vince relaxed. This was the guy who was steamed at Diamond. "Look, I don't discuss business at this time of night. You want to talk to me, do it during regular business hours."

"But this is important. I'm being cheated. Diamond has been—"

"*Leave,*" said Vince.

"That a gun behind your back?"

"You really wanna know?"

Dorsey raised his hands and started to back away.

"Shit," grunted Vince, realizing that the kid would set off the alarm system when he opened the door. "I'll come let you out." He followed Dorsey at a distance. Once out on the floor, he reached under the bar and tapped in a code to switch off the alarm.

"Sorry I bothered you," said Dorsey. Pausing halfway out the door, he turned and said, "Stay safe, now."

"What?"

"Just . . . you know. Be safe."

"What the hell do you mean by that?"

"It's just something people say."

"Get the hell out of here."

The kid hustled away.

"Irritating little fuck," muttered Vince, feeling vaguely unsettled. What he needed was another bump of coke.

12

The static electricity in the cabin made Emmett's hair stand on end. "Total bullshit," he said, watching his onboard instrumentation go dead. This couldn't be happening. Twenty years ago, maybe, but this jet had backup systems for its backup systems. He banked left, shouting at his sleeping first officer to wake the hell up and radio the air traffic controller at MSP. "We're in trouble," he said. "Tell them we're in deep shit."

Struggling against the hands gripping him, Emmett screamed, "Stop it. Let go!"

"Dad, wake up," came a voice out of nowhere. "Come on. You're having a bad dream."

Blinking open his eyes, Emmett fell back to earth with a thud. "What? Roddy?"

"You were screaming so loud you woke me up."

Except for the moonlight streaming in through the window, Emmett's bedroom was dark. His son stood over him wearing nothing but pajama bottoms.

"You been drinking again?" asked Roddy.

"I couldn't sleep. I'm so tired, but I can't turn my mind off." He sat up a little, pulled a pillow behind his back. What he didn't explain was that when he did fall asleep, the nightmares came, returning him to that single crucial moment with a terrifying immediacy. "What did I say?"

"Weird shit. Instruments. Lights. Red. Blue. Radio static. It was all garbled." Roddy eased down on the bed next to him.

It was still so vivid that Emmett couldn't seem to shut it off, even when he was asleep.

"What's wrong?" asked his son. "I got your message that you'd be late tonight. Where were you?"

"Had to go into the office." Emmett was glad that it was nowhere near the airport. The very idea of entering the Lindbergh Terminal filled him with dread. "I'm trying to wrangle a leave of absence. I needed to talk to a guy in HR. When I was done I was so wired that I went to the Y." He'd ended up in a bar, though he didn't offer that piece of information to his son. "You were asleep when I got home."

"You're scaring me. I've never seen you act like this before."

"I'm okay," said Emmett, taking hold of his son's arm, squeezing the tight muscles.

"You're not. When was the last time you took a shower?"

"At the Y after I worked out."

"Well, you need another one."

Sitting up a bit straighter, Emmett said, "Maybe we should get in the hot tub. Come on, it's cold out. It would feel good."

"It's the middle of the night. I've got school in the morning."

"Oh, yeah." He ran a hand over his face. "Sorry. I'm not thinking."

Roddy switched on a lamp. "What's all that?" He nodded to a stack of printed pages spread out on the bed next to his father.

"Just something I was reading."

Roddy picked up a page and held it next to the light. "It's on post-traumatic stress." He searched his dad's face. "Is that the problem?"

It was, in fact, part of the problem. As far as he could tell, he had PTSD in spades. Difficulty falling asleep. Feeling jumpy and easily startled. Pounding heart. Rapid breathing. Excessive sweating. Intrusive, upsetting memories. It was all there. He supposed he should go talk to a counselor or therapist. Not now, he thought, pushing the idea away. Not yet.

"You said you had a problem on your last flight," said Roddy.

Emmett gave a stiff nod.

"What was it?"

"I can't talk about it."

"I mean, like, did you almost crash the plane or something?"

"We came close."

"Jeez. Was it your fault?"

"It's . . . complex." Emmett hadn't filed a report yet. No one at AirNorth had said anything to him about it, but they would. It was only a matter of time. Questions he couldn't answer heated up inside him like a furnace. "I can't seem to concentrate."

"We all screw up," said Roddy, leaning forward, arms resting on his thighs. "Doesn't have to be the end of the world. Right?"

"No, it doesn't."

"Could you lose your job over it?"

"I don't want you to worry about anything. Everything will be fine. I can handle it."

"But I am worried," he said, sitting up straight. He picked the empty bottle of Scotch off the nightstand and held it up. "What is this? The second—third—bottle you've brought home."

"I'll stop. I promise. I took my last drink tonight." Emmett's attention was drawn to the windows. "What was that?"

Roddy swiveled around. Standing to get a better look, he said, "I think Mr. Roth's backyard light just flipped on."

"Oh." Simple explanations were good. Very, *very* good. Emmett switched the light off. He needed the darkness.

"I'm going back to bed," said Roddy.

"Son? Wait."

"What?"

He hesitated. "I have a question. I know this may sound strange, but . . . do you . . . I mean, do you believe in God?"

"Me? Yeah. Why? Don't you?"

"I used to."

"But not now?"

Wrenching his eyes away from the window, he said, "Go back to bed. I may go down and take that hot tub. I'll be quiet about it."

Standing over him, scrutinizing him one last time, Roddy said, "Chill, okay?"

Good advice, thought Emmett. He wished he could take it.

13

Early Wednesday morning, Jane had just stepped out of the shower when she heard Nolan's cell phone begin to beep. He'd given it to her last night before she left the hospital, along with his wallet, his watch, his keys, and his ring. She'd tossed it all on the top of her dresser when she got home from GaudyLights.

Racing back to her bedroom, she clicked the phone on. "Hello?"

"Oh, I must have the wrong number," came a woman's voice.

"Are you looking for A. J. Nolan?"

"Who's this?"

"Jane Lawless. I'm—"

"Oh, sure, I know who you are. You're Alf's friend. This is his sister, Fannie Lou. You've never answered his phone before, so that kind of threw me. Is he around?"

"He's in the hospital. He's scheduled for surgery this morning."

"Oh, my, no. Why? Is it the bullet fragment in his back?"

"I'm afraid so."

"I've always worried about that. Our family's been hit with so much trouble."

"I'm so sorry about your son."

"Thank you." She was silent for a few seconds. "So, tell me. What's happening to Alf? Why is he having the surgery?"

Jane explained about the pain and weakness in his leg, the tests, the specialist, and how the upshot was that the bullet had migrated and needed to be removed.

"He never called and told me," said Fannie Lou, sounding hurt.

"It was all decided so fast. I'm sure he meant to, but they kept him busy with tests and consultations."

"Truth be told, he's not the best one for keeping in touch. How long will he be in the hospital?"

"I'm not sure," said Jane. There was no point in worrying her with the potential ramifications of the operation. After coming home last night, Jane had scoured the Internet until nearly two in the morning reading everything she could find about bullet wounds to the spine. She'd done this once before, when Nolan was in the hospital the first time, right after he was shot. She'd come away then with the impression that all such surgeries were iffy at best. Her current search yielded the same results. Yet, needing to feel that she was doing something positive, she'd continued on, doing what the Internet allowed a person to do so easily—mistake information for real knowledge.

"Will you call me later today, let me know how everything went?" asked Fannie Lou.

"As soon as I know, you'll know." She wrote the woman's number on the back of a magazine.

"He's my older brother. I've always looked up to him." She had such a sweet voice.

"I'll tell him that. Say, since I have you on the line, I've always been curious about something. What does A. J. stand for? He won't talk about it."

Fannie Lou laughed. "Alfonse Jasper."

"Ah."

"Alfonse doesn't really fit him."

"Not really."

"Thank you, Jane. Alf thinks the world of you. You probably already know that. I'll wait for your call."

Still dripping wet, Jane returned to the bathroom to dry off. Mouse followed her back down the hall, wagging his tail and sitting down on his haunches whenever she stood in one place for more than a few seconds.

Concern for Nolan filled her mind as she dressed in her most comfortable jeans and ski sweater, knowing she'd be spending most of the day at the hospital.

"Come on, boy," she said, giving Mouse a scratch under his chin. "Time for breakfast."

Jane stayed with Nolan until they wheeled him off to surgery, then moved to the waiting room. She'd brought a book, a novel she'd been wanting to read for several months, but no matter how many stabs she made at it, she was too keyed up to concentrate. She alternated between idly watching TV and pacing out in the hallway. The hours crawled by.

By two, she'd met with Dr. Schulman and had been given the report on the surgery. Sitting with her in a small, airless room, Schulman informed her that the operation had gone well; the bullet fragment had been removed successfully. Nolan was in recovery, where he would stay for the next three to four hours. His vital signs were all strong.

The big question for Jane had to do with the ultimate outcome. Here, Schulman hedged. He said it would take some time before they would know how much damage the bullet had caused. He encouraged her to stay positive, especially around Nolan, and emphasized that no matter how well the operation had gone, the recovery would have its difficult moments.

Feeling less than overjoyed by his final admonition, Jane left the hospital, needing some fresh air. On the way to her car, she gave Nolan's sister a call. Instead of Fannie Lou, she got her voice mail, which was probably all for the good because Jane was tired and not in the best mood. She left a message, stressing that Nolan, or Alf as Fannie Lou called him, was in recovery and doing well. When he was feeling better, Jane promised, she would urge him to give Fannie Lou a call.

Home by three, Jane sat on the floor in the living room and played with Mouse. As she tossed the ball for him to fetch, her thoughts turned to her visit to GaudyLights last night. Before leaving, Avi, the "hot" bartender as Cordelia had called her, invited Jane back for happy hour tonight. She said the appetizer buffet was one of the best deals in town. Jane had pretty much decided that it was a no go, and yet after spending all day at the hospital, she realized she needed a break. The idea of actual food, not the unappealing hospital gruel, appealed. She was also still hoping to shake something loose and find information that would help her understand why DeAndre had come to Minneapolis. Then there was that other small matter: Jane was uncharacteristically eager to see Avi again. She didn't quite understand how she could be so instantly attracted. It wasn't her usual MO.

"I wish I didn't have to leave you alone so much," Jane said to Mouse as he burrowed his head against her chest. When she worked at the Lyme House, she could take him with her. Her office there had a couch, a small fireplace—all the comforts of home. The Xanadu Club was a different matter entirely, as was her work as a PI. "I know you like Evelyn Bratrude, but it's not exactly what you want."

Mouse sat down and lifted up his paw.

"Such a proper young pup," she said, pumping his paw and smiling. "God, but I love you." She stroked his fur with both hands. "Wish I could be two places at once. Or three or four." They played fetch a while longer. Jane ended up on her back with Mouse dropping the ball on her head. "I should take you for a walk. Maybe when I get back later tonight we can do that." She tugged gently on his ears. "You're my boy. My best boy."

Mouse nipped her nose and gave it a soft lick.

Shortly after four, Jane found herself inside GaudyLights, making her way to the long bar at the back. Exchanging the bright winter daylight for the perpetual darkness inside the club felt far more dramatic than her entrance had last night. Even with all the neon, Jane sensed a kind of chill creep inside her. She hadn't been as repelled by the place as she figured she might be. Seminaked bodies were one thing. She'd never met an attractive seminaked body, male or female, that she wasn't interested in looking at, but the blatant buying and selling struck her as gross. She assumed that the main floor was reserved primarily for heavy teasing and stripper camp. The more brazen sexual contact, the pretend—or not so pretend—grinding and stroking, went on upstairs in the VIP lounge.

The club was busier today, with two dancers onstage doing a kind of woman-on-woman slow dance to Prince's "Purple Rain." Jane stood in the shadows at the edge of the room, mesmerized. Three minutes into the song, just like last night, the music changed to Journey's "Any Way You Want It," completely destroying the spell. As the women hopped onto their poles, Jane turned and walked back to the bar, sitting down as close to Avi as the crowd around her would allow.

"Business has picked up," said Jane when Avi moved over to get her order.

"I was hoping you'd stop in. What can I get you?"

"Cola. Whatever you've got. I need a caffeine fix."

"Long day?"

"A friend in the hospital. He had surgery this morning."

Avi scooped ice into a glass and then hit it with one of the bar guns.

Feeling a tap on her shoulder, Jane turned to find her onetime sous chef, Shanice Williams, standing behind her. She still had her Whoopi Goldberg dreadlocks and tiny granny glasses. She'd also put on weight. Instead of a traditional double-breasted white chef's coat, hers was red, with French cuffs and hand-rolled buttons. The last time Jane had seen her, her white coat had been stained with tomato sauce, and her hat had looked as if someone had stomped on it with a large pair of greasy shoes. Things were definitely looking up.

"I heard you came in last night," Shanice said, pulling out one of the stools and sitting down.

Shanice was such a formal person, always so correct in her bearing and the way she spoke, that Jane couldn't help but say, "Dude. How's it going?"

She glowered.

Jane glanced at her name embroidered in black block letters, with the words EXECUTIVE CHEF, underneath.

"Slumming?" asked Shanice. "Or is this your thing?"

"Just checking out the competition," said Jane, pulling her drink closer.

"Have you tried the food?"

"The appetizers. They were good."

She puffed up at that. "You never struck me as the sex industry type."

Jane borrowed a line from Cordelia. "I am inscrutably multifaceted."

Shanice glanced at Avi, a smile touching her lips. "Oh, I get it. You're hustling the hired help. Trolling for dykes."

"Sounds like a TV game show," said Avi, leaning her elbows on the bar. "You know. *Bowling for Dollars.*"

"More like *Let's Make a Deal,*" said Shanice, smiling acidly.

"Now that you're working here," said Jane, forgetting for once to keep a lid on her snide comments, "maybe we should call it *The Gong Show.*"

Shanice stiffened.

"Anyway, I'm not a dyke," said Avi. "I'm a lesbotarian."

"What's the difference?" asked Shanice.

Avi laughed at her credulity.

"I'm merely taking a look around," said Jane. "I understand one of your dishwashers is responsible for that murder outside the club."

Her eyes hardened. "It's got nothing to do with me."

"I never said it did. Then again, you hired him."

"Oh, I get it. You're snooping. When I was working at the Xanadu, someone told me you thought of yourself as Sam Spade. We all had a good laugh."

"Is that so?"

"Someone will cure you of that notion one day."

"Why so touchy, Shanice? Makes me think you've got something to hide." Besides stealing my recipes, she thought but didn't say out loud.

The man Avi had pointed out as the owner of the club last night, Vince Bessetti, walked up and stood behind Shanice. "You're wanted in the kitchen," he said curtly. "When you're done, we need to talk."

Shanice's right eye twitched. "Of course," she said, getting up and quickly striding away.

Bessetti smoothed his goatee, studying Jane. "Have we met before?"

From a distance, he'd struck her as sophisticated, almost handsome. Close up, he looked more like a gangster. The skin on his square, rather flat face was mottled, most likely the residual effects from a bad case of teenage acne. The lizard-skin tassel loafers were the icing on the cake.

"Jane Lawless," she said, shaking his hand.

"Lawless. Familiar name. Any relation to Raymond Lawless, that defense lawyer who ran for governor a few years back?"

"He's my father."

"Your *dad* ran for governor?" asked Avi.

"He lost," said Jane.

"I liked some of his positions," offered Bessetti, slipping a hand casually into his coat pocket, "but in the end, I couldn't bring myself to vote for him."

"I forgive you." It was her standard response. She figured one unnecessary comment deserved another.

"Have you been in before?"

"My second visit."

He tapped a finger against his lips. "Seems to me I remember reading something about you owning a couple of restaurants in town."

"That's right."

He studied her for another second. "Ever thought of investing in a gentlemen's club?"

"Not really."

"Might be just what you're looking for." Nodding to Avi, he said, "Comp all her drinks." Extending his hand again, he said, "Take a good look around. Next time you're in, if you'd like, we could sit down and talk."

"I'll think about it," said Jane. Talking to Bessetti might prove interesting.

For the next hour, Jane sipped her drink, ate from a plate of standard happy hour fare, and talked to Avi as she set up drink orders.

"So you're gay," said Jane at one point.

"Card-carrying," said Avi with a grin.

She talked easily on just about any subject, no doubt one of the things that made her a good bartender. Jane wondered why she was working in a place like GaudyLights. At one point during the conversation, Avi pressed her about her unusual interest in the murder. Jane explained her connection to DeAndre Moore's uncle and her hope that she could help him find out why his nephew had been knifed—since Elvio wasn't talking.

"Elvio always seemed like a private guy to me," said Avi, scooping up another bowl of pub mix and pushing it across to Jane. "I'll keep my eyes and ears open. If I learn anything, I'll let you know."

"Thanks," said Jane, glad to have some inside help. She found herself smiling at Avi for no particular reason.

"Another Coke?"

Wanting to stay, but knowing she needed to get back to the hospital, Jane said, "I better get going." She began to gather up her coat and car keys.

"You better come back soon for more of our on-the-house drinks," said Avi with a wink. "Can't beat the price."

On Jane's way to the door, the blonde Jane had met last night— Georgia—stepped into her path.

"Hi," she said, her eyes crinkling in amusement.

"Hi," said Jane, buttoning her navy peacoat.

"You remember me?" She was dressed in a black leather bustier and miniskirt, with matching thigh-high boots.

"Of course I remember you."

"Looked like you and Avi were having one hell of a great time, laughing, talking, making merry."

"She's good at her job."

"Knows how to make the drinks strong when she wants something."

"I had a Coke."

"Is that right." Georgia guided her over to a quiet corner. "You like strip bars?" she asked, her eyes drifting down Jane's body.

"I came mainly to find some answers."

"Meaning what?"

"I'm trying to find out why that man was murdered outside the club on Sunday night."

Her expression grew wary. "You're a cop *and* a restaurant owner?"

"Just a concerned citizen."

"Yeah, right."

"Did you ever talk to DeAndre Moore?"

"We all hustled him. That's our job."

"What did you think of him? What was he like?"

"He wasn't interested in a lap dance. Once I figured that out, I didn't spend another second on him. Nobody did."

"He say anything about Elvio Ramos?"

"You may not be a cop, but you sure act like one."

"Sorry, but this is important to me."

"Then why don't you go ask Elvio?"

"He's not talking. He admitted to the murder but refused to say why he'd done it."

"And you care because?"

Jane knew she had to offer something. "I'm a friend of the dead man's uncle."

"Ah. The light dawns."

"Look, if you think of anything that might help me—" She

pulled a business card out of her billfold. "That's a number where you can reach me."

Without looking at the card, Georgia stuffed it into her bustier. "Since you're here, why don't I reach you now. I'm a lot more fun than Avi." She brushed a lock of Jane's long brown hair away from her face. "Come over to a table and have a real conversation."

"Can't. I've got a friend in the hospital. Need to go see him."

She made a pouting face. "That's a drag. Well, whatever. As long as you come back real soon." She touched a finger to her lips, then pressed it to Jane's. "Be sweet."

14

The next morning, Jane's eyes swept up and down the snowy, car-lined street as she made her way to a run-down fourplex. North Minneapolis was one of the most violent, troubled neighborhoods in the state. Many residents lived in the area out of necessity, not choice.

At one time, the fourplex had had a security system. The rudiments were still visible, though it probably hadn't worked in decades. Jane trotted up the steps to the second floor and knocked on number 209. The door opened a crack, and a young boy with soft eyes and straight dark hair looked up at her curiously.

"Is your mom home?" she asked.

Behind the boy, a woman shouted in Spanish.

"Just a minute," he said, shutting the door with a scrape and a click.

Jane waited, hearing several voices speaking Spanish. Finally the door opened again, and a woman in brown cords and a pink hoodie stood before her.

"Mrs. Ramos?"

"*Sí?*"

Jane explained who she was and asked if she could come in,

"What is this about?" asked the woman in heavily accented English.

"I was hoping I could talk to you about your husband."

"Elvio?"

"About his arrest."

"Are you . . . *la policía*?"

"No," said Jane. She knew this would be tricky. The woman had every right to tell her to take a hike. "I'm a friend. I want to help."

The woman seemed skeptical. "How you help?"

"Can I come in? Just for a few seconds."

Opening the door with clear reluctance, Mrs. Ramos stepped back.

As Jane entered, she saw three children sitting on a beat-up overstuffed couch. The boy who'd answered the door was the oldest, around ten, she guessed. The other two were girls, one maybe six and the other a toddler. Across the room, an old TV was tuned to a news show. Morning sunlight flooded in through handmade flowered curtains, yellow, blue, red—vibrant, cheerful colors. It was a pleasant room, clean and organized, but sparsely furnished with what looked like garage-sale leftovers. There was no artwork on any of the walls, no photos or paintings, only a large wood crucifix hanging above a card table.

Mrs. Ramos motioned Jane to a chair.

Before she sat down, a young man holding a scrub brush came out of the bathroom, a cleaning cloth tossed over one shoulder. He scowled at Jane, concentrating the full weight of his attention on her, a challenge in his eyes.

Shifting in her chair, Jane tried to get comfortable. "I'm investigating the murder of DeAndre Moore."

"Investigating?" asked Mrs. Ramos.

"Just a couple of questions. Did your husband ever discuss Mr. Moore with you?"

"No kill," said Mrs. Ramos, shaking her head vigorously. "He no kill."

"Then why did he tell the police he did?"

"Elvio a good man. Kind man. Family man, you know? He love us, never hurt."

"Then I don't understand," said Jane. "He told the police he knifed Mr. Moore. If he didn't do it, why did he tell them he did?"

"He love us. He say, um, he . . . need to protect."

"Protect who?"

"Us. His family."

"From what?"

"Bad things."

"Did he get money from someone for doing it?"

"We have no money."

All the forensics pointed to Elvio. With an admission of guilt, he'd sealed his fate. This didn't make any sense.

"Have you talked to Elvio since he turned himself in?"

"On phone. He tell me no worry."

Jane didn't like to be flip, but it seemed to her that if his family truly believed they shouldn't worry, they were living on Mars.

"He will be home for the new baby. He promise."

"You're pregnant?"

She nodded, smiling faintly.

"How will you pay your bills while Elvio's in jail? Do you have a job?"

"No job," said Mrs. Ramos, eyes cast down.

Jane wondered if they were undocumented. If so, she was surprised immigration hadn't already come knocking on their door. Looking around at each of the faces, she wanted to help.

"I have a green card," said the young man standing in the bathroom doorway, "but I can't find a job."

"My brother-in-law," said Mrs. Ramos. "Luis."

"Did Elvio have a green card?" asked Jane.

Mrs. Ramos glanced up at Luis.

"Yeah, he did," said the man, a stubborn fierceness in his eyes.

By the look of guilt on Mrs. Ramos's face, Jane figured the green cards were fake.

"Listen," said Jane. "If Elvio is innocent, he shouldn't be in jail. The question is, what are you going to do until he gets out? You have to eat." She switched her gaze to Luis. "I can offer you a job as a dishwasher—just like what Elvio did. Are you interested?"

His expression lost some of its edge. "Where?"

She removed her billfold from the back pocket of her jeans, drawing out a business card. "The Xanadu Club. It's in Uptown. You know where that is?"

He nodded, taking the card and examining it. "Full-time?"

"Yes. Full-time. We've got two shifts. I'll have to see where we can fit you in. Meet me at the address on the bottom at, say, eleven tomorrow. That work for you?"

"I be there," he said.

It wouldn't be the first time she'd hired someone with a fake green card—unknowingly, of course. She handed another of her business cards to Mrs. Ramos. "If you need to get in touch with me, that's the number."

"You guardian angel."

"No. No angel. If you think of anything that could help me find out what really happened to DeAndre Moore, give me a call."

"I will," said Mrs. Ramos, folding her arms protectively around her stomach and smiling, this time, with more hope.

On her way to the Lyme House, Jane picked up Mouse. Frisky as always, he bounded into the backseat of her CR-V and shook off the snow clinging to his fur, ready for anything. Once she arrived, parking in the rear lot, she made sure he was well settled in her office, fetching him clean water and a treat, then headed back upstairs to look at the reservation terminal. She spent most of her time, when she wasn't working on a case with Nolan, at the Lyme House, going less and less often to the Xanadu Club, particularly since she'd taken on Barry as a partner. His management group had persuaded her to make some changes in the day-to-day operation. She had to admit that the receipts had gone up since Barry and his team had come on board, and yet Jane wasn't entirely happy with the new situation. Spending less time on the premises, trying to keep in touch with what was going on mainly from receipts and written reports, wasn't working as well as she'd hoped.

"Hey, Brit," she said, cruising through the dining room. Brit was one of the waitstaff. She was setting up the tables for lunch, which wouldn't begin for another hour. "How's your mom?"

"Better," said Brit, smoothing a wrinkle in one of the white tablecloths. "My husband and I brought her home from the hospital two nights ago."

"Can she stay by herself?"

"With a little help from us, yeah."

"Give her my best," said Jane, sailing into the front entry. She was about to turn her attention to the evening's seating chart when Cordelia, wearing an ankle-length faux mink coat and matching hat, burst through the double front doors along with a gust of cold wind.

"You always manage to make an entrance," said Jane.

Cordelia twirled around. "Aren't I sparkly?"

"It's new, I take it."

"Brand spankin'. You're the first to see it. Well, you and Hattie and Bolger."

"Would you like something to eat? Coffee?"

"I could be persuaded."

Jane directed her downstairs to her office, saying that Mouse was already inside and would love to see her. "Don't trip over your coat."

"I am grace personified."

Joining them a few minutes later, Jane brought with her a tray of tea and hot scones, fresh from the oven, with a special brandied strawberry jam and clotted cream.

"A cream tea," oohed Cordelia.

"You built a fire."

"Wood? Kindling? Seemed like a no-brainer." Dropping down on the couch and stuffing a napkin into her cleavage, she added, "I haven't had a cream tea in forever."

They sat with the tray between them. Mouse sniffed the food as closely as he dared, eventually lying down on the rug in front of the fireplace.

"Are you ever going to tell me your secret?" asked Jane, thinking that this was a perfect time.

"Not until I have all my duckies in a row."

"Are the duckies proving difficult?"

"One or two of them. Let's change the subject. What did you think of our foray into strip-land the other night?"

"I think," said Jane, pouring more tea, "that GaudyLights isn't the treasure trove of information I thought it would be. Even so, I think there's more dirt to mine."

"So our visit was *merely* part of your investigation."

"What else would it be?"

Cordelia flashed a smile pregnant with meaning.

"It's hardly my scene."

"Okay, but you and that bartender seemed to hit it off."

Cordelia saw romance around every corner. Jane found it tiresome. "She's nice."

Cordelia nearly choked on her scone. "Nice? Come *on*, girlfriend. She's a knockout. Babe-o-delic! With those dark Rachel Maddow eyes? Wake up and smell the freakin' coffee."

"I did learn something this morning," said Jane, leaning back against the couch cushion.

"You changed the subject. I want you to know that I *know* you changed it. You rarely do that unless you're hiding something."

"Oh, give it a rest. Yes, I thought the bartender was attractive." She tapped the napkin against her lips. "Just saying."

"Do you want to hear this or not?"

"If I'm going to solve DeAndre's murder by dint of my intuitive genius, you need to keep me up to speed."

Jane struggled mightily not to roll her eyes. "I spoke to Elvio Ramos's family. His wife said that he turned himself in to the police to protect them."

"From what?"

"She didn't know, but she said he told her he was innocent."

"What would you expect her to say? That she was married to a cold-blooded killer?"

"Honestly? I think she believes it. If he turned himself in to the police to protect his family, what was he protecting them from?"

"Good question."

"Who *was* DeAndre Moore? When did he arrive? Where did he stay? Why did he spend so much time at GaudyLights?"

"Boy," said Cordelia, selecting another scone, "you've really got your work cut out for you."

"I thought *you* solved the crimes."

"After you present me with all the necessary information. I'm kind of like Nero Wolfe. I stick around the house sniffing orchids and dining well."

"So if I need to spend another night or two over at Gaudy-Lights, you won't come with me?"

"Never said that."

"Be honest. What do you think of that place? The nudity. Sex, or the illusion of sex, for money. Are the dancers victims or victimizers, whores selling their bodies or artists selling their talent?"

"I've read the odd feminist tome that makes a case for each."

"But what's your gut reaction?"

"I've got nothing against nudity and sexuality. I certainly prefer it to violence and Puritanism."

"Some would say that what these women have to do to make money *is* a kind of violence."

Cordelia picked up the last scone and thought about it. "One of the actors in last year's repertory company told me that she'd stripped when she was young. She said it was hard work, but that the money was beyond anything she could make anywhere else. She stressed that people often make assumptions that aren't always justified. If you're really interested in the topic, why don't you talk to a few of the dancers and see what they have to say."

"I might just do that." Jane spread more jam on her scone. "If I headed over to GaudyLights again tonight, would you come along?"

"Can't," Cordelia said, scraping cream off her chin with her pinky. "I need to be at the theater. Not to change the subject, but how is Nolan?"

"I talked to him this morning before I left the house. They had him up at six, gave him a bath and breakfast. The pain was bad during the night, and he had some nasty muscle spasms, but he's on a new drug that seems to be handling it. He said they were getting him up this afternoon."

"Heavens. So soon?"

"Seems kind of fast to me, too. I guess they want everyone up and moving as quickly as possible."

"What about the numbness in his leg?"

"It's still numb. The doctor thinks he'll slowly begin to get some feeling back in it when the swelling from the surgery goes down. I'm planning to spend part of the afternoon at the hospital—until he kicks me out."

"I thought I'd stop by on my way to the theater. I have a get-well present for him."

"I should warn you. All he wants is a pack of cigarettes."

"Then he's in luck. I bought cigarettes. They're Belgian chocolate."

"I'm not sure—"

"He'll love them."

Jane smiled over her teacup. "That's really sweet of you."

"I know," she said, taking a last bite of scone. "I'm awesome."

After the lunch rush was over, Jane led Mouse outside for some fresh air and exercise—his exercise, her fresh air. It was a lovely winter day, with brilliant sunlight and cobalt blue skies. The moderating temperature, balmy by Minnesota standards, was causing rivulets of water to run down the sidewalks, creating puddles that would eventually refreeze and turn treacherous.

Sitting down on the loading dock, her legs dangling over the edge, Jane unclipped Mouse's leash and urged him to run around the overflow lot. He seemed to understand the rules. He wasn't allowed to go down to the lake or disappear into the section of woods that bordered the property.

Jane was making a mental list of what she needed to check out next in the Moore investigation when she heard the door open behind her. She turned around. Instead of one of her kitchen staff, a woman in a heavy wool shirt jacket, black jeans, and chunky horn-rimmed glasses stepped out onto the deck. Jane didn't recognize her at first.

"I asked at the front desk if they knew where you were. You have a minute?"

"Avi?" said Jane, grinning broadly, despite her best efforts at nonchalance. "You weren't wearing glasses at GaudyLights."

"Contacts. Glasses make me look kind of bookish and nerdy. Thing is, I can't stand wearing contacts all the time. I thought I'd find *you* wearing chef whites."

"Not anymore. Too old."

"Oh, please."

"No, really. When I opened the restaurant I was in my early thirties. As the chef/owner, I did everything. Spent seventy hours a week here. By the time I turned forty, I'd pretty much stopped working in the kitchen."

"You never cook anymore?"

"I step in occasionally, when there's a need. My skills are still reasonably good." She paused. "To what do I owe the pleasure of this visit?"

Avi's gaze swept over the snow-covered lake, the back lot, the small section of woods. "Beautiful setting for a restaurant. Is that your dog?"

Jane whistled for Mouse. His ears immediately pricked up, and he came running back to the dock.

"Is he a Lab?"

"The prince of Labs," said Jane. "Avi—" She paused. "I don't know your last name."

"Greenberg."

"Avi Greenberg, meet Mouse."

Avi reacted with a slow smile. "That's some name. Kind of like naming a pet moose Goldfish."

Jane laughed. "You like dogs?"

"I wish I had the kind of life where I could have one." She sucked in a breath, held it. "I was hoping you'd have a minute to talk."

"You want to stay out here? We could go inside if it's too cold."

"I like the cold." She crouched, then sat down next to Jane.

"You seem so concerned about that murder in the alley outside the club—" She looked up at the sky. "The police officer who questioned me . . . I don't know. I had a bad feeling about him. Guess I don't like cops. I could see myself sitting in some windowless room for the rest of the night with Mr. Asshole hammering at me for information I didn't have. The thing is, I do have something, and I really would like to tell someone what I know. Not that it probably means anything."

"What?" said Jane.

"See, the thing is, Moore told me he'd come to town looking for his sister."

Jane's eyes narrowed. "Did he find her?"

"I think so, yes."

"Who is she?"

"He never said. He was a nice guy, you know? Friendly. Easygoing. But he also seemed . . . tense."

"Because of his sister?"

"That was my guess."

"Did he spend a lot of time at the club?"

"I worked Tuesday through Sunday. He was there every night."

"How many black strippers are employed at the club?"

"Two. Sometimes a third shows up, when she needs money."

"Did you see him spending time with them?"

"I know he talked to Sharona more than once. I also saw him with Ebony."

"Is either of them scheduled to work tonight?"

"No idea."

"I'll give the club a call. I appreciate the tip." Noticing a ring on Avi's hand, Jane said, "You're wearing a wedding band."

"Trick of the trade."

"You get hit on a lot?"

"What do you think?"

Jane adjusted her sunglasses. "I guess I don't understand why you'd want to work in a place like GaudyLights."

"All the hot babes."

"Seriously?"

"Why not?"

Jane wasn't sure how far she wanted to take this conversation. "For me, sexiness is more than just showing skin and acting seductive. The stuff that goes on at GaudyLights feels like a game to me. An act. At first the boldness of it startles you, maybe even charms you a little because it's so defiant, so—"

"Badass."

"Yeah. But it doesn't take long before it just seems silly."

"To you, maybe. You'd get an argument from most of the men." With her eyes fixed on Mouse in the distance, she said, "You might be interested to know that probably a third of the current dancers are lesbians."

"Are you kidding me?"

"Sometimes it's easier for a woman to go home to a woman after a day spent in the primeval swamps. Less to wrap your head around."

"I'll have to think about that one."

"Straights don't usually get it."

"I'm hardly straight."

"But in a way you are. See, the straight world, the good God-fearing folk, don't much like our kind. I stripped for a few years, so I'm part of the tribe. To be clear, the good God-fearing folk make up most of our clientele."

"You have no problem with what goes on at the club?"

"I have more problems with what happens on Wall Street than what happens at GaudyLights."

She had a point.

"Okay, so I have lots of problems, but they come from being an insider, not an outsider. I don't judge. The dancers come from all kinds of backgrounds. Republicans. Democrats. Working class. Middle class. Real estate agents looking to make some extra bucks because houses aren't selling. Several are single moms trying to make a good living so they have more time with their kids— more time than a nine-to-five job would allow them. To make the same kind of money they make at GaudyLights for two or three nights' work, they'd need to be on a major career path, where they'd work fifty, sixty hours every week. A bunch of the girls are putting themselves through school. Sure, we've also got the Druggernaut contingent—the stoners, the cokeheads. Stripping can be emotional quicksand, and drugs help. I didn't love every minute of it, but I have mainly good memories. The trick was, I got out before they turned bad. It was terrific money, and I made some lifelong friends. Maybe that puts me squarely in the slut category. I don't know. It's why strippers don't tell people what they do for a living. You chuck *that* little factoid into the pool of a stagnant cocktail party conversation and the ripples never stop."

"You're saying it's another closet. Like being gay."

"I won't deny some parallels."

"Why did you quit?"

"Like Dolly Parton once said, 'It takes a lot of money to look this cheap.' It also took a ton of my time. Bartending is a better fit."

"So what do you like about bartending?"

Avi glanced over at her with an amused expression. "What is this? Twenty questions?"

"Being nosy is part of my charm."

"Is that right."

"Honestly, I'd like to know."

"Well, I guess for one thing, I love that feeling of being suspended in semidarkness. Then there's the music. Always love the music. I like that everybody knows the rules at a place like

GaudyLights. Sure, it's shallow and superficial. It can also be coarse and disgusting. One thing you learn right off is that nobody on this earth is Hollywood perfect. We're nothing like the images sold to us on the silver screen. Everyone is damaged, sometimes sweaty, always needy. For me, because I live so much of my life inside my head, I see the time I spend at the club as taking a break from myself. You know what I mean?"

"Boy, do I."

Mouse trotted up with a stick in his mouth. Jane tugged it free and tossed it halfway across the lot.

"When I grow up, I want to be a writer," said Avi. "How clichéd is that?"

"I think that's great. Listen, are you hungry?"

She raised an eyebrow. "Is the food here good?"

"We're not Eleven Madison Park or Le Bernardin, but my prejudiced view is that we're the best in the Twin Cities. You like fresh oysters?"

"My God, yes."

"We got some in this morning that are amazing. Have lunch with me. If you want, I can give you the full tour of the place when we're done."

"On one condition. That it's my turn to be nosy about you."

"I'm not sure my life's been as interesting as yours."

"I'll be the judge of that."

"Do I have to answer all questions put to me?" asked Jane, getting up and brushing off the back of her brown cords.

"In excruciating detail," said Avi, rising and standing next to her, a good three inches taller.

"All my dirty little secrets?"

"Every last delicious one of them."

Jane whistled for Mouse. "That will make this a *very* short meal."

15

Instead of working out, as he always did before he left for the club, Vince sat on his stationary bicycle in his undershirt and sweatpants, trying to decide if it was time to call Emmett Washington and ring the alarm bell. After receiving no reply from his e-mail to Ken Crowder, his nerves were jangling like alarm bells. He'd made it clear that he needed to hear back from him immediately.

Crowder was a businessman, as was Vince. They both understood the necessity of simple, quick communication. He hadn't asked for a long letter, just an e-mail that said, "I'm alive."

"I'm taking our clothes to the cleaners this afternoon," said Shelly as she sailed through the room, picking up the dirty towels Vince had tossed on the carpet.

Vince jumped, startled by her sudden appearance.

"You want me to take any of your suits?"

"Probably." He couldn't believe that the mere appearance of his wife had caused his heart to pound—and not in a good way.

She stopped, looking down at him. "You upset about something?"

"Take my gray pinstripe. And maybe the navy Hickey Freeman."

"Have you had lunch? I could fix you a sandwich."

"I'll get something at the club."

On the way out the door, Shelly said, "I'm having dinner with my father tonight. If it gets late, I may stay over."

"Give him my best."

She left the room humming.

Her good mood meant she was probably high on one of her self-help books. If life could only be that simple.

Vince had no sooner switched to a different program on the stationary bike than his cell phone rang.

Rushing over to the table where he'd left it, he barked, "Bessetti."

"Hey, Vincesky, it's Ken."

Relief flooded every cell of his body.

"I got your e-mail a few minutes ago. I'm up at my cabin. Drove in last night around midnight. Hey, man, that's awful news about Rudmann."

Vince sank down on a padded bench. "You have no idea how glad I am to hear your voice."

"What's going on? You think Tatum and Rudmann's deaths are connected?"

"Yeah. Maybe."

"Too much blow, my brother. I had to get off the stuff. It was making me crazy."

"I'm probably making too much of it. As long as you're okay—"

"Never better. What about brother Emmett?"

"He's good. Drinking again, but good."

"I've been thinking. Why don't you fly out? You could catch a plane to Salt Lake, rent a car and drive up. It's only forty miles. If you didn't bring your wife, we could have ourselves one hell of a hot time. I've got connections in town like you wouldn't believe. Bring Emmett if you want."

"When was the last time you talked to him?"

"Forever."

"He got all religious when he met his wife. I don't think he'd add to the fun."

"Good to know. Scratch our soul brother."

"When are you talking about?"

"Now. Tomorrow. Next week, I don't care. I'm staying here for a month. Don't have to be back in Salt Lake until mid-March. The Sundance Festival is over. The town's back to peace and quiet. This place I bought, it's like a slice of heaven — or as close as you and me are ever likely to get. What do you say?"

"I'll have to do some checking, see what I can swing."

"You got my phone number up here?"

"Nothing to write on. E-mail it to me."

"Will do. How about you call me back tonight and let me know one way or the other. If you're coming, I need to make plans, get stuff ready."

"I'll call," said Vince. "I really need a break. I think you just saved my life."

"I'm cooking dinner tonight for Jerry and Ingrid Johnson— ever heard of them?"

"Not that I remember."

"Local celebrities. They own Lookout Pass, the famous ski resort up here. Anyway, they live just down the road and take care of my place when I'm gone. They're elderly, so they go to bed early. After they leave, I've got a bunch of guys coming over to play poker. I'll be home all evening. Make it happen, Vincesky. Life's too short."

Emmett ordered himself a double Scotch on the rocks. He felt guilty about it after what he'd told his son last night, but he needed something to steady him. Just this one last time. It was probably too early in the day for hard liquor, especially in front of a fellow pilot, and yet when the waitress had asked him if he wanted something from the bar, he responded without thinking. He couldn't do the meeting without it.

"You haven't submitted the report yet, have you?" asked Ted Kulakov, his first officer on last Monday night's flight.

"I promised we'd talk about it. I keep my promises." Emmett leaned back as the waitress set the Scotch in front of him. Ted had ordered coffee. Okay, so he wasn't using alcohol to keep himself from going under, but he looked every bit as ragged as Emmett felt.

Lifting the glass to his lips, Emmett spilled some of the Scotch on his blue oxford cloth shirt. It was then that he realized his hands were shaking. "You had any trouble sleeping?"

Ted pointed to the bags under his eyes.

"Did you talk to your wife?"

"Hell, no."

"To anyone?"

"I'm not crazy. Or maybe I am."

Their eyes met, and then, as if on cue, each looked away.

"So what are we going to do?" asked Emmett.

"Has Kingston been on your ass about the report?"

Emmett took another swallow of Scotch. "Not yet. I've been doing some research. This has happened before. As I see it, the question is, was the plane ever in any real danger? I think the answer is yes."

"Hell," said Ted. "I just want it all to go away."

"But we have a responsibility to the airline. To the passengers we serve."

"My biggest responsibility is to my family. We tell anyone the truth and our asses are on the line. I didn't mention this before, but I've been offered a job by a private party."

"Corporate jet?"

"No, it's a single guy looking for a pilot for his Bombardier Global Express. You ever seen one of those babies? They're incredible. State of the art. I'd be flying him all over the world. Big money. If we come clean about what happened and this guy hears about it, which he will, I don't have a prayer."

"Would you gentlemen like to order?" asked a waitress, stepping up to their table.

Emmett wasn't hungry. He hadn't even looked at the menu. Neither had Ted. "We're good for now."

"Can I get you another drink?"

Emmett couldn't believe the Scotch was almost gone. "Sure. Why not."

After she'd walked away, Ted said, "You're hitting that kind of hard."

"None of your business."

He shrugged, turning the coffee cup around in his hands. "When you write the report, just tell them what we told the passengers. It was turbulence."

"It wasn't."

"Okay, so . . . the airspeed indicator, then. We're not lying about that. We got conflicting reports."

"You don't put an aircraft into a steep dive because of a faulty airspeed indicator."

"We almost stalled."

"And we made the correction." Emmett closed his eyes. It was all still there, still visible, like a movie running inside his head. The loss of instrumentation. The static when he tried to radio the tower. "Do you believe in God, Ted?"

"What the hell's that got to do with anything?"

"I would think it would be obvious."

"You think God saved us?" asked Ted.

He'd completely missed the point.

"Yeah, I believe in God. Some kind of God."

"The Christian God?" asked Emmett.

"I don't know. Yeah, probably. Come on, what are we going to do?" This time, there was an edge in his voice. "We need a plausible explanation."

Emmett shook his head. "I don't have one. I don't know what to do."

Except, for all his overheated mental calculations, he did know. He'd known all along. He had to respond to this challenge ethically because it was his second chance. He'd never anticipated that life would offer him one, but it had. Once before he'd come to a fundamental crossroads, and he'd made a devastatingly bad decision. This time would be different. He would tell the truth. Before he did, however, he needed to build a case. Whether or not Ted was on board with it was of no particular relevance. Emmett had information AirNorth needed to take seriously. If Kingston didn't want to hear it, he'd take it to someone higher up.

Jane's lunch with Avi stretched for several hours, as she ordered small plates of all the Lyme House's signature dishes. She was delighted that Avi was such an avid—and appreciative—eater. After lunch, as the afternoon sun made its slow decent over Lake Harriet, they took Mouse for a walk along the wooded path, staggering a little under the weight of all they'd eaten, all the wine they'd drunk. At one point, Jane slipped on a patch of ice. Avi caught her just in time before she fell headfirst into a patch of snow-covered bushes. They held on to each other a little longer than necessary, finding themselves staring into each other's eyes. Smiling awkwardly, they hooked arms and continued on their way, talking about anything and everything. Books. Movies. Politics. Their childhoods. What made them happy and what made them laugh. Jane began to shiver, though not from the cold.

By five, they were sitting at a small dining room table in Avi's apartment, drinking Darjeeling.

"That was an amazing afternoon," said Avi, patting her stomach contentedly. "You were right about the food."

"We try."

"You're sure you want to read one of my novels? Makes me kind of nervous. They're all pretty bad."

"How many did you say you've written?"

"Since I graduated with my MFA, six. Before that, maybe three. They're dreck."

"According to whom?"

"Agents. Editors."

"So you've tried to get them published?"

"A few of them. It's a lost cause. I don't know why I keep trying."

This was the first time Avi had opened up about any source of heartache in her life. At lunch, she'd spoken of the close relationship she had with her older sister. Both parents were still alive and well, living in Pittsburgh, where she'd grown up. When she'd come out, everyone in the family had been okay with it, except for her father, a man who was deeply conservative and hadn't been all that pleased to learn his youngest daughter was gay. Yet as time went on, he'd mellowed. Given that Avi had been a stripper, she figured that people would assume she'd led, if nothing else, at least an interesting life. The truth was, her life had been deeply unremarkable, even boring. Not exactly the fodder she'd been looking for as a writer.

She seemed like an open book, easily answering any question Jane put to her. She'd been with four women, three for a couple of years, one for over five. She wasn't dating anyone at the moment. A romantic, she assumed that the woman of her dreams was out there. She fell in love easily and underscored that she saw that particular quality as a flaw.

"So, what are some of the titles of your novels?" asked Jane, lifting the teapot and pouring them more tea.

"Oh, wow." Avi scratched the side of her head, scrunching up her face in thought. "Well, *Attaboy*. That was the one I was working on when I was in grad school. Then *Skin Ticket*. *Bleeding with Humor*. And *Someone of Account*. That's the one I'm working on right now."

"What's your favorite book?"

"Always the one I'm working on. It isn't finished, so I still have hope."

"Are they literary novels? Romance? Mysteries?"

"More commercial than literary," said Avi. "General fiction, I suppose."

"Which one can I read?"

She crooked her finger at Jane and then got up and walked into her bedroom.

As Avi dug through the boxes on the shelf in her closet, Jane stepped over to a beat-up old desk, where a laptop rested next to a can of Mountain Dew. In back of the soda can was a five-by-seven picture frame. The photo was of a little girl hugging a teddy bear and wearing oversized dark glasses. Turning around, Jane saw that Avi was watching her.

"That's Gracie," said Avi, a manuscript tucked under her arm. "She's my niece."

"She's beautiful."

"Yeah." She lifted the frame out of Jane's hand and set it back down on the desk.

Jane was put off by the move, sensing a coldness grow between them. "What did you choose?" she asked, changing the subject.

"*Skin Ticket*. Be honest, okay? If you hate it, and you probably will, just stop reading and give it back."

"It's not good to be so down on your writing."

"Yeah, I know. I've had so many rejections."

"Besides the editors and agents, have you shown it to friends?"

"There aren't many people I trust."

"Distrust is a terrible habit. Do you trust me?"

Holding Jane's gaze, she said, "Not sure why I should, but yeah, I guess I must."

"I like that."

"I like it that you like it."

They stared at each other. Jane had the sense that neither of them knew quite what to do.

Breaking the spell, Avi said, "Want more tea?"

"You know, I have a friend in the hospital. I should probably—"

"Right. I remember you saying."

"I'm sure I'll be up all night reading."

"Ugh. You're going to think I'm utterly lame."

Jane brushed a hand down Avi's arm. "I'm never going to think that. I can't guarantee I'll love the book, but it will have no bearing on how I feel about you."

"Just so I know . . . you'd describe those feelings *how*?"

"Evolving," said Jane, leaning close, touching her lips to Avi's. "Definitely evolving."

16

Jane arrived at the hospital a few minutes after seven, taking the elevator up to Five West. Striding to the end of a long hallway, she turned left and made her way to the midpoint in another long corridor, all along the way feeling a sense of revulsion at the faint though unmistakable hospital stink, literally cringing when she glanced into some of the patient rooms. She'd spent way too much time in hospitals for one reason or another—her mother's final illness, friends and family who'd become ill or been the victims of accidents, a few visits of her own. She couldn't imagine what kind of personality it would take to willingly spend time working in a place like this. She was glad there were people out there who wanted to do it, because she sure didn't.

She found Nolan in bed, looking flushed, the television on across the room, the man in the bed closest to the window gone.

At her questioning look, Nolan said, "He made a prison break this morning. Lucky him."

Jane stood by his bedside, folding her hand around his. "How did it feel to get up?"

"I've been in bed all day. Seems I've spiked a temperature."

"Because?"

"An infection."

Not good news.

"It's handled. They've started me on an antibiotic, said I'd feel better by tomorrow morning." His face was drawn tight with fatigue.

"Are you in pain?"

"Some."

"Can you sleep?"

"That's all I've been doing."

She squeezed his hand. "I've got some good news. I found out why your nephew was in town."

He turned toward her. "Why?"

"He came looking for his sister."

"He doesn't have a sister."

That stopped her. "He doesn't?"

"Where'd you get this bogus piece of information?"

"One of the bartenders at the club."

"Well, either he's lying or he doesn't know what the hell he's talking about."

"He's a she. She said she talked to DeAndre several times and that's what he told her. I don't know why she'd lie to me."

"People lie all the time."

"Maybe DeAndre lied to her."

"Why?"

"What about his biological family?"

"He was an only child, thank God."

Not what she wanted to hear.

"I'm glad you're still working the investigation. Not just for my sister and her family, but for me. The longer it goes unsolved—"

"I hear you," said Jane. "I won't let you down."

"I wish I could be out there with you. My brain's so scrambled

125

by these drugs that I can't even think straight." His gaze drifted toward the windows.

She'd been sure that Avi's information was the break they'd been looking for. She couldn't imagine why she would lie. Not that Jane knew her very well. Then again, she knew DeAndre even less.

"Listen, Jane, will you do me a favor?"

"Anything."

"You've got the keys to my house, right?"

"In my pocket."

"This is small potatoes, but there's an ivy plant by the window in the kitchen that I've somehow managed to keep alive. It was one of my wife's pride-and-joys. I'd hate to think it will kick the bucket because I can't be there to water it."

"Done," said Jane.

"While you're at it, better cancel my mail. There's probably a pile inside the front door."

"I'll stop by your house after I leave. Anything else?"

Closing his eyes, he said, "Yeah. Tackle anybody who comes in here and wants to take my temperature or my blood pressure. They're sadists. Every last one of them."

Jane leaned over and scooped the mail up off the rug in Nolan's front hall. After dumping it on the dining room table, she turned on a couple of lights, adjusting the shades so they were only partway open. Checking the thermostat on the way to the kitchen, she turned the heat in the house down to sixty.

When she'd watered the solitary ivy perched on a shelf next to the window overlooking the backyard, she washed the dishes in the sink, letting them dry in the dish rack while she took out the garbage. She spent a few minutes with a shovel, cleaning the sidewalks and tossing some salt over patches of ice.

Back inside, she drifted around the quiet house, thinking of the times she'd spent here with Nolan, eating dinner or working in his basement office, the friendship they'd forged through good and bad. Spread out on the coffee table in the living room was an old family album, one Jane had never seen before. She knew so little about Nolan's early years. His wife, May, had died before Jane and Nolan had met. He'd shown her a few pictures of May, but as Jane lowered herself down on the couch, she saw snapshots of a young Nolan and his wife, long-ago images that both fascinated and charmed her. She wanted nothing more than to sit and go through the album, page by page, absorbing as much as she could about his past, and yet on the way over she'd begun to think that since she wasn't spending the evening at the hospital, she should probably head over to the Xanadu Club. It had been a couple of weeks since she'd put in an appearance.

On a whim, Jane closed the album and carried it into the dining room, where she'd hung her peacoat on a chair. She poked through the mail, finding a thick manila envelope at the bottom of the stack. The city hall return address caught her eye. Inside she found DeAndre's wallet, ring, watch, keys, and belt and a small red address book. A form letter stated that the deceased's effects had been processed and were being returned. Leaving everything on the table except the wallet and the address book, which she stuffed into her coat pocket, she took one more look around to make sure everything was in order. Feeling satisfied, she returned to her CR-V, where she took out her cell and punched in the number for the assistant manager at the Xanadu.

"Butch," said a distracted voice.

Butch who? she thought. "This is Jane Lawless."

"Oh, hi."

"Where's Rich?" Rich was the evening shift manager.

"He's . . . unavailable."

"What's that mean?"

"He's . . . you know. Busy."

"Who are you?"

"I'm the new cashier."

In the background she could hear a rock band playing, people laughing. Barry's company had done a study that showed that the Uptown crowd was more interested in rock and salsa than early jazz. Jane couldn't exactly argue since business was up.

"How's everything going?"

"Good." He didn't sound entirely sure.

"What is it?"

"Well, actually, the kitchen service has been a bit bumpy. One of the deep fryers quit on us, and the sink in the prep kitchen is all backed up. It's a mess."

"Call Hanson's Appliance for the fryer and Conrad's Plumbing for the prep sink."

"We're not using them anymore. Barry gave us the number of a guy he knows."

"A guy?"

"Yeah. A friend of his."

"Is he there?"

"Not yet."

"When did the fryer go out?"

"A couple hours ago."

"Listen, Butch. Do I have your attention?"

"Yeah."

"If this *guy* isn't there in five minutes—*five* minutes—call Hanson's. You got that?"

"Sure, but Barry—"

"I don't care what Barry said. And call Conrad's Plumbing before the backup spreads."

"Okay, boss. It's your call."

Damn right it was, thought Jane. "How many tables have we turned over?"

"We've had a waiting list since we opened for dinner. Don't see it disappearing anytime soon."

At least that was good news.

"Everything's under control. No worries. Rich's got it covered."

What Jane really wanted was to spend the rest of the night working on the Moore homicide. Restaurant owners didn't get nights off, she reminded herself, not if they wanted their businesses to thrive. Then again, that's why she'd brought in a partner. Either she trusted him or she didn't. If she didn't, why the hell was she in business with him?

"Ms. Lawless, you still there?"

She felt incredibly conflicted. "I may stop by later."

"Really? Okay. Whatever. I got a line of people in front of me here—"

"You go." She hung up, struggling to put her concerns on the back burner as she headed home.

17

After feeding Mouse his dinner of kibble and meat scraps, Jane made herself a sandwich and carried it back to her study along with Avi's manuscript. She wanted to dig in right away but felt she needed to do some work first. She ate at her desk while going through DeAndre's wallet, finding the usual: driver's license, cash, credit cards, a few photos, and a key card to a hotel room where he'd probably been staying, though there was no identifying information on either side, just a generic picture of Minnehaha Falls.

She studied the driver's license photo, one that showed a clean-shaven young man with a broad, open face, an infectious smile, and a gold link chain around his neck. His skin was lighter than Nolan's, his hair close cropped.

Turning to the address book, she found Nolan's phone number, along with phone numbers for pizza takeout and Chinese food. Several women's names had stars next to them. A few of the entries were simply first names. Jane figured that these were DeAndre's brothers or friends. Selecting one at random, a guy named Derrick, she tapped in the number. A couple of rings later, she was put through to voice mail. She left her name and cell number, gave a brief explanation for the call, and hung up. After striking out three more times, she flipped to the back of the book and tried another name. This time, she got lucky.

"Hello?" said a male voice.

"Is this Omar?"

"Who wants to know?"

She pulled her notepad closer and explained who she was and why she was calling. "You're a friend of DeAndre's?"

"Lady, we been best buds since seventh grade. I can't believe what happened to him. You say you're a friend of D's uncle Alf?"

"That's right."

"He and D were tight."

"It was a huge blow."

"Yeah. D's mom called me yesterday, told me what happened. I mean, shit like this shouldn't happen to a guy like D. His family's planning a memorial service for him next weekend. I'm scheduled to work. Gotta get that day off."

"Would you mind answering a couple of questions?"

"Like what?"

"Do you know why he was in Minneapolis?"

"Yeah."

He seemed to need prodding. "Why?"

"He was looking for someone."

"Do you know who?"

"Yeah."

At this rate, the conversation could take forever. "His sister?"

Silence. "How'd you know that?"

"I'm told he doesn't have a sister."

"That's what most people think."

"But he does."

"Her name's Sabrina. Eight or nine years older than him. From his bio family, not his adopted one."

"How come his adoptive family doesn't know about her?"

"D never told them. Sabrina was already out of the house when he was put in foster care. He said she was wild. In and out of ju-vie. He was, like, scared, you know? He didn't want his new fam-ily to think he was anything like her. I told him he was crazy, but he kept thinking that there was a chance that they might send him back to foster care if they found out."

"Did DeAndre and his sister keep in touch?"

"Saw each other from time to time—until she took off. All of a sudden. D was in a lather about it, too."

"Why'd she leave?"

"No idea. But D knew. He seemed really worried, like some-thing bad had gone down. I'm not sure how he tracked her to Minneapolis, but right after he did, he took off."

"Can you describe what she looks like?"

"Never met the woman."

"Do you know anything about her?"

"Just that she used to work in a strip club."

"As a stripper?"

"Duh, yeah."

If the sister was eight or nine years older than DeAndre, it meant she was at least thirty-seven years old. Was that too old to dance at a strip club? "Do you know where DeAndre was staying in Minneapolis?"

"Sorry. He didn't think he'd be gone more than a day or two. Said he'd call"—Omar's voice thickened—"when he got back."

"I'm sorry for your loss," said Jane, underlining the word "Gaudy" on her notepad, "and I appreciate the information. If you think of anything else that might be helpful, would you call me?" She gave him her number, waiting while he wrote it down.

"I heard he was knifed by some d-bag dishwasher. I can't help but wonder if he ever connected with Sabrina. If she had something to do with it."

"That's what I'm working on," said Jane.

"Good luck," said Omar. "If you figure it out, will you call me?"

"I will." Hearing her doorbell, Jane offered a quick good-bye.

Dashing through the house to the front door, she ordered Mouse to sit. He skidded to a stop, perched on his still-wagging tail.

Cordelia stood outside on the steps holding a white sack and a magnum of Piper-Heidsieck. "Time to celebrate."

"Celebrate what?" asked Jane.

"I've come to tell you my secret—if I don't freeze to death first."

Jane stood back. Once Cordelia had greeted Mouse properly, she tapped him on the nose and said, "No champagne for you, mister—but I didn't forget you." She dug into the pocket of her buffalo plaid hunting jacket and removed a peanut butter dog treat, Mouse's favorite. She made him sit down before she flipped it to him. Turning to Jane, she said, "Get two champagne flutes and a couple of plates. I suggest we reconvene in the living room."

"Sounds like a plan."

When they were finally ensconced on the couch, Cordelia divvied up the chocolate mascarpone cakes from D'Amico's Deli and poured the champagne.

"What do we drink to?" asked Jane.

"To my new life." She stood, jumped up on the footstool, raised her glass, and struck a Wagnerian pose.

"What new life?"

"Drink first. Explanation to follow."

Jane rose, and they clicked classes.

"Nice," said Jane after taking a sip.

"Only the best. Now build us a fire." She jumped down.

"Are you attempting to prolong the suspense?"

"I'm savoring the moment."

Jane worked quickly to get the fire going, all the while stealing glances at Cordelia, who seemed to be off in another world. Once the logs had caught, she picked up her glass and sat down on the rocker next to the hearth. "So?"

Cordelia drained her glass, then smacked her lips. "You knew my contract was up at the theater, right? That I was in negotiations."

"Yes, but you said it was nothing to worry about. You were sure they were going to offer you four more years."

"I met with the board this afternoon."

"And?"

Flashing her eyes, she said, "I tendered my resignation."

"Excuse me?"

"My term as artistic director at the AGRT will end in April. Ten years. It was a great run, but it's time for a change."

Jane was stunned. Cordelia had said nothing to her about any of this. "I know you've had your issues with the board."

"I am so done with that theater," she said, pouring them each another glass of bubbly. "I mean, every year the board gets more conservative. I like musical comedy as much as the next person, I like Tennessee Williams, Oscar Wilde, and Thornton Wilder, but come on. How many times do we have to sit through *Cat on a Hot Tin Roof* before we all puke in unison? *Blithe Spirit. Our Town. Lady Windermere's Fan.* Please! I made a suggestion last fall. I thought it might prove interesting to revive *The Cradle Will Rock,* just to mix things up a little. I mean, such a pedigree. Written by Marc Blitzstein. Originally produced as part of the Federal Theater Project during the Depression, directed by Orson Welles, produced by John Houseman. When the board got wind of it, they nearly choked to death on their communal ire."

"It's a controversial musical."

"What's wrong with controversy?"

"Might hurt ticket sales?"

"Or it might encourage them. I'm sick to death of working with such timid minds."

"Do you have another job lined up?"

Cordelia eyebrows danced. "Don't need one."

"And why is that?"

"Because I'm starting my own theater. I've been looking around for just the right property, and I think I found it. Did you ever go to the Phoenix Rising Playhouse? It's on Twelfth and Harvard Place, close to Loring Park. It was rehabbed in the early seventies by a couple of friends of mine. Very trendy at the time. They painted the interior a bunch of garish colors and duct-taped the ripped seats. Working-class chic. It was finally shut it down in 1986. It sat empty for a while, and then another group took it over—named it the Piccolo. They painted the interior black and retaped the seats. Pretty much gave away the tickets. A bunch of different theater groups used it. They closed up shop in '08."

"It's a really old theater, right?"

"It's a turn-of-the-century jewel. First floor is all shops—or it will be when we clean it up. Offices on the second. The top floor is a hundred-and-fifty-or-so-seat theater. The original name was the Criterion Opera House. Sure, it needs work—maybe a ton of work to bring it up to code—but I've got that handled. My sister, Octavia, is coming in as part owner. She's got deep pockets and is in love with the idea."

"You can't work with your sister. You'll kill each other."

"She'll be a silent partner."

"Octavia? Silent?"

"I'm planning to hire a general manager and someone to handle promotion. I'll buy the place outright and begin the renovations this spring. With a little luck, our first play should be up and running by fall."

"A repertory theater?"

"No. Not this time around. Oh, Janey, I'm so excited I feel like a kid with a shiny new toy."

Jane took a bite of the chocolate cake, feeling more cautious than positive. "This is a big step."

"It's the right one."

"You won't make as much money."

"I'm in a good place financially. Besides, money has never been my raison d'être."

"Your public profile won't be as big."

"Says who? You think this is going to be just any old theater? With my connections, we'll have major names coming to star in every production. I'm going to shake the theater world up around here, Janey. Just you wait and see." She took a bite of cake, closed her eyes, and chewed slowly. "Ambrosia."

"About Mel."

Keeping her eyes closed, Cordelia sighed and leaned back against the cushions. "She wasn't on board with the decision. We've grown apart, Janey. Hattie asked me the other day if Mel still lived across the street. That should tell you something. The final nail in the coffin was when I told her I was done at the AGRT. I never realized it before, but Mel really grooved on my gliteratti status. She couldn't believe I'd throw it all away on some pipe dream. It seems like we were arguing about it all the time. You know what it's like when we argue."

"Epic."

"Exactly. I couldn't take Armageddon every single day."

While Jane rose from the rocker to stoke the fire, Cordelia took the opportunity to refill the champagne flutes again. "Let's not talk about my love life. It stings, you know?"

"Oh, I know. This should make you feel better. Abilene and I are over."

"No."

"She took off for Aspen with her producer last Sunday. She's Abilene's new squeeze."

"That floozy."

"I thought you liked her."

"I thought she had potential. You just never know, do you? I'm sorry you're hurting, Janey. For years it's seemed like either you were miserable and I was happy, or I was miserable and you were happy. We're finally in sync."

Jane thought it prudent not to mention Avi.

For the next hour, Cordelia talked nonstop about her plans for the new theater. Against her better judgment, Jane found herself getting caught up in her friend's excitement. Her main concern had to do with the onetime toast of the Great White Way, Cordelia's wayward actor sister. If anyone was capable of tossing a stick into the wheel, she was. Cordelia had swept the issue of her sister off the table rather too quickly, in Jane's opinion. She might see Octavia as merely a financial backer, but Jane doubted Octavia saw her role that way. Octavia and her outsized ego would undoubtedly be equal parts support and threat.

"More champagne?" asked Cordelia, holding up the bottle.

"I'm good."

Finally taking a breath, Cordelia said, "Anything new on the sleuthing front?"

"Actually, there is," said Jane, glad for the chance to give Cordelia an update. "I talked to one of DeAndre's best friends a few minutes ago. Looks like he was in town searching for his sister."

Cordelia's eyes widened. "From his bio family?"

"Exactly. Her name's Sabrina. He never told anyone in his adopted family about her."

"Wow. Now that's what I call progress." Spying Nolan's family album on the table next her, she said, "What's this?" She opened the cover. "Is that Nolan as a kid?"

"It's his family album."

"I love family albums They always reek of dysfunction." Licking ganache off her fingers, she added, "I'd say he's in high school here. Look at that Afro. I didn't know he had it in him."

Jane rose from the rocker and sat down next to her. "He could have starred in *The Mod Squad*."

Starting on page four, Nolan had written names under a few of the pictures. There were several photos of Nolan's parents. A few of his two sisters, Fannie Lou and Malinda. Pictures of the house where he lived as a kid. College graduation. Several pages of marriage photos. One particularly handsome photo of him dressed in his beat cop uniform. Midway into the book came a section of shots of Fannie Lou's family.

"Those must be DeAndre's brothers," said Jane. The names James, Kellan, Antoine, and DeAndre were written underneath.

A few pages on, Cordelia pointed out that Antoine didn't like DeAndre.

"How on earth could you possibly know that?" asked Jane.

"Look at the way they're sitting on that couch. James and Kellan have their arms around DeAndre. Antoine is sitting apart. And here. They're playing checkers at the kitchen table. See the way Antoine is looking at DeAndre? He's shooting daggers at him. When the four boys are together, Antoine rarely sits next to him. When he does, DeAndre goes all rigid, won't look at the camera. And see," she said, turning pages more quickly, "it doesn't change." She pointed to a photo of DeAndre at his high school graduation, wearing cap and gown. Antoine was standing beside him, beaming at the camera. DeAndre stood stiffly, unsmiling. "Must be a story there."

Cordelia was good at reading people. She was undoubtedly right.

Toward the end of the album, they came across a few pictures of a celebratory dinner at a restaurant. Underneath, Nolan had written, "DeAndre's twenty-first birthday party." Nolan was at the table, as were DeAndre's mom, his dad, and two of his brothers.

"Antoine is nowhere to be found," said Cordelia. "You should ask Nolan about it."

"I didn't tell him I took the album."

"Ah, thievery." She stifled a hiccup.

"Are you sloshed?"

"Pretty near. I don't think I should drive."

"Want me to take you home?"

"If it's okay with you, I think I'll stay the night, just like old times. I'll give Bolger a call. He can get Hattie up and off to school in the morning." She poured herself another glass of champagne. "It's not every day I quit my job and begin a new life." Her eyes brightening, she said, "Let's order a pizza and watch a tearjerker. *Now, Voyager. An Affair to Remember. Love Story.*"

"*The Way We Were.*"

"Yes!" said Cordelia. "That's the one. What do you say?"

Jane closed the album. What she really wanted was to dig into Avi's book. She might still get a chance if Cordelia fell asleep watching the movie. "I'll order the pizza. You go find the flick."

"Division of labor. I like that."

139

18

Vince broke apart his pistol and began to clean it while willing his cell phone to ring. Why the hell hadn't Crowder called him back? It was déjà vu all over again. The joke elicited a sour smile. For about five seconds.

After scrolling through the flight options online, Vince had picked a couple that looked promising. Not too early in the morning. Nonstops. He didn't, however, book the flight. Instead, he called Crowder, hoping to give him the details, see which date made the most sense. When he was put through to voice mail, the anxious feeling inside his chest expanded so fast that it nearly cut off his breath. This time he left a testy message, swearing and saying that he wasn't going to book the flight until they'd talked. He told Crowder to call him ASAP. *ASAP.*

That had been three hours ago. It was going on eleven and still no word from him. The difference in time zones shouldn't have created a problem, because Crowder had said he'd be home all evening.

The door to Vince's office cracked open, and Shanice stuck her head inside. "Got a minute for some good news?"

"Absolutely," he said, motioning her to the chair next to the desk. Once she'd swaggered in and taken a seat he added, "I need more blow."

"Is that why you wanted to talk to me? I can't get it to you until tomorrow. Completely sold out."

He saw no reason to hide his displeasure. "Is everyone in this place a cokehead?"

"A few of your employees might as well sign their checks over to me. Most of what they earn goes up their nose."

He didn't really like Shanice. He thought her managerial skills were good, but her arrogance was hard to take. She was, however, his drug purveyor of choice. A discreet and usually well stocked dealer was hard to come by. "The good news?"

"Oh, right. Just found out that Café Bacchus is about to receive a stellar review in one of the local rags."

"One of the major restaurant reviewers?"

"No, a guest reviewer. A big name—you'll know him. It'll be a great review because—" She tapped the side of her nose.

"He buys from you."

"Didn't hear it from these lips."

Shanice had a hard-on, if he could put it that way, about being a chef. Café Bacchus was her first big break.

She leaned into the desk and lowered her voice. "Listen, since I've got your attention, I need to warn you about something."

"Such as?"

"There's a woman who's come to the club a couple of times. Her name's Jane Lawless."

"Sure, I met her. She's a restaurateur. I'm trying to interest her in investing in Gaudylights."

Shanice crossed her legs. Then her arms. "You might want to rethink that."

"Because?"

"She's been snooping around, asking questions about the guy

who got murdered in the alley. She's always meddling in other people's business. Thinks she's a PI." This time, she tapped her head. "A real head case, know what I mean?"

"And you know this how?"

"I worked at one of her restaurants. Nobody liked her."

"Well, you might be right, but I've got nothing to hide."

"I'm just telling you. We don't want her messing in our business."

"Oh. I hadn't thought of that."

"Well, *think*." She uncrossed everything and got up. Pausing at the door, she glanced back at him. "Just a word to the wise."

Vince stared, shuddering, at the spot where she'd been standing. Something about Shanice gave him the creeps.

Taking a sip of bourbon, he shook her out of his thoughts. Maybe he'd talk to Jane Lawless again and maybe he wouldn't. It was his call, not hers.

Propping his cell phone against a stack of magazines, he decided that if he couldn't fly to Salt Lake City right away it wouldn't be the end of the world. On the other hand, if Crowder didn't call him back, and soon, it just might be.

Emmett sat on the living room couch, feet resting on a footstool, his MacBook on in his lap, with papers and books strewn around him. Across the room, the TV was on, turned to the local news. He'd spent the better part of the afternoon writing the report for AirNorth, which he'd finally finished and would deliver in the morning. Roddy had called right after school and said he needed to study for a test and wanted to do it at a friend's house, where he'd been invited to stay for dinner. The fact that his son was out past his curfew again barely registered. What compelled Emmett's attention was a series of quotes that he'd found on the Internet. He was mulling them over, deciding which of them to use for his meeting with Kingston, when his son came through the front door.

"Sorry I'm late," said Roddy, dropping his backpack next to the coffee table.

Emmett glanced up. "You all ready for your test tomorrow?"

"Huh? Oh, yeah. Ready as I'll ever be." He pushed some of the papers aside and sat down on the other end of the couch so he could watch the TV.

The news anchor finished a story on the governor, switching to one about a St. Paul teen who'd hanged herself in the basement of her family's home on Wednesday night.

"Hey," said Emmett, stopping to listen. "They said she went to your school. Did you know her?"

"I'd seen her around. Knew who she was. Everyone was talking about it today."

"Why'd she do it?"

"Nobody knows."

"So sad."

"What's that?" asked Roddy, picking up a five-by-seven photograph. "Hey, that's you, right? Were you on a baseball team or something? You're all wearing uniforms."

"The Gillford Wildcats. It was a National Adult Baseball Association league. Twelve teams in all. The year before I joined the air force, I used to play for them—just for fun."

"Is that guy there"—he pointed—"Mr. Bessetti?"

"We were all young once."

"And the man with his arm draped over your shoulders. He looks like that guy who got out of St. Peter a few months ago. Can't remember his name."

"Royal Rudmann. Yeah, we were a wild bunch."

"Seriously wild?"

The question made Emmett's skin crawl. "No, just guys being rowdy. You know. All in good fun."

"Why'd you dig the picture out?"

"No reason really. Just remembering my wasted youth." In truth, the memory of that time was a like a cement block lodged inside his stomach, one that never went away.

"Your hair looks silly."

"You better think about getting to bed."

Roddy understood how important it was to keep up his grades. If he didn't, the football scholarship at LSU would be withdrawn. Emmett wasn't worried. Roddy was the one part of his life that had always worked, no matter what. If they had problems, they dealt with them and moved on.

"What are you working on?" asked Roddy.

"I finished my report on last Monday night's flight. I asked to talk to my supervisor when I submit it."

Roddy nodded.

"Nothing to worry about. I've got it covered." He reached over and clamped a hand onto his son's shoulder. "You're growing into a fine man, son. I'm proud of you."

Roddy rose and grabbed his backpack. "Gonna hit the sack. Night."

"Night," said Emmett, returning to his attention to his Internet browser. After his meeting tomorrow, it would all be over. If he got canned, well . . . he'd figure it out.

19

Avi carried a plate with a single chocolate cupcake, a candle stuck in its center, into the living room and set it down in the middle of the carpet. After switching off all but the light over the stove in the kitchen, she lay down on her stomach in the darkness and struck a match.

"Happy birthday," she whispered, chin propped on her fists, staring at the flame, watching the wax melt to within millimeters of the frosting. She finally blew it out. Some birthday, she thought bitterly. After five years, nine months, and seventeen days—then again, who was counting—spent with a woman she intended to live with and love for the rest of her life, she was on her own. Again. It was too early to get involved with anyone else, and she knew it. She was attracted to Jane, perhaps more than just *attracted*, but also concerned that her growing interest wasn't smart. It wasn't good to get too close to anyone right now since it would only complicate matters.

Before she could figure out a way to get comfortable on the carpet, her phone gave two quick rings, alerting her that someone was outside. Rushing to answer it, she said hello.

"Um, hi. Can you buzz me in?"

"Dorsey?"

"Can't seem to find my keys."

She pressed number 4 and held it. A minute later she heard a soft knock on her door. She looked through the peephole to make sure it was him. "What's going on?"

"Am I interrupting something?" he asked, pulling a half-full bottle of Jack Daniel's out from under his coat. "It's dark in your apartment."

She quickly snapped on some lights. "Where'd you lose your keys?"

"Don't know," he said, leaning against the door frame. "Probably somewhere between here and there."

"You been drinking?"

"Sharp as a tack. Nothing gets past you."

"We better call the super, see if he can let you into your apartment."

"No," he said abruptly. "Won't work."

"Why?"

He ambled into the room and slumped down on a chair. "For one thing, he's not home. He always stays at his girlfriend's place on Thursday nights."

"You know this how?"

"He told me. Shit, I need to think this through." He pressed his palm to his eye.

Avi watched him get up and weave his way past the cupcake on the carpet, heading toward the kitchen.

"The cupcake's an interesting decorative touch. Kind of worries me, though. Your friends trip over it much?" He dropped his heavy winter coat on the floor in the dining room. Underneath he had on a pair of baggy jeans, a bulky wool turtleneck, and a military green sleeveless jacket. "This apartment has the same layout as mine, except reversed. Don't suppose you've got any munchies."

146

"In the cupboard above the refrigerator."

"Crap," he said, lifting down a package of Sun Chips. "I hate these. You got anything else?"

"I'm not a 7-Eleven." She'd never seen him so much as take one single drink before.

"No problem, I'm good." He bumped past her on his way to the living room couch, where he dropped down and lifted his heavy boots up on top of the coffee table, dripping water on her magazines.

"Take those boots off," she ordered, picking up the cupcake and blowing out the candle.

"Oh. Yeah. Sorry." He removed them, rubbing his feet with a blissed-out expression.

"What the hell happened to you?"

Drinking straight from the bottle, he said, "So? Can I stay? It's either your place or I sleep in the stairwell."

"Are you kidding me? You actually think you can walk in here and just—"

"Here's what I'm thinking. I could leave the super a message, tell him I lost my apartment key, that I need another. He could leave the new one with you."

"Why can't he give it to you?"

"I may not be around."

"He could let you into your place in the morning and give you the key then."

"I don't want him anywhere near my apartment. I just need the new key." He spread his legs wide and held the bottle in his lap. "He brings it up, gives it to you, and you give it to me. Simple."

"What if he won't give me the key?"

"Yeah, I suppose that could present a problem. I'll tell him there's a twenty in it for him. That should do it."

"Why don't you want him in your apartment?"

147

"Because I'm building an intercontinental ballistic missile." He offered her the bottle.

"You're kidding, right?"

"You think?" He shrugged at her disinterest in the booze. "Seems kind of early for bed. What should we do?" He snapped his fingers. "I've got it. We'll play the truth game."

"I haven't even said you can stay." She perched on the arm of a chair. "You are something else, you know that?"

"No funny business, I swear to God. I'll sleep right here, won't make a peep."

Her instincts told her to toss him out. Her history, however, tugged her in a different direction. She'd crashed on many a friend's couch in her life and always appreciated the kindness. He was such a mess, if she told him to leave, he might freeze to death on his way to a motel. "Okay, I guess you can stay."

"You're creating good karma, Avi. Everything we do comes back to us in the end."

"I hope not," she said, shivering.

He opened the bag of chips and pulled one out, sniffed it, grimaced, then popped it into his mouth. "Okay, so here's how we play. I tell you three stories about my life. You tell me which one is true. Ready?"

She groaned as she slipped sideways down into the chair. He was slurring his words, so maybe she'd get lucky and he'd fall asleep midsentence. That way, she could just throw a blanket over him and go to bed.

"Here's scenario number one. I was born on a farm in Iowa. My parents were God-fearing Christians. I was raised up right, to love God and keep his commandments. My duty was to find a good wife, get married, and raise a passel of God-fearing kids."

"On a farm in Iowa."

"Heaven on earth."

Instead, thought Avi, you're a gay man working in a strip bar surrounded by a bunch of seminaked women. There was a certain irresistible symmetry about this one.

"Scenario number two," he said, tipping the bottle back to take another sip. "I'm an inner-city kid. Mother was a barkeep. Father was a Mafia don. Well, maybe not a don, exactly. I'm exaggerating. More like a well-paid thug. He told me he worked for the FBI, which I believed because I was a stupid kid."

"Far more colorful than the first story," said Avi.

Dorsey held up three fingers. "Third scenario. I was an orphan, smuggled out of an orphanage by a handsome male attendant who wanted to have his way with me. I escaped and was raised by wolves, thus my perfect manners."

She made a pained face.

"Don't like that one?"

"A little too Oprah."

He nearly spit a chip across the room. "Good one."

"So which is true?"

"All of them."

"How can they all be true?"

"Magic."

"You're hammered."

He held up the bottle, studied the label. "Now you."

"Oh, no."

"Come on. Give me the real story. The *real* you."

She scratched her cheek, deciding what she should say. "Well, believe it or not, I happen to be the illegitimate love child of a household name."

"Brad Pitt."

She wrinkled her nose.

"Tom Cruise. Bill Clinton. Jon Stewart."

"It's a secret."

"You're saying you're famous by proxy."

"Or I'm lying. I'll be famous in my own right one day, though."

"For what?"

"You'll have to wait and see."

For some reason, the comment seemed to turn him inward. The smile disappeared. "I went to see Elvio today."

Her eyes widened. "In jail?"

"Real happy place. I can't stand to think of him living in a pit like that for the rest of his life."

"You care about him, don't you."

"I can't stand the sight of him." He raked tears away from his eyes with the back of his hand.

"Then why did you go?"

"I had to. I needed to understand why he did what he did."

"Did he tell you?"

Dorsey's head fell forward. "Not in so many words, but I got the message."

She wasn't sure he'd remember the conversation in the morning. She took a chance. "You two were lovers, right?"

"I'm gonna be sick," mumbled Dorsey.

"Not on my couch," she said, leaping to her feet. "Get up. Up!"

He was so unsteady that she had to help him. With a hand held to his mouth, he stumbled into the hallway that led to the bathroom. Once he'd sunk to the floor in front of the toilet, she shut the door and covered her ears so she wouldn't have to listen to him retch.

That had to be it, she thought. Dorsey was gay and he had a thing for Elvio. She assumed that their relationship must have been a heavy secret to carry around, especially after Elvio murdered DeAndre.

As it happened, keeping secrets was a topic Avi knew something about.

20

In the predawn hours the following morning, wrapped in her bathrobe, with a cup of coffee in one hand and a bagel in the other, Jane finished Avi's novel. To say she'd liked it was an understatement. The language struck her as beautiful, at times even poetic. The story was fresh, the characters sad and funny, idealistic and damaged—perhaps a lot like Avi herself. Ultimately, the novel had left Jane feeling glad to be part of the human race. There wasn't much more she could ask of a novel, all of which made her wonder why such a compelling story had failed to find a publisher. Granted, Jane knew nothing about the publishing industry, but she did feel that she knew something about strong writing. She couldn't wait to see Avi tonight to tell her that her fears had been groundless. After reading *Skin Ticket*, Jane considered herself nothing less than a flat-out fan.

Later that morning, she crept into her guest bedroom carrying a boom box. She figured that, even with a slight hangover, it was time for Sleeping Beauty to wake up. After opening the shades to allow the sunlight into the room, she set the box on the nightstand. There were so many great choices on this particular CD.

She'd decided to go with Sousa's "Semper Fidelis." The opening strains exploded into the silence.

Sitting bolt upright, Cordelia opened both eyes wide and blurted, "Are we at war?"

"Aren't we always?" asked Jane.

She surveyed the room, registered where she was, gave Jane a you're-going-to-pay-for-this look, flopped back down, and pressed a pillow over her face.

Jane patted the bed for Mouse to jump up. "Like you said last night, feels like old times," she shouted over the music, sitting down at the end of the bed. "You used to stay over all the time before Hattie came to live with you."

"Turn that insane music off," came Cordelia's muffled shriek.

Jane pressed a button and returned the room to its former state of tranquillity.

"You know," said Cordelia, grunting as Mouse settled on her stomach, "I expected you'd wake me at some ungodly hour, but not with auditory torture."

"I come bearing good news."

"I don't smell coffee. Bacon. Fresh-baked caramel rolls. That's the only good news I'm interested in."

"Your nose must be broken. I've made my famous black beans in adobo sauce. Prepped a bowl of fresh salsa. When you come down, I'll make us huevos rancheros."

She arched an eyebrow. "Flour or corn tortillas?"

"Flour."

"Fresh lime juice in the salsa?"

"Would I use anything else?"

"A Mimosa or two?"

"No Mimosas. We've got work to do."

"Define work."

"I made half a dozen calls last night to DeAndre's friends. I hit pay dirt again this morning. One of them called me back."

"I'm being crushed," grunted Cordelia. "Get this beast off me."

Jane snapped her fingers and ordered Mouse to get down. "I found out where DeAndre was staying while he was in town. I've got the key to his room. We need to get over there right away and check it out."

"Shouldn't we call the police? Tell them?"

"There's no point. Their investigation into DeAndre's murder ended. I read it in the morning paper."

"Oh, joy," said Cordelia, stretching her arms over her head and yawning. "That I should be allowed to spend a perfectly good morning searching through some guy's underwear —"

"While you're dressing, I'll finish getting breakfast ready. Remember, you're the one who's always grousing that I don't let you help me with my investigating anymore. You want in? You're in."

DeAndre had chosen one of the few economy lodgings in downtown Minneapolis within walking distance of GaudyLights. Parking across the street from the venerable Grant Hotel shortly after ten, Jane and Cordelia entered through the double front doors and walked up to the reception desk.

"I need the number for DeAndre Moore's room," said Jane.

A woman in a belted tweed suit studied the computer screen through her bifocals. "Room 348."

Jane thanked her and headed for the elevators.

"This place takes the concept of threadbare to a whole new level," said Cordelia, following close behind. "By the way, did you talk to Nolan this morning?"

"No. I talked to his nurse. He still has a fever and didn't feel like talking on the phone. If he's not better by tomorrow, they'll switch him to a different antibiotic." Jane intended to visit him later in the day, after she'd met with Luis Ramos at the Xanadu Club.

When it came to Nolan, Sergeant Taylor had been solicitous, probably because of Nolan's connection to the MPD. Taylor's approach to her was far less generous or forthcoming. She'd called him a couple of times, hoping to ask him some questions, but he hadn't returned her calls. Removing the key card from her billfold, she inserted it and waited for the red light to turn green.

"The thrill of the chase," whispered Cordelia.

Jane didn't feel remotely thrilled. She felt apprehensive. Switching on the ceiling light, she moved cautiously into the room. Both of the double beds were made, and the curtains were pulled. A new pair of athletic shoes had been tossed on the floor next to the nightstand. Other than that, everything was neat.

"Smells kind of musty," muttered Cordelia, her nose twitching.

Jane wondered what DeAndre had been thinking when he left the room for the last time. Ducking briefly into the bathroom, she touched his travel kit. It was eerie to picture him in here, alive and well, with all his hopes and dreams still intact. His suitcase was open on the end of one of the double beds. She began to dig through it.

Cordelia stepped over to the desk, where a small netbook sat open and plugged in.

"This might be interesting," said Jane, removing a file folder from the bottom of the suitcase. She slipped out a single sheet of paper. "Weird."

"I love weird," Cordelia said, sitting down at the desk and powering up the computer. "Show me."

Jane handed over the paper. One word was written in the center.

ἀκαθαρσία

"It's Greek," said Jane. "Wonder what it means."

"Don't know, but give me a minute and I might be able to find out." After taking a picture of the page with her iPhone, Cordelia tapped in a number. "Mikolas?" she said, moving over to the window and opening the curtain. "Cordelia Thorn here. Listen, if I e-mailed you a photo of a foreign word, could you tell me if you recognize it? We think it might be Greek. Hey, excellent, my man. Call me as soon as you figure it out. Ta."

Jane took her turn at the desk. She scrolled through DeAndre's e-mail, surprised that it wasn't password protected. All the entries were from one person—a woman named Jazmin Lewis. The e-mail dates appeared to go back less than a week before he died, perhaps, Jane reflected, when he bought the computer in preparation for his trip. It seemed that Jazmin was teaching high school in the Czech Republic as part of a Fulbright Teacher Exchange program. "Lots of letters to and from a girlfriend," said Jane.

"Anything interesting?" asked Cordelia, pulling out each dresser drawer and looking inside.

"Listen to this. He wrote this the night he died." She read from the screen.

Jaz, hi. I gave you most of the details on the phone. Sorry I didn't tell you any of this before. It's been a secret so long that it's become my default setting. Still in Minneapolis, pretty much visiting the strip club every night. Sabrina isn't happy about it. She told me to leave, that she'd get in touch with me back home, but I can't go.

After she admitted she murdered Tatum, I felt like someone had hit me with a two-by-four. Still can't believe it.

"Who's Tatum?" asked Cordelia.

"No idea."

I'm not sure I mentioned this. The cops found her prints on the copper, which is why they contacted me. She gave them my address when she was arrested a few years back. They had her prints on file so they came to my place to find her. Thankfully, she'd already left town.

I can't believe my bio mom never said anything to me about all this. It explains so much about her, about my childhood—about Sabrina. Knowing part of the truth, but not all of it, what do I do? I came here for an answer. She said she was close, but she keeps stalling. She's sick, Jaz. Maybe she always has been and I never saw it. Sometimes she seems completely normal, but then she sinks into this awful, corrosive bitterness and there's no getting through to her. I have to try, but honestly, I don't see her changing. She's out for revenge and nobody's going to stop her.

Truth is, I don't blame her for feeling cheated, like her childhood was stolen. I feel the same way. But murder? Knowing what she has in store for those guys makes me feel like I'm a party to it. Do I contact the police? Turn her in? How can I? I owe her so much.

With the way our justice system works, or doesn't work, there's not a prayer in hell that a judge would put those men away. That's what she said, and she's right.

I plan to have it out with her tonight. One way or the other, this has to end.

I love you, Jaz. I miss you so much. Write me and let me know me what you think. I feel so alone.

D

"Wow," said Cordelia, sinking down on the bed as if in a trance. "We have to turn this over to the police."

"I agree, but I want to talk to Nolan first. The cops in St. Louis have to be looking for this Sabrina. We know where she works—we just don't know who she is. If she's thinking of murdering more people, I'll bet money she's here because one or more of the men she's after lives in town."

"Try looking up Twin Cities homicides on the Internet."

Jane logged on to the netbook's browser and typed in "Homi cides Twin Cities," and then she typed in the year. After scrolling through a bunch of articles that didn't apply, she found one that did. "Here we go."

Second Homicide for Twin Cities Metro Area

Tuesday, February 11 —The Twin Cities Metro Area recorded its second homicide of the year last night when police found a man shot to death in a motel off County Road 6 in Brooklyn Center. No one has been arrested in the shooting.

The murder victim, Royal Rudmann, 61, had recently been released from the St. Peter Regional Treatment Center.

"Damn, we're good," said Cordelia. "Look up what it says about the Tatum murder in St. Louis."

Jane searched the Internet again, popping up an article that had appeared in the *St. Louis Post-Dispatch.* She read through it, then paraphrased it. "He taught eighth-grade science. The murder occurred in the basement of his home." Returning to the Internet, she said, "It doesn't look to me like it's been solved."

"What do you suppose DeAndre meant when he talked about the police finding Sabrina's prints on the copper?"

"Maybe Taylor can tell us," said Jane.

Cordelia's cell phone rang. Glancing at the caller ID, she said, "We may have a breakthrough. Hey, Mikolas." She listened. "I et me repeat this so I know I've got it right. You say it's New Testament Greek and it means morally impure or unclean. Huh. Okay, got it. You're my man. I owe you. Later." She clicked the phone off and then dropped it in the top pocket of her jacket. "There you have it."

"Why would DeAndre be carrying around the Greek word for morally impure?"

"Beats the hell out of me."

Jane unhooked the netbook and closed it up. "We're making progress. Let's leave the rest of DeAndre's belongings in the room until I can talk to Nolan, see what he wants us to do."

"Works for me. As I've said many times before—"

"Cordelia Thorn does not haul."

"One of my founding principles."

21

Vince pounded on the front door of Emmett Washington's house. When nobody answered, he leaned on the doorbell, shouting, "Open up," straining to peer through a crack in the curtained picture window.

Emmett finally appeared, still in his bathrobe, all apologies for making him stand outside in the cold.

"Where the hell were you?" demanded Vince.

"Asleep," said Emmett, holding the door open. His eyes were red and puffy, and his breath smelled rank, like he'd been eating raw skunk.

"It's nearly eleven."

"I was up late working on a report."

Vince followed him to the kitchen, where Emmett put on the coffee.

"You heard anything more about Rudmann's murder?" asked Emmett, opening one of the kitchen cupboards and staring at a row of cereal boxes.

"No, but we've got someone else to worry about. Ken Crowder."

"I haven't heard that name in years."

"I got worried since I hadn't heard from him in a while, so I e-mailed him to make sure he was okay."

"Worried why?"

Vince was appalled that Emmett didn't get it. It was like he was walking around in a fog. Was Vince the only one who still had a working brain? Making himself comfortable at the kitchen table, he said, "It doesn't bother you that Tatum and Rudmann were both murdered?"

"Hadn't thought about it," said Emmett, rubbing his eyes.

"It's like you're sleepwalking, man. Wake the hell up."

"People get killed. Doesn't necessarily mean anything."

"They were murdered in exactly the same way."

"Gunshot, right? We got ninety billon guns in this country."

"That's an exaggeration."

"Chill out, as my son would say. I've got more important things to worry about."

"No, you don't. Something's happened to Crowder. He called me after I e-mailed him, invited me out to visit him at the vacation cabin he owns above Park City, Utah. We agreed that I'd call him back last night with the flight information. He never answered his phone."

Emmett shrugged as he sat down at the table. "He probably went out."

"You're not listening to me. He made a big deal out of what he had going on last night. He was making dinner for some neighbors, and then later a bunch of his buddies were coming over to play poker. He said he'd be in all evening."

"So he got busy, didn't pick up."

"Man, I called him a dozen times. He knows I'm worried and he knows why. There's no way on earth he would have blown me off. Unless?"

Emmett closed his eyes. "You're giving me a headache on top of the headache I already have." Before he could continue, the landline rang. Grabbing the cordless off the kitchen table, he said, "Hello?" He listened for a few seconds. "Roddy? No, he's at school. Isn't that where you are?" He lowered his head. "Sure, I'll tell him to call you, although you'll probably see him before I do. Yeah, okay. You sound kind of . . . funny? Something wrong?" He listened.

Vince drew a hand across his throat, gesturing for him to cut it off.

"Okay, right." After saying good-bye, he stared into space, seemingly dazed.

"Who was that?" asked Vince.

"Lukas Olson. He's the quarterback and captain of the football team—one of Roddy's best friends. Nice kid."

"Great. Let's get back to business. I called the cops in Park City this morning, told them that a friend wasn't answering his phone and that I was worried. They said they'd check it out."

"Okay. So?"

"An officer called me back about an hour later, said that he'd knocked on Crowder's door, walked around the place, but nobody seemed to be around. I thanked him for his time and then started looking for the phone number of Crowder's neighbors. He mentioned their names, thank God. I finally got through to the wife. She said that they went over to Crowder's house with a bottle of wine and a homemade apple pie around seven last night. Nobody answered the door. There was a light on inside, but since he wasn't around, they figured they'd gotten the date wrong."

"Huh."

"Something *happened* to Crowder between the time I talked to him yesterday afternoon and seven o'clock last night. I got a bad feeling about this."

Emmett's eyes roamed the room. "I need coffee. You want some?"

"We gotta find out."

Pushing back from the table, Emmett got up and poured himself a cup, then dug around in the refrigerator until he found the half-and-half. "How?"

"One of us needs to fly out there and see if he's okay. If he's not, you can bet we're next."

"You think this has to do with . . . you know."

"There were five of us," said Vince, forcing his voice to sound steady. Mental pictures, scenes he thought were long forgotten, kept blowing through his head. "Two are dead. Possibly three. Do the math."

"So when are you going to leave?"

"Me? No, no. You're the one who likes to fly. You need to go."

"No way. Not happening."

Completely out of patience, Vince lunged at Emmett, grabbed the lapels of his bathrobe, and bent him backward over the sink. "Listen to me, you pathetic piece of shit. We need to check this out now. Today. You're a pilot. You can jump on any AirNorth flight you want for free. There's one leaving at two this afternoon. It's not full, I checked."

"I can't. I have an important meeting—"

"Cancel it. When you get to Salt Lake City, rent a car and drive out to Park City. It's about forty miles to his house. Break in if you have to."

"I can't *do* it." He shoved Vince away. "I'm not going anywhere near an AirNorth plane."

"What the hell does that mean?"

He refused to make eye contact.

The sound of the front doorbell stopped the argument.

"You expecting someone?" asked Vince. He walked with Emmett into the living room and watched as he peered through a crack in the blinds.

"Shit," hissed Emmett. "There's a cop car in the driveway."

Vince was glad he'd parked across the street.

"Two uniformed officers are at the front door."

Ducking down, Vince whispered, "Did the police ever talk to you about Rudmann's murder?"

"Yeah, briefly. I told them I didn't know anything, and they went away. So what's this about?" He knelt down and crawled on all fours into the hallway.

"Maybe they want to talk to you again."

"I can't do it. I'm too jittery."

"Fine. They don't know you're home. You car's in the garage, right?" Hearing a noise at the back of the house, Vince stayed in his crouch and duck-walked into the kitchen. The shadow of a man's head moved back and forth behind the curtained back-door window.

After a couple of loud raps, a deep male voice called, "St. Paul police, Mr. Washington. Open up."

Returning to the living room, Vince found Emmett lying flat on his stomach. Edging over to the window, he watched as the two cops walked back out to their cruiser. They stood for a few seconds, shielding their eyes from the morning sun, studying the house, talking, pointing, then got back in the car and drove off.

"I don't know why the St. Paul police would be interested in you," said Vince. "Rudmann's murder happened in Hennepin County."

Rolling onto his back, Emmett stared up at the ceiling. "I'm never getting on a plane again."

He'd changed the subject so abruptly that Vince was momentarily thrown.

"I'm quitting. Either that or they'll fire me."

"You're not making any sense."

"I'm *scared*," he all but shouted.

163

"Of flying?" asked Vince. "Look, I don't know what's going on with you. I don't really care. Bottom line is, you have to fly to Salt Lake City this afternoon. If Crowder's dead, if someone is after us, we've got to nail down what's going on and then, if we can, figure out a way to protect ourselves. Take a flask of vodka. Breathe deeply. If you need Xanax or Valium, I'll get it for you. But you have to go."

Emmett covered his face with his hands.

"Emmett? We good? Come on, man. I need you to be strong."

After a few seconds, Emmett wiped a hand across his mouth and said, "Get me Crowder's address."

"I have it all written down. You'll call me as soon as you know anything, right?"

"You're a loathsome piece of slime, Vince. A bottom feeder. I wish to God I'd never met you."

The feeling was mutual, thought Vince, though since the die had been cast years ago, there was nothing either of them could do about it now.

22

Jane led Luis Ramos downstairs to the basement kitchen at the Xanadu Club. Since it was Friday, she assumed Fara would be working. "I want to introduce you to one of our chefs, Fara Jafari. She handles all the staff schedules."

"Thank you," said Luis, removing his baseball cap.

"She'll give you all the particulars."

"Particulars?"

"The time you need to show up. You'll need some nonskid shoes. The ones you're wearing should be fine. She'll have you sign a W-4 form. Let you know when and how you'll be paid."

"Yes."

Standing at the bottom of the stairs, she shook his hand. "Welcome aboard."

He nodded, unsmiling.

"How's your sister-in-law feeling?"

"Tired."

"I don't doubt it. Have you heard anything more from Elvio?"

He studied his fingernails. "I want nothing to do with him."

"Because of what he did?"

"Because of who he is."

Jane wasn't sure what he meant. Before she could ask, a wea-selly looking guy in a chef's coat walked up, an annoyed look on his face. She had no idea who he was.

"You need to leave. This area is off-limits to customers."

She read the name on his jacket. "Well, *Don*, since I happen to own the place, I think I'll stay."

His expression shifted to wariness. "Own?"

"Jane Lawless."

"Oh, sure. Barry told me about you." He stuck out his hand. "Don Kleimo. Barry hired me last week."

"What happened to Fara?" She ignored the hand and instead concentrated on his dirty jeans.

"It didn't work out."

"What didn't?" Jane always insisted that her kitchen staff wear the traditional black-and-white-checked pants.

"She and Barry had some issues. Not sure what. Anyway, she left and I was hired."

Jane felt her anger rising—at Barry, for sure, but even more at herself. She quickly introduced the new chef to Luis, saying that she wanted him put on the schedule as a full-time dishwasher. Don, looking flummoxed by her sudden appearance, didn't argue.

After they'd walked off, Jane made a tour of the kitchen. She stuck her head into the walk-in cooler and saw that very few of the bins were labeled and dated. Moving over to the line, she pulled open a couple of the refrigerated drawers. By this time of day, they should have been freshly stocked.

"Don?" she called, motioning him over.

He almost ran. "Yeah," he said, all eagerness to please now that he knew who she was.

"What do you call this?" She picked up a couple of limp tomato slices and a piece of wilted lettuce.

"Garnishes?" he asked weakly.

"I call it garbage."

"Barry wants us to recycle when we can. We stocked the coolers on Wednesday."

"Then you stocked it with too much. Get rid of this and replace it."

"But it's almost eleven. We're about to open."

"You serve this crap to our customers and we won't have any."

"Okay, sure. You're the boss. But I think you should talk to Barry."

"Oh, don't worry. I'll talk to him. I want all the food in the coolers checked, labeled, and dated. You got that?"

He nodded.

"What happened with the deep fryer? And with the plumbing problem in the prep kitchen?"

He brightened. "The prep sink is working great."

"What about the deep fryer?"

"We're still waiting on that."

"Did Barry's guy ever show?"

"Yeah, but he said he needed a new part. Might take a few days."

"A few *days*?"

"Yup."

"So you're limping along with one fryer. I told the guy working the register last night to call Hanson Appliance."

"I wasn't here last night."

"Well, you're here today, Don. Call them now. They're on the list in your office."

"What, I mean, like . . . what if they fix it and then Barry's guy comes with the part?"

"Have him call me. I assume you have my number."

His face turning decidedly pink, the chef nodded.

"Good. I'll see you later."

"Yeah," said Don, to her retreating back. "You take care now."

Upstairs, Jane searched for the day shift manager. She finally asked one of the bartenders where he was.

"Um, well, you'll probably find him in the men's bathroom."

"Okay, where's the cashier?" Always the second in command.

"Probably in the same bathroom."

"You're saying—"

"Like rabbits, Ms. Lawless. Every chance they get."

She'd had enough. On the way outside to her car, she gave Barry a call. His secretary, Lisa Tinker, answered.

"The Restaurant Group. May I help you?"

"It's Jane Lawless."

"Well, hi, stranger. Haven't heard from you in a while."

Don't rub it in, thought Jane. "Is Barry around?"

"Sorry, he's not."

"Could you have him call me when he gets back? It's important."

"Sure, but he may not be in until tomorrow morning."

"That's fine. Listen, there's something else. We hired a woman last fall to work as a sous chef at the Xanadu. Name's Shanice Williams. Would you still have the forms she filled out when she applied?"

"Probably."

"Could you fax them to me at my home? Is it possible for you to do it today?"

"I'll see what I can dig up."

"Thanks, Lisa. I'll be in touch."

Later that afternoon, as she sat with Nolan in his hospital room, she was still fuming.

The doctor had started Nolan on a new antibiotic. Hope was high that this would be the one to knock out the fever and the infection. His face continued to look flushed, although he seemed in better spirits. "Wanna talk about it?" he asked. "Whatever *it* is?"

"Nope."

"Boy, you are one pissed-off woman."

"Pretty much." She asked him if he was up to a short conversation about the investigation.

"You have anything new?"

She told him about the e-mail she and Cordelia had found on DeAndre's netbook. "I think you should hear it." As she read it out loud, she watched him closely to see his reaction. Nolan was a stoic. He'd learned to keep his emotions in check through many years on the homicide unit, which made it hard to tell what was going on inside him. Asking direct questions often got her nowhere. This afternoon, however, the heartbreak on his face was unmistakable.

"Why didn't he call me?" he asked, balling his hands into fists. "I could have helped him."

"Like he said, he was so used to keeping his sister's existence a secret—"

"So he calls you when it's too late. Why you and not me?"

"Maybe he was ashamed. Or maybe explaining why he'd never told you about Sabrina was too much for him right then. Talking to me was easier."

Nolan stared silently at the wall, chewing on his lower lip.

Jane understood his frustration but needed him to move away from it, if only for a few minutes. She put her question to him. "So what do I do with the netbook?"

"Call Taylor," he said, still staring at the wall. "Tell him about the hotel room, the netbook, the Greek word you found, Burt Tatum, everything."

"I was hoping I could use it as a bargaining chip. They've been investigating the Rudmann murder. They must know something about this copper thing."

He shook his head.

"But if the investigation into DeAndre's murder is closed—"

"Let Taylor be the judge of what he wants to do with it."

"What if I contacted the police in St. Louis?"

"No. Handle it through Taylor."

Since Nolan had once been a cop, he had a default response, too. "I wish I understood how Elvio Ramos is connected."

"That's important, for sure, but the central question at the moment is, who is Sabrina? We know she works at GaudyLights. We also know she's probably too old to be one of the black dancers." Switching his gaze to Jane, he added, "You've got to promise me you'll be extra careful. This is one seriously sick woman. I'm sure what she's doing is motivated, but that doesn't make it any less horrific, which is why you need to get this info to the police right away."

"I'll take care of it."

"No reason you need to stick around and babysit me."

"I thought we could play a game of Scrabble. I brought a board." She held it up.

"Go talk to Taylor. My mind's not sharp enough to beat you at Scrabble. Anyway, Nurse Ratched said I need to sleep."

She stood up next to the bed. "Is your leg still numb?"

"I'm getting a little more feeling back in it. Unfortunately, the more feeling, the more pain."

"But they're giving you pain meds to help with that, right?"

"I can't say it helps all that much. Mainly, it just put me in a place where I don't seem to care."

"I could bring you dinner. Some homemade soup?"

"Maybe when I'm feeling better," he said, reaching for her hand.

"I brought your watch, ring, and phone. I put them in the top drawer of your nightstand. Anything else you need?"

"Call me with updates."

"I will."

"And Jane? Thanks for being such a good friend."

She smiled. "Always."

Before Jane headed to city hall, she sat in her Mini and phoned Nolan's sister, giving her the latest news on her brother's condition. Fannie Lou was upset to hear about the infection, but like everyone else, she remained hopeful that the antibiotics would handle it. When they were finished, Jane phoned Kevante Taylor to let him know she was coming. She felt thwarted—or, more specifically, downright annoyed—by Nolan's confidence in him. As usual, he didn't pick up. She was put through to his voice mail, where she left a brief message explaining what she'd found.

Downtown, the cop at the front desk listened to her explain what she needed, then asked her to sit in one of the chairs while he made a couple of calls. A few minutes later, a plainclothed man who introduced himself as Sergeant Muñoz led her down a hallway to a conference room. Turning on the lights, he invited her to sit down opposite him.

She pushed the netbook across the table and told him her story. He listened, indicating that the connection between Rudmann and Tatum was something he hadn't known about.

"So you're a licensed PI," he said, studying her.

She pulled out her card and handed it over. "We know who murdered Mr. Moore, but we don't know why. That's what I've been working on. I've been trying to get in touch with Kevante Taylor. I'd hoped we could help each other."

Muñoz offered a guarded nod. "You did the right thing by bringing this netbook to us."

Not an answer. "Once of my concerns has to do with DeAndre's girlfriend. Someone needs to let her know what happened."

"Are you a friend?"

"No."

"I'll see that it's taken care of." He made a move to get up.

"Wait," said Jane.

"Something else?"

"The note DeAndre sent to his girlfriend talked about a 'copper.' Do you have any idea what that might be?"

He sat back in his chair. "I'm sorry, Ms. Lawless, but I'm not able to discuss a case that's under investigation."

So he did know something.

"Now, if there's nothing else——"

He was treating her as if she were a busybody. If Nolan had shown up with the netbook, he wouldn't have been patted on the head and sent on his way.

"If I have more questions——"

"You should direct them to Sergeant Taylor," said Muñoz. "Sounds like you have a relationship with him."

In other words, don't bother *me*. She got the message.

23

It was a three-hour, nonstop flight from Minneapolis to Salt Lake City. The flight attendant, a woman Emmett had known for many years, offered to seat him in first class. He thanked her but said he preferred the window seat over the wing. He didn't add that it would give him more to look at—and also less. The jet was an MD-80, a refit, not as new or fast as the one he'd flown in on Monday night.

Canceling the meeting he'd scheduled with his AirNorth manager had been a breeze. When he called, he learned that AirNorth had already canceled it. They were flying in someone from corporate in Detroit to talk to him tomorrow afternoon. At least he wouldn't have to wait until Monday.

Sitting in an airport bar, Emmett had downed a few Scotch and waters to get him through the takeoff. Now that they were in the air, he planned to order two more when the attendant came by. He felt woozy at the margins and intended to keep it that way. Gripping the arms of the seat, he forced his eyes to the right and looked out the window, surveying the wing, the flaps, and the small section of the engine that he could see. He scanned the airspace, his gaze roaming the cloud deck just below them. So far so

173

good. Maybe this was exactly what he needed. You fall off a bicycle, you get back on, right? When the plane hit an air pocket and dropped, he flinched and squeezed his eyes shut, listening helplessly as the first officer, another man he knew, came over the loudspeaker to explain that the ride would be bumpy for the next few minutes and that everyone should remain in their seats with their seat belts fastened.

"Is this your first time on an airplane?" asked a kindly older woman sitting in the middle seat.

God, did he look that pathetic? "I'm fine."

"These planes today are amazing. Very safe."

"You think so?"

"I fly all the time. Nothing to worry about. Just sit back and relax."

He smiled, mostly at her naïveté.

It was all so familiar. The smells. The sounds. He'd been right to assume that the flight out would not be the worst of it. It was the trip home—suspended as he would be in the heavy dark, a place where logic could dissolve in the blink of an eye—that opened up the sudden trapdoor feeling in his stomach.

The attendant came by, and he ordered two small bottles of Scotch.

Emmett had left his son a note on the kitchen table, explaining that he had to make a quick flight to Salt Lake and would be home late. He didn't add that he wouldn't be piloting the plane. He also mentioned that Lukas had called and that it sounded important.

The plane touched down at Salt Lake City International a few minutes before five. As they taxied to the jet bridge, Emmett sat up in the seat and tried to shake off his fatigue. I'm not drunk, he told himself. Unsteady, yes, but driving shouldn't be a problem. In the distance, the setting sun was half obscured by distant clouds.

He'd barely thought about Ken Crowder on the way out. The entire situation seemed so remote. If it hadn't been for Vince hitting the panic button, he'd be home tonight, not on some silly wild-goose chase. He'd probably get to Crowder's place and find him grilling hamburgers.

The ride up to Park City through the chill, leaden twilight was uneventful. Once the sun had finally set, a fuzzy seasick feeling settled over Emmett. He kept checking the navigation system on his rented Fusion, confused by some of the instructions. Coming out of Park City, he'd taken a wrong turn, but with the help of a woman at a convenience store, he was finally heading up Owl Canyon Road, not more than a few miles from Crowder's cabin.

Leaving the bright lights of the city behind, the mountain road seemed particularly dark and steep. A sign told him to slow to ten miles an hour just before the Fusion's tires rolled off the pavement onto a dirt lane covered in potholes, which eventually leveled out just as Emmett spied a two-story cabin nestled into the pines off to his right. The navigation system announced that he'd reached his destination. He'd been thinking that he might need to park a ways off from the house, just so that his coming and going wouldn't be easily observed, but when he saw the remoteness of the location, with no other houses anywhere near Crowder's cabin, he turned into a drive bordered on one side by massive boulders and on the other by a cement walkway.

Approaching the garage, he was startled when a motion-sensitive floodlight burst·on. Telling himself to take it easy, he parked, switched off the headlights, and cut the engine, then sat for a few moments staring up at the house, amazed at the size of the place.

"Cabin, my ass," he muttered.

True, there were logs. A log front door. A log balcony that ran along the upper story. Log walls interrupted by huge windows. Logs, however, did not a cabin make. This thing was a minimansion.

Second-floor lights glowed a soft yellow gold, making the interior look like an inviting port in the wilderness.

Slipping out of the front seat, Emmett was glad for the hard slap of the cold air. He made his way up the drive, his feet crunching on gravel, his blood pressure—he was sure—rising into the stratosphere. He hadn't eaten much all day, which meant that the drinks on the plane had left his stomach burning and his head banging. With any luck, this conversation wouldn't take long.

Seeing a note taped to the glass on the front door, he pulled it free and held it up to a faux lantern light.

Ken:
Where the hell were you last night? The guys and I came by at ten. Nobody home. Talked to a neighbor of yours today when I stopped over.

She said she was out walking her dog yesterday and saw a short-haired blonde come out of your door. Man, if you went off again with some skank and left us hanging, we're going to boil you in crankcase oil. *Call.*

Stan

Emmett pocketed the note and pressed the doorbell. Standing back, he flipped the collar of his jacket up against the cold, stamped his feet, and blew on his hands, wishing for the umpteenth time today that he'd told Vince no.

"Crowder? You in there?" He banged the door knocker.

As he waited, he thought back to that summer thirty-some years ago when they'd all played baseball together. Until the chaos of that one awful incident, he'd been having a great time. Crowder had been the gentle giant type, sandy haired, soft voiced, chunky, and shambling. He and Rudmann were the team leaders—and the leaders that night. They were powerful personalities. Nobody ever crossed them. Even then, Emmett knew there was something wrong with Rudmann. He was a sociopath, a word Emmett had come across years later. He had no empathy. Crowder was big and handsome, with a smile people—women especially—found irresistible. Next to them, Emmett felt like a wallflower, a hanger-on, a skinny, tongue-tied kid. He was the only black guy on the team. The fact that he was the best athlete of the bunch—and that liberal types back then thought it was cool to hang with a brother—was the only reason he'd been included.

"Come on, Ken," he called again, pounding on the door this time. "I'm freezing out here."

Before renting the Fusion, Emmett had called Crowder from the airport, still hoping he wouldn't need to make the trip up to Park City. Of course, Crowder hadn't answered. Emmett didn't leave a voice mail. Seemed kind of pointless. Until this moment, he'd never seriously entertained the notion that someone might truly be after them. It seemed too outlandish—the sort of thing that only happened in movies. Yet now, as he stood freezing in front of Crowder's house, he wasn't so sure.

Giving up for the moment, Emmett decided to do a brief inspection of the property. Coming around the side, away from the floodlights, he saw that the house was perched on heavy pilings sunk deep into the canyon wall.

"Must be an incredible view from up there," he muttered, backing up when one of his shoes started to slip on the snow. "Jesus," he whispered. One wrong step and he could easily end up on the canyon floor.

A deck ran the entire length of the rear of the house, without a stairway anywhere in sight. Unless he could fly, there was no way he could reach it. He thought back to what Vince had said to him before he left his house. *Break in if you have to.*

As Emmett crossed around to the other side of the house, the floodlight flipped back on. He was already on edge and didn't need this freakin' klieg light hitting him in the face every few seconds. He stepped up to a door at the corner of the garage and tried the handle, assuming it would be another dead end. It was. The lock, however, appeared to be loose. Glancing around to make sure he was still alone, he heaved his full weight against it. Three more tries and he was in. Light slanted through a row of small, square, high garage-door windows. An SUV was parked in one of the stalls, a canoe, a motorcycle, a snowblower, and a snowmobile in the other. Crowder apparently liked his toys.

As he made his way to another door at the back, the air around him felt like pure electricity. The top half of the door was glass, covered by blinds. Standing close, he cocked his arm and smashed the glass with his elbow. He found an oily cloth on the floor by the motorcycle's front tire and used it to knock out the remaining glass from around the edge. Slipping his arm through, he pulled back the dead bolt. He was in.

The instant he stepped across the threshold he smelled something familiar. It reminded him of the nursing home where his mother had once lived. It was the oder of urine and feces. Along with it came an unfamiliar stink—coppery, sweet, foul. As he moved through the kitchen, the metallic smell coated his nostrils and clung to the roof of his mouth.

Emmett stopped at the edge of the living room, his gaze sliding along the shag carpet to Crowder's dead body. He was sprawled on his back directly in front of the stone fireplace. Blood and excrement had soaked through his clothes, turning parts of the carpet black. Emmett barely recognized him. He'd put on at least a hundred pounds. His face was bloated in death but had also surely been bloated in life.

Holding his nose, Emmett edged closer, bending down to examine the body more closely. A chest wound had killed him.

Oddly enough, his right hand held a small piece of copper. Emmett pulled it free and examined it. A series of Greek letters had been stamped into the thin metal. The only reason Emmett knew it was Greek was that he'd been in a fraternity for a couple of years in college. He had no idea what the word meant, or why someone had so obviously placed it in Crowder's hand after he'd been killed.

Stumbling back into the kitchen with the piece of copper still clutched in his hand, Emmett bolted through the garage and burst out into the cold night air, gulping in deep breaths. He knew the smell in his nostrils was something he'd never forget.

He drove several miles down the mountain before easing the car over to the side of the road. Removing his cell, he punched in Vince's number. Two rings and they were connected.

"Bessetti."

"Vince, it's me. Can you talk?"

"Yeah. What? Tell me."

"I found him. He's dead. Shot in the chest. You can't believe how bad that cabin smelled. I found a thin piece of what looks like copper in his hand with some Greek letters on it. You know what it means?"

Vince groaned.

"I need to know."

"It means, you fucking moron, that we're fucking dead men."

24

Jane sat with Bolger and Hattie on the living room couch in Cordelia's loft that evening, watching Animal Planet, Hattie's favorite channel, while Cordelia changed out of her business duds into something more comfortable. They planned to spend another night at GaudyLights.

"You don't want to look too glamorous," called Bolger. As an aside to Jane, he added, "Unless she wants people stuffing twenty-dollar bills in her cleavage. I mean, the sane mind reels."

"What's GaudyLights?" asked Hattie, tearing her attention away from a West African pygmy hippo.

"It's a place where they have lots of colored lights and gaudy people," answered Bolger.

"What's 'gaudy'?"

Bending close to Jane, Bolger whispered, "I'll be glad when this interrogation phase is over." Lifting Hattie onto his lap, he said, "Gaudy. Hmm. Well, it means glittery. Tasteless. Flashy. Vulgar."

"What's 'vulgar'?"

As he was about to answer, the doorbell rang.

"I'll get it," said Cordelia, sailing down the steps from her raised loft bedroom wearing a striped, double-breasted men's suit with a wide tie, spats, and a broad-brimmed fedora set at a rakish angle over her auburn curls.

"Don't you look . . . gaudy," said Bolger. "Gangsta gaudy. Maybe you can start a new lesbatron fashion trend."

"I don't need a fashion critique from *you*," said Cordelia, flashing her eyes at his gray satin smoking jacket with black lapels and black satin belt.

"I love what you're wearing, Deeya," said Hattie.

Hattie still called her aunt by the name she'd given her when she was a toddler and couldn't pronounce "Cordelia."

"Thank you," said Cordelia, sticking her tongue out at Bolger. When she swung back the door, her mouth dropped open. "If I find a head of garlic and an old rugged cross will you slink away into the night?"

"I do so love your warm welcomes."

Jane stood up to see who was outside. "Oh my God," she whispered.

Standing her ground, Cordelia tried again. "How did Homeland Security ever let you back into the country?"

Octavia Thorn Lester, dripping with jewelry and wearing a black cashmere cape and black designer boots, elbowed her way into the room. "Nice to see you, too."

"Mommy," shouted Hattie, rushing to her and hugging her around the knees.

Octavia absently patted her head. "My little darling, how are you?"

"Can you stay?"

"No," said Cordelia, continuing to hold the door open. "She's on her way somewhere. *Anywhere*."

"Yes, of course Mummy can stay," said Octavia. "Jane, how nice to see you again."

Jane had never been quite sure how Octavia could pull off

looking heroic, tragic, and smarmy at the same time. It had to be a trick of the light.

"And—" Octavia turned to Bolger, inspecting him openly. "Who would this be?"

"You're Octavia Thorn Lester," said Bolger, rising as if in a trance. "You changed your hair color. Didn't you used to be blond?"

"It's a pelt," said Cordelia, finally giving up and shutting the door. "I was there when she shot the varmint. It was the year she made the cover of *Field & Stream*."

"How clever you are," said Octavia, removing her cape and revealing an off-the-shoulder midnight blue sweater and pleated gray wool slacks. "For a minute there, I thought I'd walked in on Al Capone. All you need to complete the look is a lit cigar."

"I'll borrow one of yours," said Cordelia.

"Young man," said Octavia, oozing over to the drinks cart and pouring herself an inch of Grey Goose La Poire, "would you be good enough to run downstairs to my cab and bring up my luggage?"

"My pleasure."

"You'll need a hoist and derrick," said Cordelia out of the side of her mouth.

"No, I'm traveling light this time. Just a few pieces." She followed Bolger with her eyes until he'd disappeared out the door. "Gorgeous. Gay, yes?"

"He's my nanny," said Hattie. "Wanna watch the pygmy hippos with me?"

"You're sticky, darling. Go wash your hands."

As Hattie trotted off to the bathroom, Cordelia whipped off her fedora and said, "You can't just . . . appear."

"I always *just* appear. It's part of my allure."

"Don't forget I'm your older sister. I changed your smelly diapers. You have no perceptible allure in my book."

"All right," she said, dropping the sophisticate act. "Here's the deal. I came because of our new joint venture. I'm not an idiot, which means I'm not sinking money into a theater unless I see it with my own eyes and get a chance to weigh in on the renovations. I mean, wake up and smell the greasepaint, *Deeya.* I'll be starring in the initial production, so I should have some say."

Cordelia cocked her head. "No, you won't."

"Yes, I will."

"No. I don't think so."

"Yes, absolutely."

"Over my dead body."

"You mean over your dead theatrical brainchild. I'm the one with all those lovely greenbacks. You want them, you get me— and I want veto power over which play we choose."

"We? *We.*"

"Call your real estate agent. Let's go see the space."

"Tonight?"

"You have something better to do?"

Jane motioned for Cordelia to follow her into the kitchen. When she didn't move, Jane slipped her arm through Cordelia's and dragged her. "It might not be so bad," she whispered, opening the refrigerator and cracking open a black cherry soda. She handed it over. It was Cordelia's relaxation beverage of choice. "She's got a huge name. She starred in that thriller with Michael Douglas a few years back. She's one of the biggest names in New York."

"*Used* to be," said Cordelia, glaring at the soda can.

"Don't crush it until you finish drinking it."

"She thinks she can walk in here and take over."

"If you want her backing, you'll need to humor her."

Cordelia took a few sustaining gulps. "I can do this. I am Woman."

"You take care of your sister, and I'll head over to GaudyLights."

"Oh. Right. Sorry for the change in plans."

"Can't be helped."

Squaring her shoulders, Cordelia marched out of the kitchen, ready to do battle. "I'll make that call to my real estate agent," she announced.

"Thank you, Jane," said Octavia. "As always, you're the voice of reason in my sister's life. Are you leaving?" she asked, watching Jane slip into her coat.

"I'm afraid I have plans. I'm sure I'll see you again, unless your visit is a short one."

"Oh, no. I'll be around."

Cordelia gritted her teeth.

On the way to the elevator, Jane crossed paths with Bolger. He had a garment bag slung over one arm and was wheeling an extra-large leather Pullman and carrying a valise. "Boy, she's something," he said, obviously referring to Octavia.

" 'Something' is as good a term as any."

"Not terribly maternal, though."

"Which is why Cordelia has custody of Hattie."

"Cordelia's not exactly a poster child for maternal instincts either, although she loves that kid beyond reason—pygmy hippos and all." He leaned close. "Octavia didn't pay the cabdriver, so I did."

"Just let Cordelia know. She'll take care of it."

"No, it's not a problem. It's just, she's sort of . . ."

"Entitled?"

"Yeah."

"Have fun. Looks like she'll be around for a few days."

"Do they always fight like that?"

"Prepare yourself for lots of slamming doors."

"Think I'll take Hattie to the zoo tomorrow."

"Good man."

Avi yawned so deeply that she shuddered when she finished. Spending the early morning hours listening to Dorsey puke his guts out wasn't her idea of a restful night's sleep. Thankfully, when she needed to, she could tend bar on autopilot.

She was uncapping a Leinenkugel Honey Weiss when Dorsey moved up next to her and said, "Thanks for letting me stay last night."

She set the beer and two glasses of wine on a tray. "Can't exactly say it was a pleasure."

"And thanks for getting the key from the super."

She was too tired to be diplomatic. "I don't get why you're so secretive about your apartment."

"I'm not secretive. I just don't want him going in there, okay?"

"Him and anyone else."

"It's my business," he said, turning and walking back to the other end of the bar.

"Whatever," she muttered. When she spied Jane come in the front door, her mood brightened, and then, just as quickly, sank. Jane had probably read some of her book. She should never have given it to her.

"You're busy tonight," said Jane, easing onto a stool.

God, but she was beautiful. Hair in a French braid. Wearing a black turtleneck that hugged all the right places. Avi felt her pulse heat up. "Friday night, yeah."

"Did you get my text?"

"What text?"

"About dinner and a movie."

Avi couldn't stand it another minute. "Did you read any of the book?"

"I read all of it."

"You did? And you still want to talk to me?"

Jane folded her hands on the counter. "I loved it. I'm not lying. I thought it was brilliant."

"Really?"

"Have people really been that brutal about your writing? If so, I can't understand why. This book should be published. The fact that it isn't makes no sense to me."

Now Avi wanted to kiss her.

"So what about it? Dinner? A movie?"

"A real date?"

"And a chance to talk in more detail about the story."

This was almost too good to be true. "You're on."

"When do you have a night off?"

"I'll have to check my schedule. It goes up on the board tomorrow around noon."

Georgia sidled up and took a seat next to Jane.

"Something to drink?" asked Avi.

Georgia was dressed in a see-through black lace minirobe with black panties and no bra, her lush blond hair piled on top of her head, with tendrils falling loosely around her face. Avi couldn't help but laugh at Jane's reaction. She'd actually blushed, swallowed hard a couple of times, and tried like hell to tear her eyes away from Georgia's breasts. Innocence was a hard-to-find commodity in Avi's world. "Give her a break," she said.

"Come on, play with me," said Georgia, half-whispering the words into Jane's ear.

"It's tempting," said Jane, "but I think I'll pass."

"Boo hoo. I'll be around all evening." She winked at Avi and strolled off.

"Boy, she doesn't give up," said Jane.

"It's why she makes such good money."

"That and her looks. Is she a member of the tribe?"

"She lives with a boyfriend, but she told me she swings both ways."

Jane examined the drink specials. "These are new."

"Anything appeal?"

"Make me a Waldorf. You know what that is?"

"Are we playing Stump the Bartender? Of course I do." She rattled off the ingredients.

"Hey, I have a burning question. How old are the dancers?"

"Depends," said Avi. "I've known strippers as old as forty, though that's an exception. You've got to be in great shape to do the pole moves and be on your feet all night. Most of the women here are in their twenties. A few are in their early thirties. I haven't seen actual birth certificates, but I'd say early thirties is the upper limit. You looking for the dead guy's sister? Is that why you came in tonight?"

"That's one of the reasons," said Jane, taking a sip of the Waldorf and giving Avi an approving smile.

"Did you find out any information on the sister—like how old she is?"

"Thirty-seven or thirty-eight."

"Hmm. All the black strippers are in their early twenties."

"What about that manager? The one I saw arguing with that other bartender— Dorsey."

"Diamond Brown? Yeah, she'd be around that age. So is Shanice Williams, the executive chef."

"She'd never talk to me."

"No love lost, huh?"

Jane picked up her drink. "Stay tuned. I'll be back."

For the next hour, Avi made drinks and spoke to customers and staff, all the while keeping an eye on Jane as she talked to all the African American employees of a certain age. She was smart enough to hand each person a twenty first, which at the very least bought their attention for a few minutes.

As the ten o'clock show was finishing, Georgia sauntered up and sat down on one of the stools. "You and Jane seem pretty tight."

"She's great."

"She'd be quite a catch. I hear she owns a couple of restaurants. She's a dyke, right?"

Avi nodded.

"Then what's wrong with her? Dykes who come in here want the same thing a guy wants. I've tried coming on to her more than once, and she just blows me off."

"Ever think you're not her type?"

"Are you kidding me? I'm everybody's type."

"Your ego is showing. Or maybe it's your id."

"If I want her, she's mine."

"Look, Georgia, she's a good person. Maybe you should play cat and mouse with someone else."

"I like a challenge. Besides, you know what they say. Keep your friends close, your enemies closer."

"Meaning what?"

Glancing over her shoulder, Georgia said, "I *mean*, what's with her? Talking to every black woman in the club. Don't white women qualify?"

"She's looking for someone."

"Yeah, I know. Jane Lawless, licensed private investigator."

"Funny."

Georgia propped her chin on her hand. "No, she really is."

"She's a restaurateur."

"And a PI."

"Where did you hear that?"

"She gave me her card. Nolan & Lawless Investigations."

It didn't make any sense. If Jane was a professional, why hadn't she said something about it? In that instant, the truth of the situation struck Avi like a thunderbolt.

"Something wrong?" asked Georgia.

She glanced down at an order a waitress had just handed her. "I've got nine drink orders to fill."

"And I've got a rotation coming up." Rearranging the front of her robe, Georgia sauntered back to the tables.

25

Emmett staggered off the plane at MSP Just after midnight, feeling as if he'd fought a war. Thanks to several additional Scotch and waters, a talkative passenger in the next seat, and a steely resolve not to look out the window, it was a war he'd won, though at a cost. He was drunk and too strung out to negotiate a cab ride home. He called his son on his way down the Gold Concourse and was grateful when Roddy answered on the first ring.

"I need you to pick me up."

"You sound strange."

"Everything's fine. Are you delivering pizzas?"

"Not tonight."

"You know where to come."

"Be there in fifteen."

Emmett spent the next few minutes sitting at a counter staring into a cup of black coffee. He considered ordering a burger but wasn't hungry. He needed to talk to Vince right away, get his take on what they should do about this maniac who was after them. It wasn't a stretch to think that he was no longer safe anywhere—even in his own house. He'd felt that way all week, though for different reasons.

His son pulled his rattletrap station wagon up to the curb under the AirNorth sign shortly before twelve thirty. Emmett slipped in, buckled his seat belt, and let his head drop back. The decision not to take a cab had been the right one.

"Another bad flight?" asked Roddy.

"You could say that."

"You've been drinking again. Come on, Dad. You promised you'd stop."

Emmett sighed. "I know I did . . . and I will."

"When?"

"Soon."

They wound their way though a maze of roads on their way out of the airport, finally driving under the freeway sign that read, ST. PAUL.

Emmett shut his eyes.

"Dad?" said Roddy a few minutes later.

"Hmm?"

"I need to tell you something."

"Yeah?"

"You're gonna be angry."

After what he'd been through, he doubted it would even register.

"You know that girl who hanged herself? The one from my school?"

"Right."

In the darkness, Roddy stared straight ahead. "I did know her. I'd dated her for a few months my junior year. Ended kind of badly. I got called into the principal's office today. Me and Lukas, and Brady Thompson and Darius Jones."

Brady was the star wide receiver on the football team. Darius was the nose tackle. Along with Lukas, they were Roddy's best friends. Emmett liked all of them, thought they were great kids with tons of talent and drive. They were all headed to major universities on football scholarships. "Why? Was it about the girl—or the football team?"

Roddy took an off-ramp. When he reached the top of the hill, he turned right and eased the station wagon over to the curb. Still staring straight ahead, he said, "We all got suspended."

"For what?"

"Look, Dad, you gotta understand something first. We were just having fun. We didn't mean anything by it. It started last fall. Brady—you know he's got this weird sense of humor—he began calling some of the fat girls out, telling them they needed to stop eating so many doughnuts. We all started doing it. It was a joke, you know? It was hilarious. I mean, they needed to lose weight."

"Oh, Roddy."

"I know, I know. It was mean—but they were gross. Hard to look at. Eye pollution was what we called them. Then the whole thing kind of morphed into something else. Like, one night we got to talking about all the skeezes we knew."

"Skeezes?"

"You know. Totally dubious girls. Like Lukas says—a chick with the morals of a guy."

Emmett turned to look at him. "Go on."

"Brady said he'd been asking girls out since he was thirteen just to see how far he could get them to go. Darius said the same thing. Me and Lukas, we'd never been like that, but we liked hearing their stories. That's when Brady got this idea to put together a list—all the girls we'd dated and what they liked to do—you know, like, in bed. Okay, so it was raunchy. I admit to that. But it was all in good fun. And, I guess, it was a kind of payback on the girls who dumped us for no good reason. After a while, I think Brady and Darius started making stuff up about some of the girls who wouldn't go out with them. Maybe Lukas did, too."

"What about you?"

"Well, maybe one or two skanks. You ask me, those bitches deserved it. You didn't see how they treated me. They had it coming."

"Is that how you think about women? Skanks? Bitches? Is that what I've taught you?"

"Hell, Dad, it was no big deal."

"Did anybody but the four of you know about the list?"

Roddy turned his head toward the side window. "That's the problem. I never in a million years thought Brady would show the thing to anyone else."

"Who'd he show it to?"

"I don't know. A couple friends. And they showed some other people, and someone sent it to the girls on the list. And a bunch of other students. I don't know how many."

"Lord, Roddy. When was this?"

"This past Monday. It was like the list went viral. Everybody had a copy the next day."

"Was the girl who died on the list?"

Roddy's head sank to his chest. "Yeah."

"That's why you were suspended. You deserved it. How did the principal know who'd created the list?"

"I don't know, but he did. He was hopping mad. Red faced. He screamed at us for half an hour." Turning to his dad with tears in his eyes, Roddy continued, "I think they're going to expel us. They called the fat jokes and the skank list bullying."

"It was."

"No, you don't get it. It was just . . . we never meant—"

"Roddy, this is serious."

"I *know*. If I get expelled, I can kiss LSU—and every other college that's contacted me—good-bye. LSU was my ticket. My ticket, Dad. Most guys don't have one, but I do. All I ever wanted was to play football."

Emmett couldn't believe his ears. "A girl is *dead*."

"She must have been, like, weak or unstable or something. The list, it was just silly."

"I love you, son, but I think you're the one who doesn't get it."

Through deep, heaving sobs, Roddy choked out, "The police want to talk to us. Brady's dad got him a lawyer. I . . . I think I'm going to need one, too. I was the one who dated her. That makes me their prime target. Like I wanted her to die. Like I'm somehow responsible."

Emmett slid over and put his arm around his son, holding him tight as the cries, the chest chokes, and the pent-up wails of desperation flowed out.

"This is the end," said Roddy. "I lose everything I've worked my ass off for because of this. It's not fair."

Emmett felt sick inside, as if he'd somehow passed on his own fatal flaw to his son. Roddy had made a serious mistake, the same way Emmett had, one that would forever change his life. He could hardly tell him that his fears were unfounded. Instead he said, "You're my boy. Nothing will ever change that. We'll work this out together. Okay? You and me. I'll be with you the entire way."

Solidarity with his son was all Emmett had to give. In the end, he knew it wouldn't be enough.

26

Jane's first conversation that night was with Diamond. They sat at a table, Jane with her drink, Diamond with a Perrier. Jane couldn't do much except ask questions and watch her body language as she answered. She began by explaining her connection to DeAndre Moore.

"You say his uncle was a retired cop?" Diamond tipped the Perrier bottle back and took a swallow. "That's bad news. And you're a PI."

Jane was selective about how she used that information. She'd learned to trust her gut. Some people closed up as soon as they heard the words. For others, knowing that she was an investigator seemed to impress them, as if she had more power than the average citizen.

"I understand he was looking for his sister," said Jane. "She works here."

"That right."

"Would you know anything about that?"

"Can't say that I do."

Diamond was coolness personified. If she was Sabrina, it was going to take more than simple conversational give-and-take to rattle her. "*Are* you his sister?"

Her smile was like a razor. "If I was, I don't think I'd be telling you about it. Don't much like cops—or PIs."

"That's not an answer."

"Well, hon," she said, a pleasant Southern lilt to her voice, "it's all you're gonna get."

"Did you ever talk to Moore while he was at the club?"

"No more than a few words. I saw him at the bar night after night, so I did what I always do—tried to encourage the man to get closer to the stage."

"Did you see him talking with anyone in particular?"

"Sure. The bartenders. I saw Georgia apply pressure a few times. I don't think she got him to bite. I'll tell you the same thing I told the police. I don't know nothin' about the guy."

"You like working in a strip club?" asked Jane, knowing she was getting nowhere.

"It's a job."

"Ever done any dancing?"

"No way." Nodding to Jane's drink, she said, "Are you enjoying that?"

"It's good."

"We pride ourselves on our bar. Be sure you have another before you leave."

After two fruitless hours, two more Waldorfs, and nine additional conversations, Jane finally threw in the towel. Unless these women were lying, which was possible, she figured she'd spent two hundred bucks on nothing. Strangely, she'd enjoyed the conversations. All the women seemed to be wonderful people, with interesting lives. Even the runner with the horrific breath and bad teeth, the one who kept punctuating her statements with a deep, excruciating smoker's cough, had seemed like a diamond in the rough.

Feeling uncharacteristically buoyant, Jane made her way through the back hall. As she was about to round the corner onto the night-club floor, Georgia appeared directly in front of her.

"Are you stalking me?" asked Jane, trying not to focus on Georgia's breasts but losing the battle.

"Go ahead. Look. Doesn't cost you anything."

"No? It's been my experience that very little in life is free."

"How philosophical. Me, I'm more concrete. I like to live in the moment. Don't take this the wrong way, Jane, but it seems like you should try living in the moment a little more yourself."

"Think so?"

Pushing Jane back into the deserted hall, she continued. "I've got a present for you."

"Georgia, I'm not sure—"

She placed a finger against Jane's lips, smiled like the Cheshire cat, then leaned in and kissed her.

"Um—"

"Just shut up."

"Okay." Jane responded in kind by backing Georgia up against the wall and kissing her with surprising enthusiasm, running her hands up underneath her lace robe. "Whoa," she said, standing back. She wasn't quite sure what had gotten into her.

"Don't stop."

If she hadn't thought of Avi just then, she might not have.

"Jane, come on. I won't bite. Unless you want me to." She pulled her back in. "There's a room upstairs where we can be alone. I'll take you."

Slipping a hand behind Georgia's neck, Jane looked deep into her eyes, not wanting to analyze, just to feel. Not wanting to go anywhere but right here. She pressed her body against Georgia's, her hand moving down the soft skin of her stomach.

An Asian guy in a chef's coat rushed past them, clearing his voice and giving them a disapproving look.

Falling together, giggling, then sinking to the floor, they laughed like naughty teenagers.

"Let's go upstairs," cooed Georgia.

"I don't think so."

"Aw, you are a real buzz kill. Remember I said I had a present?"

"I thought that was the present."

"Go back to the women's restroom. The middle stall. The door's shut, but nobody's inside."

"What am I supposed to find?"

"Just go."

Doing as she was told, Jane got up and crossed the hall to the restroom. Catching sight of herself in a mirror, she stopped for a second to pin a few wisps of hair back into her braid and tuck her turtleneck back inside her slacks. Feeling a little more put together, she opened the stall. Inside she found a line of white powder on a GaudyLights napkin resting on a small shelf above the toilet paper, a dollar bill rolled up next to it.

"Hell, no," she said, backing up, beginning to feel as if she'd made a big mistake.

Returning to the hallway, she found Georgia attempting to interest a bald guy with a paunch in a table dance.

Georgia winked.

"Thanks," said Jane, "but no thanks."

Georgia moved away from the guy. "No?"

"No."

Making a pouting face, Georgia returned to Mr. Paunch and her hard sell, as if what had just happened between them was nothing more than a moment of lust with a customer—albeit nonpaying—which, of course, it was.

Jane snaked her way through the tables on her way back to the bar. As she sat down, she saw that Avi was nowhere in sight. Diamond Brown had taken her place. Attempting to get her attention, she waited until Diamond came to take her drink order, then said, "What happened to Avi?"

"She left, sugar. Not feeling well."

"Do you always stand in when one of the bartenders has to leave early?"

"Couldn't find anyone else on such short notice. We need to keep the customers happy."

Down the bar, Dorsey was watching their interaction with a smirk on his face. Shanice Williams, who sat across from him nursing a glass of wine, looked positively menacing.

"If you're interested, Avi cut out about an hour ago," said Diamond. "Can I get you something? You're drinking Waldorfs, right?"

"No thanks," said Jane, feeling deflated. She'd been looking forward to spending the rest of the evening with Avi, maybe getting a bite to eat after her shift was over. When she turned around, trying to figure out what to do with the shank of the evening, she found Vince Bessetti steaming toward her through the crowd.

"You got a couple minutes?" he asked. Even a few feet away, he wreaked of men's cologne.

She shrugged. "Sure."

"I pulled some figures together."

"Figures?"

"You said you might be interested in investing in GaudyLights."

"Oh, right. Sure, I'd be happy to look at them."

"Why don't you come back to my office. It's a little loud in here to talk."

Glad to get away from the pounding music, Jane followed him down a dimly lit hallway directly behind the nightclub's main floor.

"In here," he said, unlocking a door and shoving it open with his foot. "There's a chair next to the desk. Make yourself comfortable. I'll just be a second." He stepped over to a filing cabinet and began searching through the top drawer.

For some reason, the room didn't feel quite solid. Glancing at her watch, Jane saw that it was a quarter of one. It was odd that she didn't feel as tired as she normally would at this time of night. She was concerned about Avi, but it was probably too late to call, especially if she wasn't feeling well and had gone to bed when she got home. Jane figured she would text her, ask her to call in the morning, just to make sure everything was okay. Maybe she'd take her some homemade chicken soup tomorrow. The idea made her smile.

Waiting for Bessetti to find what he was looking for, she surveyed the office. It was fairly large, with a comfortable-looking couch, a flat-screen TV, and a few chairs. Most of the furniture was boringly utilitarian. A calendar of nude women hung on the wall next to a couple of GaudyLights posters.

"Who designed the posters?" asked Jane.

"A friend of a friend," said Bessetti absently, still digging through the files. "I was sure I'd put the pages right in front."

Scanning the desktop, Jane sat up straight when she saw a piece of typing paper lying on top of a stack of magazines with the same Greek word written on it that she'd found in DeAndre's hotel room. Moving closer to get a better look, she was surprised when Bessetti said, "Find something interesting?"

She looked up, unable to read his expression. "No. Well, yes. This is Greek, right?"

"It is," he said, his eyes locked on her.

Something had just happened, she wasn't sure what. In a split second, the warmth in his manner had turned subzero.

"You read Greek?" he asked.

"Me? No."

"But you knew they were Greek letters."

"I was in a sorority at the U of M. They'd revoke my membership if I couldn't recognize Greek."

He sat down, dropping a file folder on the desk. "I'm curious," he said, placing his hands flat on the folder. "You've lived in this town for what—fifteen, twenty years?"

"All my adult life."

"All your adult life," he repeated, tasting the words as he spoke them. "If you're so interested in strip clubs, how come it's taken you so long to visit us?"

"I wasn't the least bit interested until I indulged in a whim the other night." She could tell by his tone that the question had an important subtext—the real question. She wasn't sure what it was. Deciding to take a chance, she nodded to the page with the Greek letters and said, "If you don't mind my asking, where'd you get that?"

He pulled it in front of him and smoothed the rumpled surface. "From the police. They found a thin fragment of copper with those letters stamped into it."

Copper, thought Jane. Was that what DeAndre had written about? "Found it where?" she asked.

"A friend of mine was murdered."

"Here in town?"

"In Brooklyn Center."

The answer turned her upside down. It had to be Royal Rudmann. "I'm sorry to hear that," she said. "Was he a longtime friend?"

"You could say that." Leaning back, he went on. "So, have you given any thought to how much money you might like to invest in the club?"

"I'd need to look at your figures first, have a conversation with my lawyer and my accountant."

"Say, a hundred thousand?"

"It's possible. No promises."

"Do you have any questions I could answer? You might be interested in a tour."

"Not tonight. Like I said, I'll need to take a look at your figures first."

He flexed his fingers. "That's reasonable," he said, shoving the file across the desktop. "Do me a favor. Stick around long enough to see the 1:00 A.M. floor show. We always reserve the best for last."

"I'll do that," said Jane, rising and shaking his hand. "Thanks for the information."

27

Jane found herself an empty table near the front and watched the final show. Georgia was one of the dancers and gave her . . . all on the pole. Standing a good fifteen feet away along the side wall, Shanice ignored the show and instead glared at Jane. Jane had the sense that if she'd had a mustache to twirl, she would have been twirling it. Jane found it strange, even a little pathetic, that she still held a grudge.

Shortly after one thirty, Jane left the club, bundling a wool scarf around her neck as she wound her way through the back parking lot. After so much loud music, the minimal traffic noise outside seemed like utter silence. She had so much on her mind that she barely noticed her surroundings as she trotted to her car. It had been hours since she'd had anything to drink, thus she felt it unnecessary to take a cab. She'd found a parking space at the far south end, and thankfully, because she'd driven her Mini, she'd been able to squeeze into it.

Coming out of the lot a few minutes later, she turned onto Washington Avenue, then west, working her way through the side streets in the north loop. As she was about to pull onto 5th, flashing lights lit up her rearview mirror. At first she figured the cop car was trying to pull around her, but it eventually penetrated that the cruiser was following her.

Moving to the curb, she lowered the window.

The cop sauntered up and leaned over to talk to her. He was around her age, burly, with small, unfriendly eyes. "You got a taillight out."

"I do? Sorry. I'll be sure to have it repaired."

He glanced inside the car. "Let me see your license and registration."

She flipped open her glove compartment to get the registration and handed both over.

Using his flashlight to examine them, he said, "Step out of the car, please."

"Something wrong?"

"Just step out."

She wasn't sure what was going on.

Once she was standing in the street, he said, "I'd like to examine the inside of your vehicle."

"Why? No."

"Step to the back of the car, please."

"What's this about?"

"The back of the car, ma'am."

Grudgingly, she moved, waiting while he ducked inside. He emerged a few seconds later holding a plastic sack. "What's in this?" he asked.

"I have no idea. I've never seen it before."

Opening the sack, he took a taste. "Turn around."

"Not before you tell me what's going on."

Pushing her roughly against the rear fender, he cuffed her hands behind her back. "You're under arrest for possession."

"Of what?"

"Looks like about half a gram of cocaine."

She sucked in a breath, trying to force away the panic in her chest. "It's not mine."

"Then what was it doing in your car?"

"I don't know, but I didn't put it there."

"Sure," he said, grabbing her arm and leading her back to his squad. "It's amazing how often I hear that. Like it's magic that the stuff just—poof—appears."

"You had no right to do a search without my permission."

"Got a visual, lady. It was on the floor in plain view."

"If it was in plain view, I would have seen it, and I *didn't*."

"Take it up with the judge."

Before she knew what was happening, she found herself staring out the back window, watching the lights of downtown Minneapolis rush past as she was driven away to be booked.

Vince scanned the empty parking lot, relieved to see that all the vehicles were gone. Springing down the steps to his car, he couldn't seem to shake the feeling of being watched. As the owner of the building and the lot behind it, he'd commandeered the best parking space for himself. On this bleak winter night, however, it was little solace.

This had been one of the worst days of Vince's life. Right along with the knowledge that someone was out there trying to kill him came a heavy, almost suffocating paranoia. It wasn't simply an excess of cocaine. Someone really was out to get him. Every unexpected sound or sudden movement sliced into him. He did have one thing going for him, a piece of critical information that the others never knew. His killer, whoever he or she was, liked to do his or her handiwork up close and personal. Tatum, Rudmann, and Crowder had all been murdered inside, where they lived, which meant it was unlikely that someone would take a shot from a distance. As long as Vince could protect himself, as long as he knew it was coming, he had a leg up on the others.

He began to scrape a thin coating of frost off his windshield, then groaned when he noticed that his tire had gone flat. Bending down to take a closer look, he found a pocketknife stuck in between the treads.

"Shit, shit, shit," he said, straightening up and smacking his hand on the hood. Hearing a car and then the crunch of tires on snow, he looked up in time to spot a red sedan pull into the alley. As it rolled up next to him, the window came down and one of his strippers called out, "Need some help?"

Before he could answer, she was out the door.

"No problems here, Georgia. Just get back in your car and go home."

She stepped closer. "Jeez, hon, that's nasty. Your tire's completely flat. Is that a knife?"

"I can handle it."

"Want me to call the cops?"

When he noticed that her hands were hidden inside the pockets of her jacket, all expression died on his face. He pulled his Walther from his coat pocket. "Just back up and get the hell out of here."

She raised her hands. "Sure. Whatever."

He kept the gun on her, sweating inside his coat's heavy fleece lining, until she drove away.

"Jesus," he said, almost collapsing against the trunk. As he stood trying to catch his breath, he felt a twinge of pain in his chest. "No way," he said, staggering back to the steps. With all the exercise he did every day, all the desserts he'd passed up, all the lousy protein shakes he sucked down instead of burgers and fries, no way was he going to die of a freakin' heart attack. He waited, gripping the railing, until the feeling passed, then went back inside, resetting the security code and returning to the safety of his locked office.

Feeling humiliated, raw, and dead tired from a night spent being booked, fingerprinted, stripped of her clothes, ordered to wear a jumpsuit, drug tested, and moved from one small claustrophobic box to another, Jane stood next to her father at the arraignment the following morning. Initially, she'd been loath to phone him, thinking that this was the last thing he needed, but she became more and more frightened by the impersonal, brutal, and seemingly all-powerful bureaucracy all around her, and because he was a defense attorney, albeit a semiretired one, she made the call. When they'd first been allowed a brief conversation, she could see her own horror mirrored in his eyes. They were both doing their best to calm each other's fears.

After pleading her case, the judge set bail. An hour later, she was released ROR.

Her father drove her home and stayed downstairs in the kitchen making them breakfast while she went upstairs to shower and change into clean clothes. It felt so good to be in her own house that she could have kissed the floors, the walls, the furniture. Thinking that there had to be a better way to show her euphoria, she kissed Mouse instead.

At the kitchen table, over cheese omelets, toast, and coffee, Jane finally began to process what had happened.

"It was a setup," said her dad.

"Could that police officer have been part of it?"

"I hate to say it, but yes. It wouldn't be the first time some bent cop targeted an innocent person, most likely for money, or because he owed someone a favor."

"But why?"

Ray spread strawberry jam on his toast, thinking it over. "You said you've been spending a lot of time at GaudyLights?"

"Because of DeAndre Moore's murder."

"That place is a snake pit. You can bet someone there was behind it."

Jane thought back to the cocaine Georgia had left in the bathroom stall last night as a present. If she'd taken the bait and used it, the coke would have been in her system when the police did the drug test. That was a little too close for comfort. Had Georgia set her up?

"What happens now?" she asked, holding the coffee mug in both hands.

"The next court date will be six weeks from now. This is a felony, Jane. We're talking *serious crime*. If you're convicted, even if you don't go to jail—and that's a big 'if'—you could lose your liquor license for both restaurants, as well as your PI license. You might have to pay a significant fine. The conviction would be public knowledge. Fact is, the charge might already be."

All of a sudden, Jane didn't feel quite so hungry. "What should I do?"

"I made some calls while you were upstairs. I've got my people working on it. For the time being, stay out of GaudyLights. Understood?"

She nodded.

"You need to get some sleep. Don't try to analyze what happened until you're rested. You'll just be spinning your wheels."

"Good advice."

"I'll call you when I know anything. Might take a while."

Jane studied her father's strong face, seeing the affection in his eyes and feeling steadied by it. His hair, once a chestnut brown like hers, had turned silver and then, in the last couple of years, white. He was still a handsome man with a formidable voice and an imposing manner, but he was smaller somehow. Age was playing all of its dirty tricks, the ones even a practiced lawyer couldn't refute.

"Thanks, Dad."

"Eat your food."

28

No rest for the wicked, thought Emmett, gazing up at the white colonial with dark green shutters that Vince Bessetti called home. On his way over, Emmett had been mentally riffing on that little biblical aphorism. He'd concluded that he didn't want to rest. In the Bible, the words "rest" and "death" were often synonymous. The wicked were doomed to hellfire. Thus, no rest for the wicked was just fine with him if it meant more time before his ultimate consignment to eternal damnation.

Vince's house was twice the size of his own house, with a three-stall garage and a wrought-iron fence that encircled the property. Standing at the front door, Emmett thought back to Vince's middle-of-the-night phone call. He'd demanded that Emmett come by his house today at 10:00 A.M. sharp. He'd whispered, then shouted, then whispered again, acting like a man coming apart at the seams. He kept repeating that they had to make a plan. They couldn't just wait around while this stalker picked them off. Emmett was glad to let Vince take the lead on it, especially after what he'd heard from his son last night.

It had been a busy morning. An old friend, Gavin Rand, a criminal defense attorney, had stopped by just after eight. Sitting down at the kitchen table, Emmett allowed Roddy to tell his story. As he listened, a few details his son hadn't mentioned before leaked out. Not only had Roddy and his friends been bullying other students, but after football season was over, they'd been doing a lot of drinking. Even using something called ketamine—a substance Emmett had never heard of before.

Once Roddy was finished, Gavin asked him questions, waiting through Roddy's stumbling answers. He eventually agreed to take the case. He stressed that if the police came to the house, Roddy should not allow himself to be interogated without Gavin and his father present, and he made it clear to Roddy that what he'd done wasn't the least bit funny. It was morally wrong and had probably contributed to his onetime girlfriend's suicide.

Emmett regretted that he didn't have much money in the bank, but if he had to, he intended to take out a second mortgage on the house to pay his son's legal expenses. Gavin was a friend, but he didn't work for free. After gathering all the information he needed, he shook their hands. Roddy retreated to his room once Gavin had left, clearly ashamed and unnerved.

When the door to Vince's house finally opened, Emmett was jarred back to the present. A chunky women in a tan twinset and slacks peered at him suspiciously. He was wearing his pilot's uniform. He had the sense that she might not have opened the door if he'd been wearing street clothes.

"Can I help you?" she asked, taking in his cap and the braids on his jacket.

"I'm a friend of Vince's. Emmett Washington. He's expecting me."

"Oh, yes. Mr. Washington. I'm Shelly Bessetti, Vince's wife. He didn't mention that you were—" She stopped short of completing the sentence.

Emmett wasn't sure if she was about to say *black* or *in the military*.

She invited him in.

As he was standing in the foyer, Shelly shouted up the stairs, "Vince, honey. Mr. Washington is here." Turning back to Emmett she said, "Would you like coffee?"

"No thanks, I've already had plenty."

Vince, still wearing his bathrobe and slippers, bounded down the stairs. "We'll be down in the workout room," he said to Shelly. He led Emmett through the kitchen to a stairway at the back of the house, and they descended the steps into the basement.

"Take a seat," said Vince, nodding to a leather couch.

As Emmett sat down, taking in all the expensive equipment, Vince perched on the edge of a workout bench. "I spent the night at the club," he said. "Just got home a couple of hours ago. Had to get Shelly to drive me."

"How come?"

"Somebody stuck a knife in one of my front tires."

"You think it was—"

"Damn straight I do. I been thinking about hiring myself a bodyguard."

"Oh. Not much of a solution for me."

"Why not?"

"Can't afford it."

"Seems to me you can't *not* afford it."

There was no use arguing with him.

"You got a gun?" asked Vince.

"Hell, no."

"Here," he said, stepping over to a safe in the corner. He spun the dial and opened it, removing a revolver with a simulated wood handle. "It's a .22 caliber. Not much firepower, although it's better than nothing. If I were you, I'd go to a gun store and buy myself a cannon."

"Okay," said Emmett, taking the gun and stuffing it in his pocket. He felt numb, overwhelmed, unable to process.

Vince must have noticed something in his reaction, because he said, "What's wrong with you?"

"Didn't get much sleep."

"You think I *did*?" He hunkered back down on the bench. "Look, here's the key, what's going to keep us safe. Don't let anybody into your house. This maniac likes to kill up close. If you're alone, lock the doors and keep the gun handy."

"And hire a bodyguard."

"Right. I've already called a service. They're sending a guy out today, or at the latest tomorrow morning."

"Are we looking for a man or a woman? Remember that note on Crowder's door?"

"Yeah, the blond woman. Maybe it is a woman."

"Her daughter?"

"Hell, it could be the woman herself."

"Or maybe someone dressed up to look like a woman."

"Possible, I suppose."

"It's not fair." Emmett put his head in his hands. "I had nothing to do with what happened that night."

"Yeah, right."

"You four . . . you deserve to be punished."

"And you don't?"

"I was collateral damage."

"Hell, it was all so long ago." Vince rubbed his eyes, his forehead, raked a hand through his hair.

"It's pretty clear what that Greek word means."

"That we're scum. Yeah, I get it."

Jane assumed that Mouse, after being cooped up in the house alone all night, needed a walk. She put him in the backseat of her

CR-V and drove him over to Lake of the Isles. The fact that her Mini had been impounded by the police galled her. She liked the CR-V okay, but she hadn't had it long enough to form an emotional attachment. She still remembered with great affection the rusted green Saab she'd driven around for years, a time in her life when almost every dime she earned was funnelled back into her restaurant. It was funny how life seemed so much simpler back then.

Hooking a leash to her dog's collar, Jane walked him halfway around the lake. On her way back, she remembered that she hadn't checked her cell phone messages. Sitting in the front seat with the motor running and the heat turned up to broil, she switched it on and found three voice mails and four texts from Cordelia. Things must not be going well with Octavia. One call was from her executive chef at the Lyme House, one from a wine distributor, and the other from Barry Tune, returning her call. Nothing from Nolan, which didn't surprise her. Nothing from Kevante Taylor either. And nothing from Avi.

Jane thought about calling Cordelia and Nolan to let them know about her arrest, but with a head that felt like it was stuffed with cotton, she figured it was better to wait. She couldn't stand the idea of going over it again in the kind of detail they would demand.

She might not have wanted to talk about her arrest, but she couldn't stop thinking about it. In fact, she felt as if she were at the center of a mind blizzard. There were so many angles she needed to consider. Had someone planted the cocaine in her car just to mess with her, or had this been DeAndre's sister's way of telling her to back off? If the latter was true, then maybe she was closer than she thought to uncovering who Sabrina really was. She tried as hard as she could to remember the conversations she'd had last night, but her memory, always something she counted on, seemed to have failed her.

One particular matter bothered her like nothing else. If she was convicted of drug possession, her father had said, her liquor license could be revoked. She'd never even considered the fact that working as a professional PI might put her restaurants in jeopardy. If she couldn't serve alcohol, she might as well close her doors. Not many days ago, when she received her PI license from the state of Minnesota, she'd been sure she could have it all. She was a restaurateur and a private investigator. Now it looked as if she might lose both.

Back at the house, Jane found a pillow and a quilt and stretched out on the living room couch. There was one person she did want to talk to. She tried Avi's cell. When she was put through to her voice mail, she left a message.

"Avi, hi. It's Jane. I came back to the bar last night to talk to you, but Diamond Brown said you'd gone home—that you weren't feeling well. Hope you're feeling better today. I had kind of a train wreck of an evening, myself. Maybe, if you don't work tonight we could get together for dinner, or even just a drink. I'll be unavailable for the next few hours. When you get this, leave me a message or a text and I'll get back to you."

Jane was about to flip her phone closed when it began to vibrate. Checking the caller ID, she saw that it was Nolan's sister. She decided to take it.

"I'm so glad you answered," said Fannie Lou. "Alf finally called me, but only once. Is that infection better? Is he finally on the mend?"

Jane filled her in about the second antibiotic, saying that the doctors still felt it was the right one.

"Oh, my. It all sounds so serious."

Jane was worried, too—one of many worries, but one that kept bobbing to the top. She didn't feel, however, that her concern was something she needed to pass on to Fannie Lou.

"Will you ask him to call me?"

"I'm sure he will, when he's feeling better. Since I have you on the line," said Jane, "can I ask you something?"

"Sure. Anything."

"Did DeAndre have a girlfriend?"

"Do you mean Jazmin? He broke it off with her when she left to go to Europe. I think he was angry that she would leave him for an entire year. She's teaching in the Czech Republic. She's very lovely—and very civic minded. I thought they made a wonderful couple."

From what Jane had found in DeAndre's hotel room, the e-mail on his netbook, they'd apparently patched things up. She said as much to Fannie. "Somebody should probably contact her, let her know what happened."

"I'll call her mother."

"This next question may sound strange. Did DeAndre ever talk about a sister?"

"My Lord, no. He was an only child. We have that in writing."

"Was he close to his adopted brothers?"

"Oh, yes. Well, he and Antoine—we all call him Twan—would mix it up sometimes, but they loved each other, I know they did."

"Will Antoine be coming to the memorial?"

"He has such a miserable boss. I hope so."

"What's he do for a living?"

"Works for Carson & Keppler funeral home in Chicago. He has a degree in mortuary science."

"He's an undertaker?"

"Odd career choice, I know. My other two boys still live in town, thank the dear Lord. They're my rocks since my husband died."

"Is there anything I can do for you?" asked Jane. "I know this is a terrible time."

"You're sweet for asking. No, just get that brother of mine on the horn."

"I promise I'll do my best."

"That's all you can do. Thank you, Jane. Let's stay in touch."

Turning off the phone before it could ring again, Jane closed her eyes, hoping she could turn her mind off as easily as her cell.

29

Avi sat on her bed, cell phone in hand, a finger over the DELETE key, wondering how she could have misjudged Jane so totally. It had to be the same old problem, one that had dogged her since high school. When it came to physical attraction, she saw only what she wanted to see. She would take her needs and conjure up an illusion to fill them, thus utterly failing to understand her new love interest for who she really was.

A friend had once said to her, "Once is a mistake. Twice is a pattern." If that was true, what was four times? A blueprint? Even now, when she found herself attracted to a woman, she would convince herself that this time it would be different. That's how it had gone down with Jane. She might be a liar, she might have zero interest in Avi, and yet Avi couldn't see anything but the fantasy Jane—the good-looking entrepreneur, the wealthy, caring, funny, and literary-minded woman of her dreams. Admit it, she told herself. Jane had approached her for one reason only: to strip her of what was left of her pride, to take away everything she'd been able to salvage of her life, and ultimately to turn her over to the police and send her to jail.

Pressing DELETE, Avi consigned Jane's text message to oblivion.

When her landline rang, she reluctantly set the cell phone down and raced out to the kitchen to answer it.

"Hey," came a female voice. "It's Georgia. Let me in."

Except for Dorsey, nobody from GaudyLights had ever come to her apartment before.

"Avi? Are you there?"

"Yeah. I'll buzz you." She pressed the button, holding it for several long moments, then went to open the door.

Georgia stopped in the hall, a couple of feet away from the threshold. Looking tentative, she said, "My boyfriend kicked me out."

"That's . . . awful," said Avi, surprised to see her looking so ragged, so . . . unglamorous and normal.

"Dorsey told me where you live. I hope you don't mind. I needed a friend to talk to."

"Am I a friend?"

"Aren't you?"

Georgia had hit on Avi so many times that Avi considered it laughable. She was like a sexual wind-up toy, coming on to any warm body in her path. "Come in."

"Really? It's okay?"

"Of course."

Depositing herself on the couch, Georgia lowered her head, her long blond hair falling over the hands covering her face. "That bastard. He's been cheating on *me* and he throws *me* out."

"If your name is on the lease——"

"Freakin' douche. He knows how tight money is for me right now. This is my last few months in law school." Running a finger under her nose, she added, "It's his place, not mine. Every dime I make goes to pay for my degree."

And for clothes, and hairstyling, and shoes, and makeup, and perfume, and body glitter, and a membership at Life Time Fitness, thought Avi. It was simply more proof that it cost a lot to look like a cheap whore.

"I don't know what I'm gonna do," said Georgia, her face growing mottled and her eyes tearing up.

"What about your family?"

"My dad's dead. My mom doesn't speak to me anymore."

"Other family?"

"My sister lives in Portland."

"Friends?"

"I don't have time for friends."

"Well," said Avi, "I suppose you could crash here for a while, just until you find someplace else to stay." This was a variation on how she'd gotten in trouble last time. Not that it worried her. She wasn't the least bit interested in Georgia.

"Are you kidding me? You'd let me do that?"

"It would only be temporary, right?"

"God, you're a saint," said Georgia, scraping tears off her cheeks. "I'll find a way to repay you, I promise."

"You'll need to pony up some cash for food."

Georgia pulled her purse off the shoulder of her belted camel-hair coat. Digging around inside, she came up with a fairly thick wad. "Here," she said, peeling off two hundred dollars in twenties. "Will that do it?"

"More than adequate," said Avi. "Unless you're a big eater."

"To be honest, I am. I eat like a horse."

"You never diet to keep yourself slim?"

"I must have a supersonic metabolism."

Avi hated her on general principles.

"I've got a bunch of stuff in my trunk," said Georgia, leaping to her feet, all traces of anger and sadness gone.

"Need some help?"

As Avi retrieved her coat from the closet, a knock came at the front door. It was then that she realized how much she'd grown to like her privacy since coming to Minnesota. Today was turning into a zoo.

"Dorsey," she said, surprised to see him standing in the hall. He was holding a lumpy-looking blanket.

"Can I come in?" he asked, glancing furtively over his shoulder.

His pinched, nervous expression struck her as hilarious. "Why do you always look guilty?"

Georgia moved up behind her. "Hey, Dorse," she said, smiling seductively. "I hear the FBI's been asking questions about you. Something about an MX missile?"

Stepping inside, Dorsey ordered Avi to shut the door.

"You need to learn some manners," said Avi.

"You're so jumpy you're making me jumpy," said Georgia.

Lowering himself into a chair, he held the lumpy blanket carefully in his lap.

"What have you got there?" asked Georgia, her tone teasing.

Dorsey fixed Avi with a serious look and said, "You wanted to know why I've been so secretive? Why I never let anyone into my apartment?"

"You mean the missile thing was just a ploy?"

"This is *not* funny," said Dorsey. He opened the blanket, revealing a small, curly-haired black dog. The eyes were bright and playful, the demeanor calm and gentle.

"What's that?" asked Georgia, backing up a couple of steps. "Is it a dog? I'm not a dog person."

"Your loss," said Dorsey. "I found her out back of the apartment right after Christmas. I figure she must have been a gift, but when her owners discovered she couldn't hear well, they dumped her."

"She's deaf," said Avi, crouching down to get a better look.

"Not completely. I took her to the vet. She's only deaf in one ear. Hardly ever barks. I keep her in the bathroom when I'm gone. That way I'm sure she won't hear anything and start yapping."

"I see one big problem," said Avi, caressing the dog's head. "This is a nonpet building."

"I know. I just got busted. The super told me to get rid of the dog today—or else. He told me to take it to the humane society and have it put down. I'll never do that. *Never*. I thought . . . maybe you'd keep her until I can find her a good home. Unless you know someone who'd take her."

Avi shook her head. "Nobody."

"The super will never know she's moved in here. Just put her inside your coat when she needs to go out."

"Wait a minute," said Georgia. "That's a whole lot to ask. I mean, how many times a day do you have to take her outside?"

"A few. She's completely house trained. She scratches at the door when she needs to go out."

By the pained look in his eyes, Avi could tell that giving up the dog was hard for him.

"I'll keep her. Just until we can find her a home."

Georgia was about to object when Avi said, "I'd think you'd understand what it's like to be in a fix and need a place to stay." That shut her up.

"What's her name?" asked Avi, lifting her off Dorsey's lap.

"Gimlet." Glancing up at Georgia, he said, "Well, I am a bartender, after all."

"I like it," said Avi. "Gimlet, welcome to my home."

"I'll run back and get her food, her toys, her bed and blanket."

"You cut quite the father figure," said Georgia, biting the nail on her pinky.

"Bag it," said Dorsey. "Avi, you're a saint."

"So I'm told," she said, holding the dog up and kissing her muzzle.

When she'd signed up for sainthood, she hadn't realized that it came with such a heavy price. Always wanting to be Joan of Arc was another reason her life was such a disaster.

30

When Emmett entered the AirNorth offices on Saturday afternoon, he'd expected his supervisor and friend, Jerry Kingston, to be in the room when he talked to the senior management honcho from Detroit. He trusted Jerry and hoped he'd be an advocate for his many years as an airline pilot. Instead, he was ushered into a meeting room with only one man present. The man rose stiffly, introduced himself as Dan Coulter, shook Emmett's hand, and then nodded to a chair on the other side of the table. His cold manner immediately put Emmett off.

You can do it, Emmett told himself. You have to. This is your one shot at redemption—at meeting a challenge head-on, not cowering or selling your soul just to be one of the guys. This time you can't just drift with the herd because it's easier. The herd was wrong then and it's wrong now. For once in your life, you *have* to stand up for what you believe is right.

Coulter adjusted his glasses before removing a copy of Emmett's report from the file folder in front of him. Sliding it across the table, he said, "Is this the report you submitted?"

Emmett glanced at it. Nodded. He'd brought a stack of supporting materials with him, data he'd been unable to submit with the official report but something he wanted this man—and all of senior management—to see.

"I wonder if you could summarize your report for me, just so that we're both on the same page. I don't need all the details, just the . . . relevant information."

Emmett straightened his tie. Cleared his throat. "I was piloting flight 2091 from LAX to MSP last Monday night. We were about three hundred miles out when an unidentified aircraft came straight at us out of a thick bank of clouds. I was able to make an evasive maneuver, an emergency descent to avoid a collision. After regaining control of the aircraft, the UAF—unidentified aerial phenomenon—reappeared in front of us at approximately eleven o'clock and stayed there for the next few minutes. I got a good look at it during that time. So did my first officer. I asked my FO to radio the control tower at MSP and see if they could identify the craft on radar. Unfortunately, our radio had gone dead— as had much of our instrumentation."

"Describe this so-called UAF."

"It was huge, the size of a football field in length, triangular, with red lights at each of the three tips, and underneath, a white light directly in the center of the craft. All of these lights were pulsing. About a hundred miles from the airport, the craft pulled away from us and accelerated. It was gone in an instant."

"You say your first officer saw this, too?"

"There's no way he could have missed it."

"Passengers?"

"I doubt it. It was out ahead of us. I don't think passengers would have had the correct angle."

"And what do you think this so-called craft was?"

Coulter couldn't have made it any clearer that he didn't believe the report.

"Do you want me to say it was a hallucination?"

"Do you think it was?"

"Can two men hallucinate the same thing?"

Making a bridge out of his fingers, Coulter leaned back. "I had your first officer in here earlier today. He said he didn't see anything. He thought you might have had a little too much to drink, which was why you put the plane into an unexpected dive."

With as much gravity as he could muster, Emmett said, "I have never flown a plane drunk in my life. Never."

"That term can mean many things to many people."

"I had not been drinking before the flight. What I'm telling you is the truth."

"So your senior officer is lying."

Emmett wasn't given to making brash statements, but Coulter had left no choice. "Yes."

Tapping two fingers together, Coulter gave himself a couple of seconds. "Okay," he said. "We'd like you to talk to one of our psychologists."

"You think I'm crazy. Or that I'm making it up."

"Those thoughts had occurred to us."

"Because UFOs don't exist."

"Oh, I think they exist—in people's imagination. The plane lost altitude unexpectedly, that much we know. You simply picked an illogical way to cover it up."

"I'm not lying."

"I'm afraid that we're looking at possible termination, Mr. Washington, if you won't agree to see one of our doctors."

"Before I submit to this witch hunt, I want to make a couple of statements."

Coulter made a go-ahead gesture with his hand.

"First of all, airlines and the FAA need to stop covering up incidents like this, stop sweeping them under the rug and then blacklisting the pilots who have the guts to tell the truth. We almost collided with that aircraft, Mr. Coulter. We managed to avert a disaster, but it was close. Someday there will be a huge, catastrophic collision that nobody can deny. This is a safety issue."

Tapping his fingers on the table, Coulter said, "Do you have a second point?"

"I want you to include this in my file." He shoved across a fairly thick report.

"What is it?"

"It's a PDF of a paper written in 2001. 'Unidentified Aerial Phenomena.'"

"Forgive my bluntness, but I don't know why we should be interested in some crackpot's ideas about flying saucers. I can see that you believe in what you're saying, but belief isn't proof."

"This is a catalog of military, airline, and private pilot sightings compiled by the French NARCAP international technical adviser, Dominique Weinstein. He's not a crackpot. He believes, as I do, that a culture of airline bias causes pilots to underreport safety-related encounters with UAPs. I'm talking about near misses, like we had, disrupted avionics, close pacing by unidentified aircrafts, even collisions. You people *have* to start taking this seriously."

"I'm afraid, Mr. Washington——"

"Look," said Emmett. He pulled out another page. "I could have been sitting on your side of the table last week, just like you, mocking me for what I'm saying. Or pitying me because I'd gone off my rocker. UFO believers are all freaks. Nutcases. But all that changed when I witnessed an unknown object nearly collide with my aircraft."

"As I said, I understand that."

"Just listen a minute. You have to hear this. 'All Apollo and Gemini flights were followed, both at a distance and sometimes also quite closely, by space vehicles of extraterrestrial origin—flying saucers, or UFOs if you want to call them by that name.

Every time it occurred, the astronauts informed Mission Control, who then ordered absolute silence.' That was reported by Maurice Chatelain, former chief of NASA communications systems. Is he crazy?"

"You made that up."

"Check it out for yourself. I hope you do. Now this: 'At no time when the astronauts were in space were they alone. There was a constant surveillance by UFOs.' That was NASA astronaut Scott Carpenter," said Emmett. "Wouldn't he be in a position to know? Why would he lie?

"And another. 'Unknown objects are operating under intelligent control . . . It is imperative that we learn where UFOs come from and what their purpose is. I can tell you, behind the scenes, high-ranking military officers are deeply concerned about UFOs.' That was Admiral Roscoe Hillenkoetter, former director of the CIA.

"And finally: 'Extraterrestrial contact is a real phenomenon. The Vatican is receiving much information about extraterrestrials . . . from nuncios in various countries such as Mexico, Chile, and Venezuela.' The man who said that was a Vatican theologian, Monsignor Corrado Balducci. The pope ordered him to establish a commission on the subject because he believes it's something the Catholic church is going to have to address in the near future. If the pope thinks these sightings have some validity—"

"I'm not a religious man," said Coulter. "What the pope thinks or doesn't think has no bearing on my life."

"I have other quotes, too. Richard Nixon. Ronald Reagan. Mikhail Gorbachev. Barry Goldwater. Senior military officials in France, England, Iran, Chile. The prime minister of Japan. Men on our National Security Council. Why do American citizens always start snickering like teenagers when you bring up the subject of UFOs?"

"Of course, this is all very interesting," said Coulter, pushing away from the table. "However, the reason I'm here is to tell you that the board has already made its decision."

"Why doesn't that surprise me."

"You have two choices. Your supervisor will make an appointment for you with one of our staff psychologists. After we have a chance to talk with him, we'll make our final decision. In the meantime, you will be assigned to a desk."

"Or?"

"Or, you and AirNorth part company."

"And that's it?"

"That's it."

"Nothing I've said makes any difference."

"I'm afraid not."

On the way to the door, Emmett dropped the page of quotes in front of him. "Will you pass this on to the board of directors?"

"Of course," he said.

Like hell, thought Emmett. This meeting was for one purpose only—to get the ball rolling toward his eventual termination. He couldn't say it was a surprise, and yet now that it was over, the unfairness of it made him feel like putting his fist through a wall.

31

Jane woke in the late afternoon to the sound of Mouse's barking. Rubbing the sleep out of her eyes, she sat up, noticing that the light outside was beginning to fade. Between the ringing doorbell and the pounding, Jane was fairly sure she knew who was outside.

"Just a minute," she called, pushing aside the quilt and swinging her legs off the couch. "Good boy," she said, giving Mouse a quick back rub.

"I left you about six billion messages," said Cordelia, steaming into the front foyer. She handed Jane the mail she'd obviously pulled out of Jane's mailbox, then removed her leather gloves and slapped them into her hand. "I called your restaurants. They hadn't seen you. I called your brother. As usual, he wasn't home. I finally phoned your dad."

"Come in," said Jane.

"Don't change the subject." She marched into the living room and stood over the couch, glaring at the pillow and the quilt. "You've been sleeping. I woke you." Clasping Jane in a nearly bone-crushing bear hug, she said, "Your dad told me about the arrest. I know all. Understand all. I'm here for you, Janey. Whatever you need."

"If you understand all, maybe you can explain it to me."

After one final squeeze, Cordelia backed up and sat down. "You'll never guess what I heard on the radio as I was driving over."

"Don't make me guess," said Jane. Lowering herself onto the rocking chair by the fireplace, she ran her hands through her long, disordered hair, feeling a headache coming on.

Cordelia looked as if she were about to burst. "There's been another murder at GaudyLights. Well, not *at* GaudyLights, per se, but connected."

"Who?"

"Vince Bessetti."

Jane got up to turn on a lamp. She was still groggy and needed a moment to make what Cordelia had just said real in her mind. She also wanted to be able to see Cordelia, wreathed as she was in turquoise jewelry and a heavy dose of turquoise eye shadow. "How did it happen?" she asked, resuming her chair.

"All they said on the radio was that he was outside by his grill when the shooting occurred. His wife was inside the house and heard the gunshot. By the time she came outside, he was dead."

Jane remembered the Greek word she'd seen on his desk last night. "It was Sabrina. It had to be."

"That's my guess. You're likely one of her victims, too, because you're getting too close."

Jane tried to push away the crushed feeling in her stomach. "In what universe am I getting too close? Certainly not in this one. I have no idea who she is."

"You must know more than you realize."

Jane looked down at the pile of mail in her lap.

"Let's regroup," said Cordelia. "Jeez, I should have brought my bulletin board."

"I think we can regroup without it."

"Sure. We're all professionals here. Now. Here's what I was

thinking on the way over." She counted the points on her fingers. "DeAndre Moore came to Minneapolis to find his sister—and to get an answer to an important question, whatever that means. He found her working at GaudyLights. Her real name is Sabrina. She admitted to him that she'd murdered a man, most likely Burt Tatum, in St. Louis, and that she wasn't done. The murders may have something to do with her childhood. DeAndre was knifed by Elvio Ramos. We're not sure why, though he's admitted to the crime and is in jail. The day after DeAndre died, we think, his sister cornered Royal Rudmann in a motel room in Brooklyn Center and shot him to death. Vince Bessetti is her third victim. Will there be others?"

"Oh, God," said Jane, looking everywhere but at Cordelia. "What if nobody can stop her? What if she keeps killing?"

"Maybe Bessetti's death is the end of it. Let's hope so. Now, we have one significant clue—a thin piece of copper with the Greek word for moral impurity stamped into it. Something she leaves behind at the scene of the crime. Her calling card. I've been giving this some serious thought." She folded her arms protectively over her stomach. "What if she was gang-raped?"

If Jane had to guess, she'd bet it was something like that, too.

"We already know she plays nasty, which means she's probably the one who planted the coke in your car as a way to get you to back off."

"You might be right."

"No maybe about it."

Jane had taken off her watch before she showered and had forgotten to put it back on. "What time is it?"

"Quarter after five."

"We missed the local news."

"I called Bolger and told him to DVR the news at five and six."

"Good woman." Flipping through her mail, Jane found a letter from the Restaurant Group, Barry Tune's company. "Wait."

"What is it?"

Removing several sheets of paper, Jane read through them quickly. "It's the job application Shanice Williams filled out last fall when she applied to work at the Xanadu. I asked for it to be faxed to me. Barry's secretary must have dropped it in the mail instead. Says here she's thirty-eight."

"You think she might be——"

"It's possible." Jane had figured that Shanice's thinly veiled animosity toward her was all about being fired. Now she was wondering if it wasn't something else.

Eying Jane curiously, Cordelia barked, "What?"

"*What* what?"

"You're acting all antsy. Do you need to be somewhere and don't have the guts to tell me to shove off simply because I spent my perfectly good afternoon trying to track you down and then came over here with nothing but love and concern in my heart?"

"I need to make a phone call."

"To whom, may I ask?"

"Avi."

"Ah."

"I need to see if she's working tonight."

"You're *not* going back to that hellhole, Janey. Your father would have me drawn and quartered if I let you get anywhere near that place."

"Avi left early last night because she got sick. I just want to make sure she's okay."

"Good. Because you're coming with me tonight."

"I am?"

"My real estate agent was finally able to contact the owner of the old Criterion Opera House. We're being given an official tour. I want you there to protect me."

"From your sister?"

"From myself."

"What time?"

"Nine. On the dot."

"Okay. I'll be there."

When Jane got off the elevator on Five West shortly after six, she immediately spied Nolan's favorite nurse, Carla Stanhope, standing in the nurse's station. Jane approached and waited until Carla was done on the phone, then asked, "How's he doing tonight?"

Carla's serious expression didn't alter. "Not much change."

"When was his last pain med?"

"About an hour ago. He's probably asleep. You know, Jane, he called you his daughter this afternoon. I thought—"

"He got mixed up. I'm his niece."

"Right," she said, elongating the word.

Jane had the sense that she'd figured out it was a lie.

"If he's your uncle, why do you call him Nolan?"

"He doesn't much like Uncle Alfonse."

"No?" She thought about it for a few seconds, then laughed. "Understood."

"He can be pretty gruff."

"I think he's a sweetheart."

"Me, too," said Jane, "but don't tell *him* that."

Carla circled around the end of the counter and walked Jane down the hall.

"Is it okay if I wake him?"

"I think so, but I wouldn't stay long. The infection has weakened him."

Jane had assumed the second antibiotic would knock out the

234

infection and he'd be fine in a couple of days. "Do I have anything to worry about?"

Standing by the door, the nurse lowered her voice. "Let's just give it some time. A few prayers wouldn't hurt."

The comment shook her hard.

"Let me know if he needs anything," said Carla, walking off.

Jane entered the darkened room. In the bed next to the window lay a man with his leg in a brace. He was watching the TV attached to the wall. Jane gave him a friendly nod as she drew the curtain around Nolan's bed. He was asleep, snoring lightly. His cheeks looked hollow. Jane almost didn't recognize him. Not sure what to do, she checked the water in his pitcher and found that it was almost empty. She left for a moment to fill it. When she returned, she saw that his eyes were half-open.

"Nolan," she said, smoothing his hair. "It's Jane."

He looked up at her, tried to focus, to wet his lips. "Water."

Jane poured him a glass and then bent the straw toward his mouth.

"Better," he said.

"How are you feeling?"

"How do you think?" he asked, lifting his hand to gaze at the IV needle.

"They still think this antibiotic will work."

"Love those doctors," he whispered.

"About as much as some people love cops."

"I'm retired."

"Once a cop, always a cop. Isn't that what you always say?"

"Sounds like me," he said, closing his eyes.

She hated to see him so sick. The only good part was that she wouldn't be subjected to the third degree about her drug arrest. "Your sister called. She wanted to know how you're doing. I told her you'd call her in a few days, when you were feeling better."

He gave a little nod.

"I think I should let you sleep."

"Your dance card filled tonight?"

"Not really."

"It should be." He opened his eyes and gave a weak smile. "Afraid you're like me. A loner."

"Think so?"

"It's sad."

"What's sad?"

"You're young, so beautiful. You shouldn't be alone."

"I'm not. I have you. *Uncle*."

He laughed, coughed. "We're family, huh?"

"In every way that counts."

"Listen to your uncle, then. Go find someone. But," he added, reaching for her hand, "make sure she's smart, otherwise you'll lose interest."

"Good advice."

"Get out of here."

"I'll be back tomorrow."

"I'll be here," he said, his eyes drifting shut.

The words nearly dissolved her. "You better be," she whispered.

32

Jane called GaudyLights on the way out of the hospital. She'd called before she left the house, but the line just rang and rang. This time, a recording announced that the club would be closed due to the death of Vince Bessetti, the owner. The sexy voice invited her to check back tomorrow, when the club would return to normal business hours. So much for mourning the dead.

Feeling at loose ends, and more than puzzled that Avi hadn't returned any of her calls or texts, Jane drove across town, all along the way trying out various scenarios. Avi was under the weather and didn't want to talk. Her phone was out of juice and she didn't know it. She had a cold so bad that she'd lost her voice. None of the explanations satisfied.

Finding a lucky parking space on the opposite side of the street from Avi's apartment building, Jane could see from her car that Avi's unit was lit from one end to the other. Shadows thrown against the shades told her that she was home, and that she wasn't alone.

Dodging patches of ice as she dashed across the street, Jane bounded up to the steps to the front door just as a young man emerged from the building. Seeing the keys in her hand, he held the door open.

"Thanks," she said, amazed at her good luck.

"You betcha," he responded.

"Yah sure," she whispered, taking the stairs two at a time. She listened at Avi's front door for a few seconds before knocking. When the door was pulled back, Avi's startled face greeted her.

"Jane."

At least she hadn't forgotten her name.

"Can I come in?"

"Ah, okay." She didn't sound—or look—too thrilled.

Stepping inside, Jane saw Jason Dorsey sprawled on the couch, about to light up a joint. On the table in front of him was a half-empty bottle of Bombay Sapphire, a nearly full bottle of SKYY Ginger vodka, and a ceramic bowl filled with several dozen pills of various sizes, shapes, and colors.

"Join the party," said Dorsey, sucking in a lungful of smoke. He held it in, a silly grin on his face.

"You didn't return any of my calls," Jane said to Avi.

"No, I didn't, did I."

"Any particular reason?"

Out from the bedroom walked Georgia, dressed in a sheer lace minirobe, a black thong, a minimal black lace pushup bra, and fluffy white slippers. She was cradling a small dog in her arms. "Well, the marines have landed," she said, grinning at Jane. "Long time no see, gorgeous."

Jane blinked at Avi. Her first response—*What the hell is that woman doing in your bedroom?*—must have been written all over her face.

Avi smiled but said nothing.

Beginning to get the picture, Jane said, "What did Georgia tell you?"

"I don't kiss and tell," muttered Georgia, her pout about as fake as her breasts. She looked older and less glamorous out of the dim light. She came into the living room and made herself comfortable on one of the chairs, crossing her legs and dropping the dog to the floor.

"You didn't tell?" asked Jane. In one corner of the room, she noticed a suitcase with the name Dietrich on it.

"Tell what?" asked Avi.

"Look, can we talk? Alone?"

"Want a drink?" asked Georgia. She poured herself an inch of the vodka.

The dog scampered over to Jane and stood up on her hind legs, pawing at her jeans.

"She likes you," said Georgia.

"She?"

"Gimlet," said Dorsey. "She's a poodle puppy."

"I can see that," said Jane. The dog was all black curls and eager eyes.

"You could give a dog a good home," said Avi.

"I could?"

"You already have a dog. Another one wouldn't be a big deal."

"But," said Dorsey, coughing out smoke, "I mean, I thought she could stay here for, like, a little while longer."

"You know I could get tossed out if the super finds her in here," said Avi, hands rising to her hips. "You might be willing to risk getting tossed out, but I'm not."

Taking another toke, Dorsey said, by way of explanation, "The super just busted me. Said if I didn't get rid of her he'd get rid of me."

"She needs a good home," said Georgia. "How can you look into those deep brown eyes and refuse to help?"

Jane crouched down and picked the dog up. She seemed bright, sweet. Her sharp little puppy teeth gnawed gently on Jane's knuckle. She couldn't have been more than ten pounds, if that. "How old is she?"

"The vet thought about four months." Dorsey tapped ash into a Coke can. "She's starting to lose her baby teeth. I found one in a chew toy last week. She has a hearing problem. I think that's why she was dumped."

"I don't know what to say," said Jane. The dog certainly was adorable. Then again, taking a new critter into her life wasn't something she should do without careful consideration.

"She's house trained," said Avi.

"Do you really want me to take her?"

"Why not? Yes, I do. As a favor to me."

Everyone in the room was staring at her. "Well, okay. Sure," she said. She set Gimlet down and watched her scamper over to Dorsey. If the dog didn't work out, she could always find her a different home.

"It's not like I want to give her up," said Dorsey, cuddling her in his arms. His lips trembled, and for a moment he looked as if he might cry. "I love the little runt, you know? Hard not to."

Jane stood up and stuffed her hands into the pockets of her jeans. With everyone's attention drawn to Dorsey, she moved closer to Avi. "Come on, talk to me."

"This really isn't a good time," said Avi. "You can see that I have company."

"I know, but like I said, you haven't returned any of my calls."

"Don't mind us," said Georgia, poking a finger through the pills in the bowl. "We can entertain ourselves."

"Out in the hall?" asked Jane, nodding to the door.

Reluctantly, Avi followed her.

Trying to act nonchalant, Jane closed the door softly and then said, "What's up with Georgia? Does she always dress like that

240

when she's at your place? And, I mean, what's she doing in your bedroom?"

Avi shrugged. "Her boyfriend kicked her out. She needed a place to stay, so I offered my couch—until she can get set up somewhere else. It's hard for her with work and law school. She doesn't have much free time."

Jane thought she looked like a woman with a great deal of free time. She also assumed that the suitcase in the living room belonged to Georgia. "Can we sit on the stairs?"

"I'd rather stand."

The coldness in her manner left Jane at a loss. "Did I do something to upset you?"

"Upset me? Let's see, whatever could that be?"

"I must have. I'm sorry. I'll do anything I can to make . . . whatever it is right."

"Just stop, okay. I'm not a complete fool."

"If you could just tell me—"

"Oh, that's marvelous. Stop acting. We both know why you're here. Why you wheedled your way into my life."

"I'm here because I thought we were—"

"I thought we were, too," said Avi. "You're good, I'll give you that. Problem is, you have no idea what the real story is."

"What *story*?" asked Jane, touching her arm.

Avi shook her hand off. "Come in and get the dog, and then get the hell out of my life." Turning away, she hesitated. "Just tell me one thing. Are you going to turn me in?"

"Avi, listen to me, *please*. I don't know what you're talking about."

Her back stiffened. "All right, if that's the way you want to play it, I can't stop you. But you're making a mistake. A big one. You think you know what's going on, but you've got it all wrong, Jane. Maybe to you I seem like I'm the bad guy, but I'm not. I'm the victim."

33

Less than a minute after Gimlet appeared in his life, Mouse was in love. The two dogs chased each other all over the house, up and down the stairs, through the kitchen to the rear hall, through the living room into the dining room and back to the kitchen. Then they'd start all over again. At this rate, Jane would never need to take Mouse out for another walk. If he didn't have a heart attack from trying to keep up with a puppy, he'd be in great shape simply from playing.

For the moment, as Jane sat at the desk in her study, Mouse was lying on his back in one of his beds—now his *and* Gimlet's—his feet stuck in the air, with Gimlet licking his ears, his eyes, his mouth. He was in heaven, and so, it would seem, was Gimlet. There was no way Jane could ever hope to separate the two of them. Thus Gimlet was officially a new member of the family.

Returning her attention to the computer screen, Jane continued to search the William Mitchell College of Law Web site, looking for a student directory. When she finally located one, she couldn't get into it without a username and a password. Frustrated, she called her father's paralegal, Norm Toscalia, and was put through to his voice mail. She asked, as she had many times before, for his help. She was trying to verify that a woman named Georgia Dietrich was a student at the college. Jane suspected that her law school story was a bunch of baloney. Still reeling from her conversation with Avi, Jane was determined to prove that Georgia was a liar and a fake. That didn't mean Avi would fall into her arms and swear undying devotion, but hopefully it would, at the very least, help her understand that Jane was on her side. She thanked Norm for his help and said that if he was able to find anything, he should call her back on her cell.

What mystified Jane most about Avi was that she seemed to think Jane was about to turn her over to the police—if she'd read Avi's rather terse comments correctly. Why Jane would want to do that was a mystery. She figured she'd give it a few days, and then, perhaps when Avi had calmed down a bit, she would contact her again. After so many abortive attempts at romance, it astonished Jane how quickly she'd fallen for Avi—and how hard that fall had been. If, after a respectable period of time, Avi blew her off again, that would be the end of it. It wasn't a decision that would go down easily, but Jane would have to accept it, though she refused to let Avi go without one hell of a fight. She was, to put it succinctly, over the moon about her and wasn't likely to fall back to earth anytime soon.

Inwardly aching and feeling more than a little lost, Jane walked back to the kitchen, both dogs at her heels. She was pouring herself a final cup of coffee before she hit the theater when her landline rang. Checking the caller ID, she saw that it was her dad.

"Hi," she said, holding the receiver between her shoulder and her ear. "Anything new?"

"Your drug test came back."

"Good. No cocaine, right?"

"No cocaine. But the report came back positive for amphetamines."

She set the cup down. "You mean like speed? Come on, I've never used anything like that in my life."

"It got into your system somehow."

"They mixed up my report with someone else. That has to be it." Then it hit her. She had felt odd. Her mood. Her energy. She'd been so upbeat, with a strange sense of . . . she couldn't think of another word but euphoria. Everything was brighter, all the women prettier, the conversations fascinating "Someone drugged me!" She was instantly furious.

"I'm having another test run. Hopefully, we can narrow down what the actual drug was. Did you drink anything?"

"Three Waldorfs."

"Who made them?"

"The first one I ordered from a bartender I know. I'm sure it was clean. The other two were ordered while I was sitting at one of the tables. From a waitress. Actually, one of the dancers served me the second drink."

"Why?"

She wasn't about to tell him how many times Georgia had come on to her, or that she'd eventually succeeded. "I figured she was just being playful. Her name's Georgia Dietrich." It had to be Georgia. Did she do it to make Jane easier to seduce? Would she try to use their sexual connection as a wedge to split Jane and Avi apart? Maybe she didn't kiss and tell, and maybe she did. But why? Most important, was being drugged at the club connected to the cocaine planted in her car?

"I'll have her checked out. How about the third drink?"

"The same waitress I ordered it from brought it to me. I'd never seen her before."

"Do you know who mixed them?"

"Either a guy named Dorsey or the floor manager, Diamond Brown."

"I should have more info on the amphetamines soon," said her dad. "Stay *out* of that place, you hear me?"

"I already got the message."

"Did you get some sleep?"

"I'm fine. I'm heading over to Cordelia's new theater in a few minutes."

"Her what?"

"It's a long story. I'll tell you about it when we've got more time."

"One more thing. Are you still investigating that murder?"

She told him that she planed to stop by city hall on Monday to try one more time to talk to Kevante Taylor.

"Wait on that, Janey."

"Why?"

"For one thing, I don't want you talking to Taylor unless I'm with you. More than that, though. We need to keep your investigation and this drug arrest separate—at least in the minds of the police."

"I don't think they are separate."

"I don't either." He paused. "I'll be in touch."

Before leaving the house, Jane gave Mouse a stern talk, instructing him that he was in charge of Gimlet when she was gone. She gave them each a treat, kissed their heads, and then left through the back door—the quickest route to the garage. For the first time since Mouse had come into her life, she didn't feel guilty about leaving him. He wasn't alone anymore. Like her, he'd fallen in love.

Pulling up to the dark theater shortly after nine, Jane dashed across the street and was met in the lobby by a woman in a fur coat.

"Hi, there," said the woman. "I'm Cordelia's real estate agent, Amanda Brooks. You must be Jane." She smiled uncertainly.

"That's me."

"Listen, I'm running late. Cordelia and her sister are already inside. They're . . . kind of intense, don't you think?"

"They can be."

She handed Jane her card. "I have another showing in twenty minutes, and I need to get across town. Just close the door when you're done. It locks automatically. And, if you don't mind, tell Cordelia that the seller is *very* motivated. Got that? *Very* motivated."

"I've got it."

"She should call me as soon as she makes a decision. The sooner the better."

"Is someone else putting in a bid?"

"On this place?" She shuddered. Taking one last look around, she said, "Good luck. You'll need it."

Jane couldn't help but laugh as she watched the woman scuttle out. Entering the third-floor theater from the rear, she came upon a scene that both surprised and fascinated her. Wearing a belted black sweater, gray skinny jeans, and black pumps, Octavia stood in the center of the stage looking up at a spotlight shining down on her. The interior acoustics must have been good, because Jane could hear everything that was being said. She'd seen Cordelia and Octavia go at it many times before, but never onstage. Standing in the shadows at the back, Jane felt as if she were eavesdropping on rehearsals for a Mamet play.

"And how *is* the prince?" asked Cordelia.

"My husband is not a prince," said Octavia, still staring up at the spotlight. "He's a count."

"A vampire, no doubt." Stopping to reorganize the drape of her white toga with gold edging, she continued. "What was it? Your seventh marriage? Eighth? Could it possibly be your ninth?"

"Why didn't you come to Italy? Yours was the first invitation I sent."

"You really think I should show up for every ceremony? I'd go broke."

"Is a little sisterly affection too much to ask?"

"Vlad must miss you," said Cordelia. She stopped circling long enough to adjust the belt on Octavia's sweater. "I would think you'd want to get home to Transylvania before he turns into a bat and flies away."

"I'm not the only one who's been unlucky in love. Should I count up your failed romantic forays? We could start with the latest, Melanie Gunderson. You say it's no big deal, that you saw it coming and prepared yourself for the worst, but I know you. She left you shattered. Mangled. Pulverized."

"You make her sound like a blender."

Octavia repositioned her belt the way it was before Cordelia had fixed it.

"Besides, my love life is off-limits."

"But mine isn't?"

Cordelia drew her arm wide and projected toward the last row of the balcony. "Your life, such as it is, my dear, is utter tabloid chaos. If the *National Enquirer* can discuss your comings and goings openly, surely *moi* can. May I point out," she added, crisply enunciating each word, "that you said you have been gone from Italy for over a month. That brings up the next question. How much longer will you grace us with your presence?"

"You can't act for shit, you know that?"

"Gloria Swanson in *Sunset Boulevard* is what I'm aiming for. The question remains."

"Am I that awful to be around?"

"Do you really want an answer?"

Octavia kept looking up but now shielded her eyes from the light. "The count wasn't who I thought he was. How was I supposed to know that he saw me as a meal ticket?"

Cordelia dropped her arm, and her act. "It's always something, isn't it?"

"It is."

"People are forever letting you down."

"They are. But"—she bared her teeth—"we always have each other."

"Is that supposed to lighten my load?"

"Why is everyone always leaving me?" demanded Octavia. "This theater. It could be a new beginning for both of us."

In the darkness, Jane cringed. She knew Cordelia hated the term "new beginning."

"I've got an idea," said Octavia.

This time, Cordelia stood still as Octavia moved around her. "We agreed that we'd both take a fifty percent share of the business, right?"

"Only after you removed that travel-sized waterboard from your luggage and threatened to strap me to it."

"But if we divide it equally, what happens if we have a disagreement?"

"Us? Impossible."

"It's an important question. What do we do when one of us wants one thing and the other wants something different?"

"Paper, rock, scissors?"

"We give a ten percent share to Jane. That way—"

"Wait a minute," called Jane, rushing down the aisle toward them. "Leave me out of it."

Cordelia tapped a finger against her chin. "I like it. Of course, since she's my best friend, one would expect that she'd generally side with me."

"Not if she has a brain," said Octavia. "You have a working brain, don't you, Jane?"

"Thanks for the kind words, but not interested." She could tell she was being ignored.

"Now that we've got that settled," said Cordelia, "let's move on. My real estate agent said that the old chandeliers were still in the basement. Wanna go look?"

"Lead the way," replied Octavia.

"So," called Jane to their retreating backs, "you verbally torture each other for a few minutes and suddenly you're Laverne and Shirley?"

"Snow White and Rose Red," Octavia called from the bowels of stage left.

"What about my tour of the premises?" Jane called back to the empty stage. "I don't have all night, you know." Actually, she did, though she had no intention of telling them that.

Checking her phone, she saw that she had a text message. "Score," she whispered, seeing Norm Toscalia's name.

Checked with William Mitchell @
Georgia Dietrich. Not Registered.
N.

"I knew it," said Jane. Georgia was phony clear through. She was a manipulator. The skunk at the picnic. Jane couldn't wait to give that little piece of information to Avi.

Sitting down in one of the seats, Jane pulled out her notebook and began to go over her chicken scratches. Noticing that there was one item without a check by it, she tapped in the number she'd found for the Carson & Keppler funeral home in Chicago, Antoine Moore's employer.

Several rings into the call, a woman's voice answered. "Carson & Keppler. This is Melody."

Jane's plan was to make it sound as if she knew Antoine. "Melody, hi. It's Jane. I'm looking for Twan. Is he around?"

"You just missed him."

"Nuts. We were supposed to get together for a drink later. Look, I don't have his cell number with me."

"Happy to help." The woman repeated it, and Jane wrote it down.

"Thanks," said Jane. "Have a good evening."

She couldn't believe it was that easy. Tapping in the number, she waited through several more rings until his voice mail picked up. A deep voice said, "You've reached Twan. If you're part of the problem, hang up now. If you're part of the solution, leave your name and number."

She hoped she was part of the solution.

"Antoine, my name is Jane Lawless. I'm a friend of Alf Nolan, your uncle. I need to talk to you about your brother DeAndre. It's important that we talk as soon as possible. Call me anytime, day or night."

She repeated her number and then hung up. She had no way of knowing if he'd call back, or whether, even if he did, he'd have anything to add to what she already knew, and yet she had to cover all her bases.

34

Sometimes a woman had to perform triage on her own life. That was why Jane was at the hospital before dawn on Sunday morning. With so much in limbo—her drug arrest, the identity of De-Andre's sister, the possibility of more murders, the fate of her relationship with Avi—Jane's first priority today was Nolan. A nurse had called around four thirty in the morning, saying that Nolan had spiked a 103-degree temperature and that Jane might want to come down to the hospital. Jane didn't ask any questions. She got dressed, took care of the dogs, and then hopped in her car.

Standing at his bedside, watching him breathe, in and out, slowly, steadily, she wished she believed in prayer. She felt so helpless. When a nurse came in to check his vitals, another nurse came in directly behind her holding a syringe. "Dr. Schulman ordered a different antibiotic."

"A third antibiotic?"

"It's newer. We're hoping this one will be more effective. This is his second dose."

Jane waited while she gave him the shot.

By noon, she was standing at the window, watching a light snow begin to fall.

"Jane," came Nolan's raspy voice.

She rushed back to the bed. "Hey," she said, "you're awake. How do you feel?"

"Like I've been hit by a freight train."

She pressed a hand to his forehead. It didn't seem quite as hot.

"What time is it?" he asked.

"Noon."

"How long have you been here?"

"A while."

"How long?"

"Since five."

"A.M.?"

A nurse came in. "Well, look at that," she said, checking his plastic water jug. "Your eyes are open."

"Can I have something to eat?"

"Are you hungry?"

"Something hot would be good. Soup? Toast?"

"I'll order it up." She took his pulse, his temperature. "You're down almost three degrees. That's major progress. Maybe we've finally found the right drug." She patted Jane's back as she left the room.

"You must be hungry, too," said Nolan, lifting his eyes to Jane.

"I'm good."

"I don't know why you stick around when all I do is sleep."

"It's a quiet place to think."

"What are you thinking about?"

"You."

The edges of his mouth turned up. "Maybe you should take off. I'm sure you've got stuff to do."

"I'll stay a while longer."

"Okay, until I'm done with lunch. Then you shove off, right? I'm not going anywhere. You don't have to worry."

252

"I'm not worried," she said, cupping her hand around his. "You'll be up and out of that bed in no time at all."

"Damn straight, I will. Damn straight."

Jane trudged through the freshly fallen snow up to the front door of Vince Bessetti's house and rang the doorbell. A thirtyish woman in jeans and a bulky blue sweater appeared a few seconds later.

"Mrs. Bessetti? My name is Jane Lawless. I'm a private investigator." She handed the woman her card. "I was wondering . . . I know this is a bad time, but I was hoping I could ask you a few questions."

"Is this about my husband's death?" she asked, her expression tight with fatigue. "The police have already been here."

"I'm working on something else," said Jane, "but it's related."

"Oh, I suppose," she said, sizing Jane up before she let her in.

They sat down at an elegant dining room table. Jane could hear the TV on in another room.

"Did you know my husband?" asked Shelly.

"We'd met at his club a couple of times. I've been looking into the murder that happened there last weekend. The man's name was DeAndre Moore."

She shifted in her chair. "I thought the police caught the man who did it. A cook or something."

"One of the dishwashers admitted to the stabbing. The young man who was murdered was in town looking for his sister. I have reason to believe that she may be behind the murder of several men, including your husband. I think it's also possible, even likely, that she works at GaudyLights."

Shelly crossed her hands on the table. "Go on."

Jane handed her a copy of the Greek word she'd found in De-Andre's hotel room, the same one she'd seen on Vince's desk two nights ago. "Have you ever come across this word before?"

She glanced at it but refused to take it. "The first time I saw that word was last week after a friend of Vince's, a man named Rudmann, was shot. The police stopped by to question Vince about it. They left a piece of paper behind with that word on it. I asked him what it meant, but he didn't seem to know."

"You saw it again?" asked Jane.

"Yesterday. Vince had just gone outside to get the Green Egg going on the patio. He seemed anxious that I follow right behind him with the steaks, which I told him I would, but then the phone rang as I was putting the meat on a plate, so, I mean, I had to answer it. It was my father. While we were talking, I heard a couple of pops. I didn't think much of it. When I finally got outside—it couldn't have been more than a few minutes—I found Vince lying in the snow behind the grill. It's very secluded back there. His blood is still all over the snow," she said, raising a trembling hand to her mouth. "What do I do about that? It's still *there*."

"Honestly," said Jane, "I don't know."

Shelly brushed roughly at her bangs, trying valiantly to rein her emotions back in. "I thought he might still be alive, so I got down right next to him and tried to find a pulse. That's when I noticed that he had something in his hand. It was a thin piece of metal, small, about an inch long and half an inch wide. That Greek word was stamped in the center. When the police came, they took it away with them."

"Did they tell you what it meant?"

She shook her head. "I asked, but no one ever never answered."

"I'm wondering," said Jane. "Have you ever heard your husband talk about a man named Burt Tatum?"

"Tatum?" she repeated, hesitating. "May I ask where you got that name?"

"From a note DeAndre Moore wrote to his girlfriend. Apparently, his sister murdered this man while she was living in St.

Louis. She took off before the police could arrest her. When she resurfaced, she was living in Minneapolis and working at Gaudy-Lights."

Once again, Shelly lifted a trembling hand to her mouth.

"I think Burt Tatum, Royal Rudmann, and your husband were her victims. I'm concerned that there might be more."

"Wait just a second," Shelly said, getting up and leaving the room. When she returned, she handed Jane a piece of yellow legal paper. "I found this on my husband's desk last night."

Jane read the names printed on the sheet out loud. "Royal Rudmann. Burt Tatum. Ken Crowder. Emmett Washington. Me." She looked up. "Do you know Crowder or Washington?"

"Not Crowder, but Mr. Washington came to our house yesterday morning. He's an airline pilot, flies for AirNorth."

"Does he live in town?"

"St. Paul. I looked up his name in Vince's Rolodex. The house is on Fairlawn, I remember the number because I used to live at 10927 Cottonwood Avenue in Spring Lake Park."

Jane took out her notebook and wrote it down. Rudmann was dead. Tatum was dead. Vince was dead. There still might be hope for Crowder and Washington. "You've been a big help. You might want to call the police and give them this information."

"If you think it would help." She glanced away, wiping a tear from her eye. "We wouldn't have made it, Vince and me. It's hard to admit, although in a strange way, it's easier now that he's gone. He didn't love me the way I loved him. I kept trying to work on myself, to make myself into the kind of woman he wanted."

"That's a tough way to live."

"Tell me about it."

"What happens to GaudyLights?"

She twisted her wedding ring. "My father gave Vince the money to start the place. Since he never paid my dad back, I guess he

255

owns it now. Far as I'm concerned, I never want to hear that name again."

"Makes sense to me," said Jane.

"I'm glad you stopped by. The police didn't have any answers. Sometimes it takes a woman to figure things out, don't you agree?"

Jane smiled and extended her hand. "I do."

Pulling away from the curb with Patty Griffin's "When It Don't Come Easy" playing on the radio, Jane headed straight for I-94, the freeway that would take her across the river to Emmett Washington's home. She had no idea how long it might be before Sabrina made another move. Rudmann's and Bessetti's murders had happened less than a week apart. Crowder was apparently another man in her crosshairs. Who knew if he was still alive or how to find him?

Washington's house, a small one-story bungalow, sat close to the street with a single-stall garage tucked underneath and winding steps leading up to the front door. An aging, rusted station wagon stood in the drive. She rang the doorbell several times. When it seemed unlikely that anyone was going to answer, she removed a notepad from the pocket of her peacoat and wrote him a message. She asked him to call her ASAP, saying that she had information about Vince Bessetti's and Royal Rudmann's murders—and that his own life might be in danger. She left her card, with her cell number and her home number, stuffing both pieces of paper through the mail slot, hoping he'd call her sooner rather than later.

On her way back to Minneapolis, Jane called Sergeant Taylor and was, as usual, put through to his voice mail. She left a message, telling him what she'd learned. Her dad might have counseled no contact with the police, but Jane felt that, with several men's lives hanging in the balance, she couldn't just sit on what she knew.

She hoped the police were getting close to arresting DeAndre's sister, because, as it stood right now, she was still flailing in the dark.

Georgia sauntered out of the bathroom wrapped in Avi's white terry-cloth bathrobe, vigorously towel-drying her hair. "I decided to work tonight after all," she said, dropping down on the couch right next to Avi. "Have to be there at five thirty."

Avi thought Georgia smelled great. She also thought she was sitting uncomfortably close. "You said you were going over to your boyfriend's place to get the rest of your stuff tonight."

"*Ex*-boyfriend." Georgia reached for a joint and lit up. "Did they call you to come work?"

"Yeah, I'll be there."

"What about Dorsey? Now that we're all living in the building, we could carpool."

"I suppose I could go ask him." It was an excuse to get up and put some distance between them. Even though she wasn't all that attracted to Georgia, she wasn't made of stone.

On her way out the door, Georgia called, "Tell him from me that he should come out of the freakin' closet—because *everybody already knows*."

Avi doubted that Dorsey would welcome the comment. She strode down the hall, relieved to be away from Georgia for a few minutes, and tapped lightly on Dorsey's door. "Oh, hi," he said a few seconds later, opening the door a few inches. "What's up?"

Now that the dog was no longer an issue, she couldn't understand his need for secrecy. "Can I come in?" He shrugged and stepped back, but not so far that she could get more than a few feet inside. "Are you still hiding something?"

"Me? Nothing but that intercontinental ballistic missile." He smirked.

"Georgia and I were wondering if you'd like a lift to the club tonight?"

"I bought a car, so I'm good."

"You did? When? What kind?"

"A couple of days ago. It's an old Chevy Camaro. Not as cool as your wheels, but it suits me just fine. Hey," he said, continuing to smirk. "You and Georgia seem pretty tight. Has she moved in for good?"

"She's a roommate, Dorsey. Nothing more."

"Right. *Right*."

Disgusted by the smirk and the attitude, she left him to his opinions and returned to her apartment, where she found Georgia in the kitchen gazing intently into the refrigerator. "Quick question," she asked, standing in the kitchen doorway. "Do you always sleep this late?" It would make life kind of awkward, especially if Avi wanted to get up early and bang around making herself something to eat. Or listen to music. Or watch TV. The only TV set was in the living room, which was where the couch was.

Georgia didn't reply. Instead, she moved over and rested her arms on Avi's shoulders. "If I slept in the bedroom, I wouldn't bother you as much."

"Where would I sleep?"

"With me." She nuzzled Avi's neck.

Feeling suddenly way too warm, Avi said, "What are we doing?"

"What do you think? I've had a thing for you ever since you came to work at GaudyLights. Never thought somebody would get to you before I made my move." Her hand dipped under Avi's sweater.

"Your . . . *move*? You've done nothing but make moves."

"I kept asking myself, why can't I get you out of my head? Now I don't have to."

"I'm not sure this is such a good idea."

258

"You think too much."

"I do?"

"You and Lawless. Same problem, simple solution."

"This isn't—"

"Come on," said Georgia, tugging Avi's hand, pulling her toward the bedroom. "Let's have some fun."

35

Emmett slumped at his kitchen table, coffee cup in hand, gazing dispiritedly at the article in the morning paper about Vince's murder. He was next. He didn't have the money to hire a body-guard, as Vince had wanted to do. Maybe a hired thug could have saved Vince's life, though the point had been rendered moot. Emmett figured his hangover made his thinking sluggish, although he'd felt this way for days. Even getting up to pour more coffee seemed to require superhuman effort.

Hearing Roddy shamble into the kitchen, he glanced up and saw that his son was still in his pajamas.

Roddy removed a carton of milk from the refrigerator. "I'm thinking I might go over to the mall. All I do here is sit around and stress out."

Gavin Rand, the lawyer Emmett had hired to help Roddy, had set up a meeting with the police for three thirty Tuesday after-noon. It would be Roddy's first interrogation.

Pulling the box of Oats & Honey Granola off the cupboard's top shelf, Roddy poured some into a bowl and topped it with sev-eral glugs of milk.

"You okay about Tuesday?"

"Do I have a choice?"

Gavin had spent several hours prepping him last night. They'd gone over the questions the police were likely to ask. Emmett could see by the strain in his son's eyes the toll this was taking on him. Roddy was finally beginning to see that he'd done something wrong. As a dad, Emmett wanted to protect him, to shield him from the worst of it, but there was no way he could. Roddy would have to walk through fire to get to the other side. At least he wouldn't have to do it alone, as Emmett had.

"I'm leaving in a few minutes," said Emmett. He'd already showered and dressed. He'd put on his best suit and tie, hoping he could hide behind the image of a well-dressed man.

"Okay. Whatever." Roddy shuffled quietly out of the room.

Emmett felt tears burn his eyes. A mere two weeks ago he could have honestly said that his life was good, that he was a blessed man. Now every part of that life was in chaos.

Half an hour later, after slipping into his heavy topcoat, he grabbed his wallet and his car keys and made his way down the outside steps to his car. He'd parked on the street yesterday afternoon, too enervated by his conversation with AirNorth management to even open the garage door. Popping the trunk, he reached in to retrieve the window scraper and snow broom. It was really coming down, big fluffy flakes floating onto his face and hands. He'd left his gloves inside and had no desire to return to the house to get them.

He tackled the back window first. The snow was light, easy to remove. As he stepped around to the front, he glanced down and saw that his tire was flat. When he bent over to get a better look at the pocketknife shoved into one of the grooves, his knees almost buckled. The stalker had sent the same message to him that he'd sent Vince: *You're next.*

Returning to the house, Emmett stood in the living room and called Roddy's name. "I need your car keys. My tire is flat."

"But . . . the mall—" came Roddy's voice.

"You'll have to walk. Or wait until I get home."

Grudgingly, Roddy appeared and handed over his keys.

Shortly after two, Emmett drove into the parking lot of the Fellowship Baptist Church, the one he used to attend regularly when his wife was alive. He and Roddy attended only sporadically these days, although Emmett still considered himself a committed Christian.

Standing in the first-floor outer office, waiting for Reverend Willie Young, Emmett broke out in a cold sweat. He nodded to the receptionist, hoping she hadn't noticed.

"Emmett Washington," said Reverend Willie, coming out of his office with a big grin on his face. He pumped Emmett's hand. "Didn't see you at services this morning."

"Yeah, well—"

"Come on in, man. Come on in."

"You sure you've got the time?"

"All the time in the world for you, my brother."

Willie Young was a few years younger than Emmett. His hair was still dark, though his once muscled body had gone to seed. He looked as if he'd eaten too many cookies at his parishioners' homes. Looks aside, Reverend Willie was one of the kindest, most positive, most spiritually centered men Emmett had ever met. It seemed only right that he should come to him now.

The reverend's desk was covered with books and papers. Neatness wasn't one of his strong suits. Instead of sitting behind it, he ushered Emmett over to two wingback chairs next to a series of windows. "Can I get you a cup of coffee?" he asked.

"I'm fine," said Emmett.

"So. What brings you here on this wintry afternoon?"

Emmett drew his hands together in his lap. "Before I get into that, can I put a question to you?"

"Of course."

He cleared his throat and then asked what the reverend thought about UFOs.

"Do you mean, do I think they're real?"

"Yeah."

He laughed. "No, I'm afraid I don't, Emmett. Do you?"

"So you think people who say they've seen them are lying?"

"Well, I guess I'd say it's more on the order of a vivid imagination."

Emmett should have expected the answer, and yet he'd held out hope that it might be different. "But, I mean, what if they *were* real? What would that do to your faith?"

"It would do nothing to my faith, Emmett, because they're not real."

"But if they were."

"Listen to me. God has a plan for us. Humans are special. In the entire universe, this is the only planet that's filled with intelligent life. The Great Creator God chose to create man in his image on this earth, and only this earth. That's what the Bible tells us and that's what I believe. Don't let yourself get sucked into any of these crazy ideas. Stay on the godly path. 'For strait is the gate, and narrow is the way, which leadeth unto life.'"

"Thanks," said Emmett.

"Happy to help. So what is going on?"

Emmett fidgeted, changing positions in his chair. "My son."

"Roddy? How's he doing? I always admired that kid. So much going for him. Smart. Athletic. He'd be in high school now, right?"

"A senior."

"My goodness. Is he planning to attend college?"

"He was."

The smile on Reverend Willie's face turned uncertain. "Something's changed?"

"Afraid so."

"That's the real reason you've come."

"I didn't want to just pick some unknown counselor's name out of the phone book. I felt I needed to talk to a friend."

"I'm glad you think of me as your friend."

Emmett began slowly, explaining about the loss of Roddy's mother, how he'd tried to be a good father, even though he sometimes failed. He went on to talk about his son's football scholarship, his passion for sports, the time he put in at the practice field and the gym. Only when Roddy's character was firmly established did Emmett move on to his friends, the bad decisions he'd made because of their corrupting influence. Alcohol had been part of the problem. The other guys liked to drink, and Roddy had gone along with it, even begun to like it. Emmett spoke briefly about the bullying, the list, and finally the girl who'd hanged herself. He underscored again and again that Roddy was a good kid, a star athlete, a top student. This was an aberration. Deep down, it couldn't be who he was. Emmett kept talking, kept making the case that his son had made bad decisions, sure, but they'd come out of a young man's need to fit in with his buddies. Drinking after losing a baseball game, when you were mad as hell, was nothing new. Everybody did it.

"This list . . . it was drawn up after a losing baseball game?" asked the minister.

"I have no idea when they put it together."

"Then . . . who lost the baseball game?"

"You're not listening. My son plays *football*." He went on, talking about the girl, how bad Roddy felt about what had happened, about his part in it. He understood now that women should be respected, never called skanks and bitches. Even a woman who had been teasing them, trying to seduce them. "You know what men are like? They have too much to drink—"

264

"Men?"

"It's just . . . like I said, he never meant for anything bad to happen. The other guys, they were mainly responsible. They were the reason he lost his bearings. Temporarily lost his sense of right and wrong." He ran a hand over his eyes. "Sure, okay, so he might have been there with too much beer in his belly. Pissed at the world. You know how it is. It was dark. The beer and the game and his anger got all mixed up. Every guy on the team agreed she was a slut. It was hard to ignore all the rumors. Married and divorced. With a kid out of wedlock. Liked it rough. I didn't necessarily believe it, but, I mean, she sure enjoyed the flirting. She kept setting 'em up and we kept pounding them back. Suddenly it was closing time and they were telling us we had to leave. None of us wanted to go. I wish I could remember exactly what went down next." He mashed the palm of his hand against one eye, struggling to see the scene and at the same time resisting the vision. "We got her to walk across the road to the woods. Pretty night, you know? Summertime. Soft breezes. Except I was hot. Sweating. Stumbling. All I know is, I wasn't part of it. I watched, sure. I should have stopped it. For sure I should have stopped it, but . . . you know. Things get away from you sometimes. And then . . . she was just lying there in the grass, so quiet. I thought she was dead. We all ran back to our trucks, drove away from that roadhouse like the devil himself was chasing us."

Feeling a hand on his knee, Emmett looked up and wiped the tears out of his eyes. The reverend was leaning toward him.

"We seem to be talking about you now, Emmett. Not your son."

"Me? No. Hell, no. I came here to talk about Roddy." Rising from his chair, feeling a sudden need for air, he said, "This was a mistake."

"Please, don't go," said Reverend Willie, standing with him. "I believe it's important that we keep talking."

"I can't," said Emmett, patting his pocket for his car keys. "I . . . I got confused," he said, turning toward the door. He needed a drink. He had to get home. "I never should have come."

The Xanadu evening crew was working on dinner prep when Jane walked in shortly after four. Tables were being set, the bar was being restocked, and everything was abuzz. Jane spied the shift manager, Rich Gillett, standing over by the wait station in the main dining room, looking at the POS computer. Without alerting him to her presence, she made a hard left into the hallway that led to the restrooms. Not more than ten seconds after entering the women's bathroom, she was back out, hollering for him.

"Jane, I didn't see you come in," he said, blinking his nervousness.

"I want those bathrooms cleaned up right now. They're filthy."

"Sure."

"That's all you've got to say?"

"I'll get someone right on it."

"Don't you check the bathrooms as a matter of course before we open for dinner?"

"Usually."

"So today is . . . what? Atypical in some rare, anomalous sort of way?"

"No. I mean—"

"Get it done, Rich," she said, brushing past him on her way downstairs to the kitchen.

The Xanadu's food was less gourmet than the Lyme House's. It was a basic turn-and-burn steakhouse. Jane always set high standards, which was what made the difference between her place and all of her competitors. As far as she could tell, that edge had been lost.

Checking the cold room, she found that most of the tray pans had been dated and labeled. That was some progress. Stepping over to the line, she opened one of the lowboys. "Don," she said, crooking her finger at the same chef she'd had the conversation with yesterday.

"Oh, hi, Jane. I didn't see you there."

"This," she said, holding up a sliced tomato, "is a garnish. This," she added, holding up another tomato slice, one that looked dry and wilted, "is garbage. Are you able to comprehend the difference?"

"About that," he said, adjusting the instant-read thermometer in the pocket of his chef's coat. "I talked to Barry. He said I should use my discretion."

"You're talking to me now, Don. Clean out this top crap and replace it."

"If that's what you want."

"Would you like to be served that piece of tomato on your burger? Those dry-looking chopped onions? That wilted lettuce?"

"I guess not."

"You like your job here, Don?"

"I love it."

"Then try a little harder."

"Yes, ma'am. Say, Jane, I hear you had a little"—he sniffed, touched his right nostril, and grinned at her—"problem Friday night."

She caught the meaning and the sarcasm. Apparently bad news traveled fast. "Get back to work."

Walking through the prep area looking for Luis Ramos, she found him in the corner, his body bent over a deep sink. As she walked up he nodded to her.

"How's it going?" she asked.

He wiped his hands on a rag and turned to face her. "Okay."

"Your sister-in-law feeling any better?"

"She have . . . nausea. Is that . . . right word? Sick a lot. I try to do . . . to help."

"I don't suppose you've heard any more from Elvio."

Luis spit on the floor. "He is filth."

"Because of what he did?"

"Because of who he is."

It was the second time he'd said that. "I don't understand."

"He . . . faggot. I always know, but don't say. I take care of Rosa now. I . . . the man."

"I see," said Jane.

"Thank you for my job."

"Is everyone treating you okay?"

His eyes flicked to the head chef. "I like you. I tell you truth, yes?"

"Please."

"He trouble." He nodded at Don. *"Un hombre malo."*

"In what way?"

"I see him. He sell food to workers from that room." He pointed to the cold room.

"Sells food?"

"And do cocaine. Saw him after we close last night. He chop . . . um . . . what you say . . . lines? On bar top. Offer around."

Jane glanced in Don's direction and saw that he was watching them, a hard look in his eyes. "Thanks," she said.

"I go back to work."

"Good. Thank you. I appreciate the tip."

On her way back through the kitchen, she stopped next to Don, who was talking with one of the line cooks. Without waiting for him to finish, she said, "You fire Luis for any reason—*any* reason—and I'll fire you. I find out you're harassing him, you're gone. You got it?"

"Sure."

"Clean out the lowboys, Don. I'll be back."

After delivering that last line, she felt a moment of pure Arnold Schwarzenegger as she trotted up the steps to the dining room.

36

After putting on the coffee, thinking that once she was done shoveling, something hot would be welcome, Jane opened the back door and stood on the porch, watching the dogs leap through the snow. As usual, with the white stuff came higher temperatures. This time of the year the low twenties felt almost balmy.

As she pulled the shovel out from behind a sack of ice melt, she saw a figure move slowly up the drive and stand next to the fence. She opened the back screen to get a better look. "Dorsey?" she called. In the growing darkness, with a hoodie under his jacket pulled up over his head, she couldn't make out his face. He was the right height, the right general size.

"Yeah, it's me," he called back. "Gimlet seems to like it here."

"You want to come in? Have a cup of coffee with me?" The shoveling could wait.

He hesitated. "Sure," he said finally. Gimlet raced up to him when she spied him pushing through the gate. "Hey there, you," he said, picking her up and carrying her into the kitchen.

While he took off his coat and removed his boots, Jane got down two mugs from the cupboard.

"I've been standing outside your front door," he said. "I wasn't sure if I should knock, if you'd mind me seeing her. When I heard them barking, I just had to come see." Gimlet squirmed in his arms, licking his face, his hands, nipping at his nose.

Seeing the clear delight in Dorsey's eyes, and the deeper sadness underneath, Jane couldn't help but feel sorry for him. "You miss her."

"More than I thought possible." He glanced around. "But she's got a good home here. At least that's something."

"You can come visit her anytime you want."

"Thanks, but I think seeing her almost makes it worse."

Jane poured the coffee. She set the mugs on the table and then sat down.

"Avi was right. It was silly of me to think I could keep her."

"I'm curious. Do you know Avi well?"

"We started out work friends. I got hammered the other night and ended up crashing on her couch. The next morning, I don't know why exactly, but it was like something had changed. She really opened up to me. I think she figured she'd finally met someone as screwed up as she was."

Jane let that one pass. "I was kind of surprised to see that Georgia had moved in."

"She's in a league of her own."

"Because?"

"I don't understand people like her. I've seen her manipulate tons of guys to get what she wants. Money. Attention. Flattery. The thing is, nothing ever seems to make her happy—or satisfied. She's always on the make. She's like . . . a black hole wind-up doll." Blowing on his coffee, he added, "I shouldn't have said that."

"You don't like her."

"Not much."

271

"Are she and Avi—"

"Who knows. I feel sorry for Avi if they are. You like her, right?"

Jane nodded.

"Look, Avi thinks I'm a gossip, and maybe I am. All I'm saying is, it strikes me that Avi is a sucker for somebody who says they need her."

"You mean Georgia."

"Among her many . . . obvious . . . skills, that woman knows how to find just the right nerve to touch to get people to do what she wants. I saw her work the same magic trick on one of the managers when I first started working at GaudyLights. She moved in with him. I guess he finally wised up and threw her out."

Now she had her sights set on Avi.

"Avi's pretty steamed at you," added Dorsey, taking a sip of coffee.

"But I don't know why."

"You never told her you were a PI. Now she thinks her ex hired you to find her."

"Her *ex*?"

"Have you ever seen the car she drives?"

Jane tried to recall. "A Porsche?"

"You think she bought that on a bartender's take-home pay?"

Jane shrugged.

"She stole the car from her ex-girlfriend. She cleaned out one of her bank accounts, too. It's a really depressing story. Ask her about it."

"I will." A ringing telephone interrupted them. "Help yourself to more coffee," said Jane, removing her cell phone from her back pocket. "This should just take a second."

"Hey, Janey," said her father. "I finally got the results back from that second drug test."

272

"And?"

"It's MDMA, otherwise known as ecstasy."

"You're kidding me. I've never taken that in my life."

"Not knowingly, but you had it in your system the other night."

"I'm sorry to cause you all these problems."

"It's not you, honey. It's the company you keep. Besides, I'm your father. That's what I'm here for. I'll keep you posted."

As Jane stuffed the phone back into her pocket, she decided to take a chance. "Somebody slipped me ecstasy the other night when I was at GaudyLights. You know anything about that?"

"God, no." He gazed down at Gimlet and scratched her head. "It's no church, that's for sure."

"Do any cops frequent the place?"

"Cops are some of our best customers. Why?"

"You know any of their names?"

"Not last names."

"Any have a rep for dishonesty?"

"No idea."

She stirred some cream into her coffee. "I hired Elvio Ramos's brother at one of my restaurants. That family is going to be in tough shape without at least one breadwinner."

"Luis's a good man. He'll help out."

"You know him?"

Dorsey's head snapped up. "No. Well, I mean, we've met."

"You and Elvio were friends, right?"

He gave a casual shrug. "We talked at work."

"Did Luis ever come to the club?"

"Can't recall."

"Where'd you meet him, then?"

"Um . . . I guess it must have been GaudyLights."

"Luis said something to me the other day. Kind of surprised me. He called Elvio a faggot."

Dorsey shifted in his seat. "Really?"

"Said Elvio didn't deserve a good woman like Rosa."

"He's probably right."

"Was Elvio gay?" asked Jane.

He crossed his legs, trying to get comfortable. "How should I know?"

"I'll bet you do. You like to watch, to listen. I'll bet you know everything that goes on around that club."

"Not everything—but, yeah, I do keep my eyes open."

"Which means you probably know the truth about Elvio."

"He was a good man. I know that much."

"A good gay man?"

Dorsey shrugged. "Yeah, I suppose you could say he leaned that way."

She crept out on a limb. "Were you in love with him?"

"Me? Hell, no."

"But you were attracted to him."

"I don't have to answer that."

She didn't reply. Instead, she let the silence work for her.

"What I do is my own business." He picked up the coffee cup but put it down when he realized that his hands were trembling. "I'm not gay, if that's what you're suggesting, but I understood his pain."

"Why did Elvio murder DeAndre Moore?"

"Honestly, I don't know. I wish I did." He didn't move for several seconds. "I didn't love him, but I did feel sorry for him. That's all I can tell you." Grabbing his scarf and jacket, he moved quickly to the door. "I've probably said too much." He took one final look at Gimlet, then let himself out.

Gimlet stood looking up, whining softly. Jane reached over and scooped the puppy into her arms, holding her close. "You'll see

him again. Don't worry. He loves you way too much to stay away."
She hoped she was right, for his sake and for Gimlet's.

Emmett sat on the floor of his living room with the lights off, the
gun Vince had given him in his lap. Roddy was in his room playing
a video game, oblivious to anything but his own problems. That
was as it should be. For the rest of the night, Emmett intended to
stand guard. Whoever was out there wasn't going to catch him
unawares. Tomorrow, he would put his plan into motion.

Seeing car lights flash against the curtains, Emmett crawled
across the room to look outside. A small SUV had parked in front
of the house. The lights snapped off. The door opened. A moment
later a thin figure in a peacoat emerged and climbed the stairs up
to the front door.

Sitting back against the wall, Emmett waited, the gun heavy in
his hand. The doorbell rang. Willing the person to go away, he
drew his legs up to his chest, ready to move swiftly if he had to.

Again the doorbell sounded. Then came knocking. "Mr. Washington," called a woman's voice. "My name is Lawless. I need to
talk to you."

Roddy appeared in the hallway. "What's going on? Who is that
outside?" Pulling a Fudgesicle out of his mouth, he said, "Why are
you sitting on the floor in the dark?"

Emmett grabbed Roddy and pulled him down, then held a finger to his lips. "Go back to your room," he whispered.

"What's that in your hand?"

"Out. Go."

"Mr. Washington," the voice came again. "I think you may be in
danger. If you're in there, will you at least speak to me? You don't
have to open the door."

"What's she talking about?" asked Roddy.

"Keep your voice down," said Emmett. "Do what I tell you. Go on, get out of here."

"No."

"Mr. Washington? I'm the one who left my name and number in your mail slot this afternoon. Call me, *please*. We need to talk. It's *very* important. I believe you're in danger." She rang the bell again.

"Dad?"

"Shhh."

"Is that a gun?"

Crawling back to the curtains, Emmett parted them ever so slightly and watched the woman walk back down the steps to her car.

"Tell me what's going on," demanded Roddy.

"Were you planning to go anywhere tonight?"

"Yeah. Maybe. Why?"

"I want you to stay home." Turning to face his son, Emmett added, "I'll tell you everything, I promise, but not tonight. Right now I need to be in here by myself."

"Something bad's gonna happen, isn't it."

"Not if I can stop it."

"With a gun?"

"With whatever it takes."

37

On her way back to Minneapolis, Jane made a quick decision. Instead of spending the rest of the evening working at the Lyme House, she had a different destination in mind. A thought had begun to nag at her while she was driving over to Emmett Washington's place. It was something that should have leaped out at her sooner, but with everything on her mind, she'd failed to see it. This might be the key she was looking for, the proof that her drug arrest had been a setup. She hoped she wasn't too late.

Pulling into the parking area behind GaudyLights around ten thirty, she was surprised to find so many empty parking spaces. Maybe it had something to do with the good citizens of the Twin Cities getting ready for work in the morning, or maybe it was the residual effects from Sunday morning church attendance. Whatever the case, she had her pick tonight.

Jane cut the engine and jumped out of the Honda holding a small flashlight and a paint scraper. She walked briskly back to the rear of the lot. Crouching down, with the flashlight held in her teeth, she began to carve snow away from the packed mound that sat next to where she'd squeezed her Mini in on Friday night. She was working on the theory that the cop who'd stopped her because of that broken taillight had probably smashed it himself. It took a few minutes and some careful digging, but she finally found what she was looking for. Buried close to the ground not three feet from where the Mini had been parked were pieces of shattered red plastic. Not quite sure what to do with the evidence, Jane opted to call her dad.

"Ray Lawless," came his rumbling voice.

"Hey, Dad. You watching *Law & Order* reruns?"

"Cute. What's up?"

She explained what she'd found and asked what he thought she should do about it.

"Nothing," came his instant reply. "Leave the parking lot *now*. I don't want you anywhere near that evidence."

"You saying the police will think I planted it?"

"I never second-guess what the police will think. Just to be on the safe side, I'll call one of my investigators, get him right on it. He'll call the MPD after he takes a look. Good work, honey. I should have thought of that myself."

"Will this get me off?" She knew it was a dumb question.

"I wish it were that easy. Then again, it can't hurt. Now you get out of there."

"I'm gone. Bye." She stuffed the phone into her pocket as she ran back to her SUV.

A few minutes later, after finding a lucky parking spot on the street, Jane walked into GaudyLights, feeling far less gullible than she'd been a couple of nights ago. She knew full well that her father would be livid if he learned she'd ignored his direct orders to stay away, but she had her reasons. Threading her way back to the bar, she found Avi talking to a gray-haired guy seated at the counter, laughing, listening, doing the job she did so well.

"What are you doing here?" asked Avi, stopping midsentence.

"We need to talk."

"I'm not interested."

"Excuse us," said Jane, glaring at the man until he vacated the stool. Since he was one of only three people sitting at the bar, Avi didn't have anywhere else to go. Even so, she moved away.

Jane followed.

Each time Avi shifted her position to clean up a spill or organize part of the backbar, Jane moved right along with her. "I'm not leaving until you listen to what I have to say."

"I told you. Not interested."

"I didn't know anything about your ex-girlfriend until Dorsey told me this afternoon."

"Not listening."

"It's the truth. Just stand *still* for a second!"

Avi seemed startled by the anger in Jane's voice.

"I came because I care about you. Way the hell too much, it would appear." She paused, sinking her hands in her coat pockets. "Come on, cut me some slack. Just give me five minutes. You owe me that much."

"I don't owe you a damn thing. We just met a few days ago. Who the hell do you think you are, coming in here like—"

"I *think* " Jane bit at her lower lip, knowing what she wanted to say, what was in her heart, but unsure how Avi would react to it. In the end, she couldn't help herself. The words just burst out. "I think I'm falling in love with you."

Avi's eyes widened. "Love?"

"Yeah. Would that be so bad?"

Avi backed up a step.

"I'm not after you. Your ex didn't hire me. I swear. I'm not going to turn you over to the police. I only want to help—to understand. Can't you give me that much?"

Standing her ground, Avi said, "Why didn't you tell me you were a PI?"

"I should have. You don't know how sorry I am that I didn't. It's just . . . I don't always announce it. Sometimes it helps, sometimes it creates a barrier. But I did tell you why I'd come to the club. I never lied. In fact, you were the one who set me on the right track, telling me about DeAndre Moore's sister. You trusted me. You still can. I never expected to find someone like you in a place like this. You have to know I'd never hurt you."

"I thought I did."

"Nothing's changed. I don't know what happened between you and this woman—"

"Her name is Sarah." Avi reached for a bottle of Bombay Sapphire. "I'm not supposed to do this, but here goes." She poured herself a shot.

"A *gin* shot?"

"So I like gin." She downed it in one neat gulp.

Jane eased onto a stool. Their relationship, such as it was, had reached critical mass. Avi would either talk to her or walk away.

Pouring herself another shot, Avi cleared her throat and said, "I loved Sarah and she used me. It's an old story." Downing the second drink, she wiped a hand across her mouth. "We'd been dating for maybe four months when one night—I was making us dinner at her apartment—she told me she'd been offered a job in Cleveland. It was a great job. The only problem was, she didn't have the money to move across country and set up housekeeping in a new city. She had a baby, a four-month-old little girl. She said the salary would be far more than she'd ever made, though not enough to cover day care. She was adamant about not wanting Gracie to spend her days with strangers.

"I was bartending back then and, as always, writing in my spare time. I didn't go out much, so I had a little money in the bank. I told her I could afford to get us to Cleveland and, if she'd let me, I'd take care of Gracie full-time as long she paid for rent, food, etc.

280

She acted like she wasn't sure she should let me make that kind of sacrifice. Two days later we were packed and on our way."

Jane cringed inwardly at what she assumed was coming next.

"I mean, I was in heaven. I thought Sarah and I would be together forever. She was promoted quickly through the company hierarchy. I was so proud of her. Less than a year after we moved to Cleveland, we were able to buy a house. She did a fair amount of traveling every month. I didn't mind. By then, Gracie was like my own child. We did everything together. Four days after Gracie entered first grade, Sarah announced that she wanted out. I discovered, after the fact, that she'd been dating someone behind my back—keeping me around, basically, as a nanny. When I found out, I snapped. I packed a bag, jumped in one of 'her' cars, wiped out the only bank account my name was on, and took off. I figured it was only a matter of time before she'd come after me. I had no rights because we weren't married. She used me, then shoved me out the door with nothing and nowhere to go."

Jane reached across the counter and took hold of Avi's hand.

"I don't need your pity."

"It's not pity. I'm just so sorry you had to go through that."

"I hate her."

"So do I."

Wiping tears from her eyes, Avi said, "I'm a fool."

"We've all been fools." Squeezing Avi's hand, Jane said, "Do you forgive me?"

"I guess . . . maybe . . . I should ask you the same thing."

"I don't suppose you'd consider blowing off your shift and having a late dinner with me."

Before Avi could answer, Georgia sauntered up and planted her arms on the bar, cuddling up next to Jane. "Looks like you two are having quite a powwow."

"It's private," said Jane, easing away from her.

"Now, don't be like that. We're all sisters around here."

Jane thought this was as good a time as any to torpedo Georgia's bogus story about being in law school. "Speaking of William Mitchell—"

"Were we?" asked Georgia, one eyebrow rising.

"I understand you're not registered there."

"You're not?" asked Avi.

"I know it was, perhaps, an error in judgment to allow Avi to think I was attending William Mitchell. In my defense, I plead vanity. I didn't correct her because WMCL has more status, in my opinion, than the U. If you'd like me to have the U of M registrar send you a note—"

A middle-aged man in a cowboy hat and snakeskin boots stepped up to the bar and put his hand on Georgia's back. "Come on back to my table, darlin'. I need some looking after."

"Well, my pleasure," said Georgia with a sly smile. "Later, ladies."

Not quite sure what to say after she'd walked off, Jane asked, "Do you . . . like her?"

"Sure," said Avi.

"The same way you like me? Assuming, that is, that you do."

"Of course I do. The answer is no."

"I feel a 'but' coming."

"Not really. It's just . . . she's a lot more vulnerable than people think."

"Okay, so she's vulnerable. Can't she go be vulnerable someplace other than your apartment?"

Smiling, Avi said, "Of course."

Turning to watch the dancers on the stage, Jane said, "I suppose I better get out of here before my father sends in the marines."

"Huh?"

"Call me in the morning."

"God, but I want to kiss you."

"We'll put that on tomorrow's agenda. Top of the list."

"The very top," said Avi, an unexpected wistfulness in her voice.

38

On Monday morning, Emmett sat across from his banker, Carl Chumway, waiting patiently while the vice president read through his application. He'd been banking at Guarantee Savings for over twenty years and was considered one of their triple-star customers.

"This all seems to be in order," said Chumway, stapling some pages together.

"As I said, I need the loan right away."

"For your son's legal expenses. I understand all that, Emmett. Even so, it may take a couple of days."

"Can't you put a rush on it?"

Chumway removed his glasses and sat back. "I'm sorry about your son's problems, I really am. I've got a son, too. What was it he did?"

"Our lawyer advised me not to discuss it."

"Very sensible." He nodded to Emmett's uniform. "Still like working for AirNorth?"

"Couldn't be happier."

"I imagine you're looking at retirement in the near future."

"Not for a few years."

"Hard to give up a job you love."

"It is."

Emmett hated these pretend conversations, the kind that mimicked real human interaction. He could have applied online, but Chumway knew him. He'd worn his uniform because people were impressed by it.

"Well," said Chumway, standing and extending his hand, "I'll do whatever I can to expedite the matter. Call me later today. If your lucky stars line up just right, I may be able to have a check for you sometime tomorrow."

"Wonderful," said Emmett, tucking his cap under his arm and pumping Chumway's hand.

On his way out the door, he thought, next stop, the car rental company.

Still riding high from last night's discovery of her shattered taillight—and optimistic about her relationship with Avi—Jane rose early and drove over to the Lyme House, arriving just after seven. She spoke briefly with Nolan's nurse, learning that his temperature was almost normal. He'd had a good night and was hungry for breakfast. She planned to stop by before lunch.

On her way up the back steps to the kitchen, the cell in her pocket started to buzz. Not even bothering to look at the caller ID, she answered it. "Jane Lawless."

"Ah, hey. This is Twan Moore returning your call."

"Oh, hi. Thanks so much for phoning back." She sat down on the stairs.

"I assume you wanted to talk about DeAndre. Mom told me Uncle Alf was trying to figure out what he was doing in Minneapolis. Am I calling at a bad time?"

"Not at all. And yes, you're right about my reason for the call."

"First, you should know that D and me weren't close."

285

"I wondered about that. I was looking through one of your uncle's family albums and—"

"You could read the smoke signals. Yeah, you're not the first person to point that out."

"How come you two didn't get along?"

He sighed. "This is so weird to talk about, now that he's gone. I guess it was partly just kid stuff. Sibling rivalry. I was closest to him in age, and I wasn't all that happy when Mom and Dad decided to adopt him."

"Sure, that's understandable."

"He lived with us for a couple of years before the adoption. He was, like, this attention magnet. My brothers played with him, my parents fawned over him. Me, I felt left out. And then, I remember I'd ask him questions about his mom, about what his life was like before he came to live with us, and he'd give me these really evasive answers. Made me think he had something to hide, you know? Turns out he did. Hey, wait. I've got some popcorn in the microwave. It's beeping at me." He returned a few seconds later. "Burned it. Jeez, I can't even boil water without torching the entire kitchen. That was supposed to be my breakfast."

"If you want to call me back—"

"Nah, let's do this. Where was I? Oh, yeah. See, D was a liar. Even before the adoption, I used to hear him talking to someone on the phone fairly frequently—always when Mom and Dad were gone—but he'd never tell me who it was. He'd take the receiver into, like, a closet or the bathroom and close the door, so I couldn't hear the conversation. That went on for years.

"One day I remember thinking, I'm gonna follow that little twerp after school, see where he goes—just for the hell of it, you know? He ended up at a McDonald's sitting with some older chick. She looked like a hooker—glam clothes, long red hair, platform shoes, the complete deal. I stood by the order counter for a while, trying to figure out how I could sit close enough to them to hear what they were saying without being seen. It wasn't gonna happen. So that night, I cornered him outside by the garage, demanded to know who the chick was. At first he wasn't gonna tell me. I threatened to beat it out of him, but he still wouldn't talk. That's when I told him I'd tell Mom that he was meeting hookers after school. That changed his mind real fast.

"Turns out, the chick was his sister—Sabrina. He said he had to keep her a secret because he figured Mom and Dad might not adopt him if they knew he had a fucked-up relation like her. He said she was wild but he loved her. She did what she could to keep in touch with him, to give him a little money when she had it. He also said that with his ma sick because of drugs and booze, she was all he had left of his real family. I didn't like that—him calling her his *real* family. So I told him, I'll keep your secret if you do what I tell you from here on out, without any backtalk. If I get nailed to clean the basement? You'll do it. If I was supposed to pick up groceries after school, I passed it off to him. Basically, he was my slave."

"And he always did what he was told?"

"Well, as time went on, I guess I mellowed, but we were never gonna be close."

"He never told anyone about Sabrina, even when he got older?"

"Nope. It was such a long-standing secret that I guess he just decided to keep it. It was easier than telling the truth."

"You mentioned that his sister had long red hair and dressed like a hooker. Can you tell me anything else about her?"

"Hell, I don't remember what she looked like. It was too long ago. Except, and this is the real kicker, she was white."

Jane felt as if all the air in her lungs had suddenly been sucked out. "White? I don't understand."

"Apparently his mom was white, but D's father was black. D

287

wanted to connect with him. Sabrina kept telling him she was gonna find him, but far as I know she never did."

All along, Jane had been looking for a black woman. This changed everything. "You've been a huge help," she said.

"In retrospect, I have to admit that I should have treated D nicer. Guess I'm never gonna get the chance to apologize now. Sucks, you know? Really friggin' sucks."

Yawning and stretching as she walked out of her bedroom, Avi was surprised to find Georgia seated at the dining room table, typing on a laptop, with books, papers, file folders, notebooks, and handwritten notes spread from one end of the table to the other.

"What's all this?"

Georgia didn't look up. She kept typing as she said, "Hope you don't mind. I needed a place to work. Big day today." She was already dressed in a business suit, her hair up in a tight bun, her makeup about as tasteful as Avi had ever seen it.

Pushing out of the chair, Georgia sailed into the kitchen. She reappeared a few seconds later with an apple and her leather briefcase. "I should be home early. I don't work tonight and neither do you, right? Thought I'd take us out to dinner. Something nice. Sound like a plan?"

Avi was still groggy. "Um, I don't know. I might have other plans."

"Cancel them. I'll call you later. If I have time." Her amused eyes flashed.

"You seem excited."

"You think?" She kissed Avi on the lips on her way to the door.

Sinking down on the couch, covering her face with her hands, Avi muttered, "Lord, what am I going to do?" After last night, Jane had moved from double-crossing bottom feeder to official girlfriend. What was Georgia? A friend? A friend with benefits? Sleeping with her had been a bad move all around, except that Avi didn't really regret it. She was getting used to this being alone business, and now, suddenly, she seemed to have acquired two relationships. "A plethora," she whispered, running her hands through her hair. "A superfluity," she shouted to the empty apartment. "A profusion." Heading for the bedroom to get dressed, she added under her breath, "A glut."

Avi threw on a sweater and jeans, slipped into a pair of winter boots and a heavy jacket, grabbed her keys and phone, locked her door, and breezed down the hall. She needed groceries, and this was as good a time as any to go get them. When she spied Dorsey's door, she walked up to it, held up her hand to knock, then stopped herself. She paced up and down the hall, thinking. When she stepped up to the door the second time, she called. "Dorsey, it's Avi. I need to talk to you. It's important." When he came home from work, he never went to bed. He'd fix himself something to eat and sit in front of the TV watching old movies. He'd told her he rarely hit the sack before five, which was why he never got up until early afternoon. "I know you're in there. I'm not leaving. I'm going to bang on this door until it drives you nuts. You might as well talk to me." She waited another full minute, pressing her ear to the door and listening. "Dorsey? Damn it." She gave the door a kick. It finally occurred to her that it was theoretically possible that he wasn't ignoring her, he simply wasn't home.

She pulled out her keys and gazed down at them. Okay, so she wasn't always entirely ethical. He'd been so ridiculously secretive about his apartment that when the super had delivered her the new key, she'd had an extra one made. Pressing it into the lock, she opened the door.

"Dorsey?" she called, moving cautiously inside. "It's Avi. Are you here? I came to look at that missile of yours." Crossing toward

289

the bedroom, she forced a laugh. "That's a joke. We need to talk, okay?" She opened the door a crack. The bed was a mass of sheets and blankets, but no Dorsey.

"Has Elvis left the building?" she called, closing the door behind her. "Dorsey?" She ducked into the bathroom. "Nobody home, huh?" She made her way into the kitchen. The place was a disaster. Clothes draped over the furniture. Dirty dishes everywhere. The garbage can overflowing. The refrigerator was covered with a haphazard collection of photos—all of Gimlet. Apparently nobody else was important enough to rate a featured role on the fridge. "Well, we've learned one thing," she whispered. Dorsey's secret wasn't that he was an international spy. No, it was much more prosaic than that. Dorsey was a slob.

Crossing back to the bathroom, she was appalled to see short beard hairs all over the sink. "Pig city," she called to no one in particular. She opened up the medicine chest, thinking that she'd take a look to see what drugs he was taking—legally or illegally. He didn't seem all that interested in Georgia's stash the other night, though you never knew about a guy like him.

Instead of drugs, she was surprised to find a ton of makeup, from lipstick to brushes to eyeliner to foundations to several different kinds of moisturizers. On the lowest shelf she discovered something even more strange—several different-colored braids of dark wool crepe hair. Next to them were more brushes, a bottle of spirit gum, and a small scissors. She knew they were used in theater productions because she'd been in a play in high school. What Dorsey was using them for was another question.

She drifted back to the kitchen, where she sat down at a square wood table. Several small, shiny pieces of copper—rectangular, thinner than a penny—caught her attention. Some sort of foreign-looking word had been stamped into the center.

The front door opened.

Avi panicked. Looking around wildly for a place to hide, her eyes fell on the broom closet. Hoping like hell that Dorsey didn't have it stuffed to the gills, she made a dash for it, wedging in with great difficulty next to a brown paper Target sack. Try as she might, she couldn't get the door to close all the way. Through the crack, she saw Dorsey stride down the hall and duck into his bedroom. He came out a moment later holding a gun.

She stopped breathing.

Sniffing the air, he looked around as if he suspected something was amiss. He continued to stand in the hallway, just inches away, but finally shook it off and disappeared back toward the living room. Just as quickly as he'd come, he was gone.

Avi pushed the sack out in front of her, her knees screaming as she dislodged herself. The sack fell over, spilling several boxes of tampons onto the linoleum.

"Oh, really?" she whispered, dashing over to the window above the sink. Dorsey wasn't hiding the fact that he was a slob, he was hiding that he was a freakin' *woman*!

Straining to see through a maze of dying plants, she watched him emerge from the building, the gun nowhere in sight. He ran up to a black Chevy Camaro and got in.

Dorsey was a woman masquerading as a man. Why? A woman with a gun. Where the hell was he——she——going? Was it possible? Could DeAndre Moore's sister, the mysterious Sabrina, be white, not black?

Racing through the apartment and down the stairs, Avi burst outside and headed for her Porsche. As she got in, she saw that the Camaro had just turned right onto Franklin. She gunned her motor and took off after him. Feeling a surge of excitement, she pulled out her phone and punched in Jane's number.

As the Camaro turned onto I-94, with Avi in hot pursuit, Jane answered.

"Hey, Avi, I was hoping you'd call."

"Just listen. Is it possible Sabrina is white?"

"How'd you know that? I just found out."

"It's Dorsey. At least I think it is. He's a woman."

"He's what?"

"Just trust me. I saw him—her—whatever, leave the apartment building with a gun. Right now he's on I-94 heading east and I'm following him."

"Heading east? Jesus, I think I know where he's going. But Avi, no. If he is Sabrina, it's too dangerous. Pull off. I'll take it from here."

"I'll call you when he stops, let you know the exact location."

"Avi, please. Listen to me."

"Later."

39

Jane grabbed her coat and tore out to her car. Tapping in 911 on her cell as she gunned the SUV out of the lot, she put the call on speakerphone and tossed the cell onto the seat next to her.

"911. Is this an emergency?" came a woman's voice.

"I think someone's about to be murdered."

"Give me your address."

"No, not me. The man's name is Emmett Washington. He lives in St. Paul."

"Are you with Mr. Washington?"

"No, but I'm headed over to his house. Can't you look up the address?"

"You're headed to the house but you don't know his address?"

"Look, I don't know him personally. I've been to the house, so I know where it is, but I can't remember the address. He's in danger. It's connected to two murders in Minneapolis—Vince Bessetti and Royal Rudmann. Can you send someone to Washington's house right away?"

"Your name?"

"Lawless. I'm a private investigator. I've been working on this case for over a week."

"You're a private investigator and your name is *Lawless*. Is this a joke?"

Jane was beginning to wonder about her karma with cops. "Look, maybe I could talk to your supervisor."

"One minute."

Jane couldn't believe it. The woman had put her on *hold*.

Emmett was almost done. The rental car was packed. He'd stopped by the post office to have them stop his mail. The check would be waiting for him when he got to the bank on his way of out town. He'd ordered Roddy to be home by noon. He hadn't told him why. There would be plenty of time for that when they were in the car on their way to Canada.

After he finished vacuuming, he drifted through the house, surprised at how little he cared about leaving. He had a passport, as did his son. They'd be on the other side of the border before anybody knew they were gone.

After yanking the cord on the refrigerator, Emmett carried a cooler of food down the inside steps to the garage, setting it down next to the back bumper of the rented van. As he turned to run back upstairs, his attention was drawn to shards of broken glass scattered on the cement.

"Hello, Emmett."

He whirled around.

"I had to break the window to get in. Sorry about the mess."

A young man stood by the hood of the car, a gun held casually in one hand.

"Who—"

"Who do you think?" he asked.

"I'm not sure—"

"I'm her daughter."

"But you're—"

"An optical illusion? Yeah. It's fun. Sometimes I'm a man. Sometimes a woman. I saved you for last. In case you're wondering, yes, I'm going to kill you, and I'm going to enjoy it. But first—" He motioned with the gun. "Upstairs. *Now*."

Jane roared down Fairlawn toward Washington's house. Avi's Porsche was parked on the opposite side of the street. Pulling up next to it, Jane lowered her window.

Avi did the same. "That's Dorsey's car over there," she said, nodding at the black Chevy.

"He inside?"

"I got here just as he broke a window and went into the garage." She pointed.

"I wonder if there's an inside stairway."

"Must be. They didn't come out. I saw them both through the picture window a few minutes ago, but then they disappeared."

"Listen," said Jane, swiveling to look both ways down the street. From the west a rusted gray and white Park Avenue came rumbling toward them. "I called 911 on my way over here. A squad car should arrive any second. If it doesn't get here in the next minute or two, I want you to call 911 again. Give them your name, the address, and tell them that the owner of the house, Emmett Washington, is being held inside at gunpoint. You got that?"

"Sure, but what are you going to do?"

The Park Avenue stopped in front of Washington's house, and a young man wearing a varsity jacket and carrying a backpack jumped out. He waved to the guy in the driver's seat.

"Don't forget to call," said Jane, parking her car the wrong way in front of Avi's. Dashing across the street, she caught the young man just as he was about to head up the steps to the front door. "Excuse me," she said.

He turned partway around. "Yeah?"

"Do you live here?"

"Who wants to know?"

"My name's Jane Lawless. I came by a couple of times yesterday hoping to talk to your father."

"Oh, yeah," he said, turning all the way around. "I heard you last night. I'm Roddy Washington."

Jane motioned him into the shady part of the driveway. She didn't want to be observed from the picture window. "Look, I don't have time to sugarcoat this. Your dad's inside the house with a woman who wants to kill him. Is there another way in other than the garage or the front door?"

"In the back," he said. "We've got a deck off the dining room. There's a sliding glass door."

"Do you have a key?"

"Yeah."

"Give it to me."

"You going in?"

"That's the plan."

"Not without me."

Jane didn't have time to argue. She followed him up one of the neighbor's walks and through a rear gate, standing behind him as he pushed back the sliding door.

"Let me go in first," she whispered, her eyes pleading.

"Okay, but I'll be right behind you."

Holding a finger to her lips, she stepped inside. A deep voice was crying, a man begging for his life. Edging up to an archway, she saw Dorsey—Sabrina—standing in the middle of the living room, a gun held at her side. Washington sat on the floor, his back against a wall, his legs drawn up to his chest.

"Let's rush him," whispered Roddy.

She gave her head a stiff shake. Pointing at a door toward the back of the dining room, she mouthed, "Where?"

"Leads to a pantry, then into the kitchen."

She motioned for him to follow.

"I'm not interested in any more of your lies," said Sabrina. "I came here to tell you something, so shut the hell up and listen."

Jane and Roddy crept silently into the kitchen.

"Did you know she had a kid?" asked Sabrina.

"I didn't know her at all."

"I was eight years old. *Eight*. She took me with her when she worked. Couldn't afford a babysitter. I'd sit in a cubby under the bar with a coloring book, some crayons, and a flashlight. She'd pass me stuff to eat. Maraschino cherries. Orange slices. Olives. Sometimes a cup of peanuts. I loved that cubby. It was my special place. I felt safe there—until the night you guys came in. You were loud and said bad words. I could tell my mom was afraid, that she was trying to be nice so you'd leave her alone. When it was time to go home, she told me to stay inside the roadhouse until she got the car unlocked. I was supposed to run out and get in and we'd drive home. Except when I came out, I saw you dragging her across the road into that patch of woods. I ran across and ducked down behind a tree. I saw everything."

"Then you know I never touched your mother," said Emmett. "I should have stopped the other guys, sure, but it was four against one. I was drunk. I was weak."

Jane felt Roddy move up next to her. As she turned from the scene in the living room to face him, she couldn't miss the horror in his eyes.

Sabrina went on. "You all took her, one at a time. Again and again and again. When it was over and you'd all driven off in your trucks, I thought she was dead. She didn't move for such a long time. I gathered up her clothes, her bra and underpants. I'm not sure how we made it home that night. She went to bed and didn't get up for three days. On the fourth day, I came home from school and found her in the shower. She spent hours in that shower rubbing her skin raw."

"I'm sorry," screamed Emmett, "but it wasn't me."

"It wasn't?" asked Sabrina. "You're saying you were simply at the wrong place at the wrong time?"

"They were my friends, sure, but I wasn't like them."

"No? Let's think about it. Five guys. Four white and one black. Funny how that works. My mom was white. I'm white. Nine months after my mother was gang-raped by everyone but you, she gave birth to my brother, DeAndre. By the way, he was black."

Before Jane could stop him, Roddy rushed into the living room. "That's not true," he screamed.

Sabrina turned and pointed the gun at his chest, stopping him dead in his tracks.

"My father never touched your mom. Did you, Dad? Tell him. *Tell* him."

"It's sad that you never got to know your half brother," said Sabrina, swinging the gun between Emmett and Roddy. "He was a wonderful, talented man. I told him that, one day, I'd find his father. He wanted that so much. I wanted it, too, but for different reasons."

Emmett was crying now, his face pressed hard against his knees.

From outside the house came a voice over a loudspeaker. "This is the St. Paul police. Mr. Dorsey, I'm John MacAvoy. I'd like to talk to you. Just so you know, the house is surrounded. You can't get away. I don't want this to end badly, Mr. Dorsey. I'm asking you to throw your weapons out the front door, then come out with your hands up. Nobody is going to hurt you, I promise. We just want to talk."

"Like hell," said Sabrina, edging closer to the picture window.

"Four police cars and a paramedic van. They must think I'm going to blow up the entire neighborhood."

"What are you gonna do?" asked Roddy, inching toward his dad.

"Good question. Never been in this situation before." She felt for the curtain cord and pulled it. "Gotta think this through. You got anything to drink in this house?"

"You mean like alcohol?"

"Yeah, I *mean like alcohol*."

"I think my dad has some Scotch in the kitchen cupboard."

"Go get it," she ordered

Roddy raised his hands and backed his way into the kitchen. As he opened the cupboard, Jane moved up next to him. "See if you can get him to come in here," she whispered.

"How?"

"Leave through the patio door and slam it on your way out. That'll get him moving."

"What's taking you so long?" called Sabrina.

"I'm coming," said Roddy. "I'm not leaving," he whispered to Jane.

"Stop arguing and just do it."

He struggled with the idea for a moment but finally disappeared into the pantry. A second later, Jane heard a loud thump. She hid next to the refrigerator.

"What the hell?" called Sabrina. She came into the kitchen, holding the gun in front of her.

Jane lunged at her arm, spinning her around as she tried to force the gun out of her hand. Sabrina pulled away and fired wildly. Lunging a second time, Jane dragged her down onto the floor. This time, the gun skittered across the linoleum. They fought to reach it, squirming against each other, each looking for an advantage. With her fingers mere millimeters from the handle, Sabrina screamed and rose up. Jane bucked away from her as Roddy dragged her free and fell on top of her, his hands squeezing her neck.

"Roddy, don't," said Jane, trying to pry his hands off. "She's not worth it."

"Piece of shit," snarled Roddy. "Filthy piece of shit."

"Listen to me." She grabbed his head and pressed her fingers close to his eyes, forcing him to look at her. "If you want to help, flip him over, pull his arms behind his back, and then sit on him. Don't let him up." Roddy outweighed Sabrina by a good seventy-five pounds.

Standing with some difficulty, Jane scooped the gun off the floor on her way into the living room. Emmett was still on the floor, though now he was on his side, curled into a fetal position.

Jane opened the front door and tossed out the gun. A second later, she stepped outside. From then on, everything moved quickly. Three officers charged up the steps past her and into the house. Jane stood to the side holding her arm, realizing for the first time, as blood oozed through her fingers, that she'd been shot.

An officer came up to her and asked if she was okay.

"I think so," she said.

"Let me help you." He put a strong arm around her waist and helped her down the steps to where another officer, this one in plainclothes, was waiting.

"Ms. Lawless?"

"Yes?" She was feeling a little woozy.

"I need to talk to you about what happened up there."

"Good, I'd like to talk to you, too."

"The paramedics should take a look at you first."

As Jane crossed the street, Avi ran up and threw her arms around her. "I was so scared."

Jane's arm didn't hurt so badly that she failed to notice the warmth and passion of their first real kiss.

"You're bleeding."

"A shot clipped me when I was fighting Sabrina for her gun."

"Is she—"

"She's alive."

"And Washington and the young man you talked to—"

"Everyone's okay." That wasn't entirely true, but true enough for the moment.

"You going in there like that was one of the bravest things I've ever seen."

"Could also be stupidity. Of course, if brave gets me a few gold stars, I'll cop to it."

Avi kissed her again and held her tight.

Jane had to ask. "You're . . . not put off by my being a PI?"

"No way. I think it's beyond cool." Cupping Jane's face in her hands, she narrowed her eyes and said, "What are you thinking?"

"Just something silly."

"What? Tell me."

"That of all the gin joints in all the towns in all the world . . . I walked into yours."

"*Casablanca*. How romantic."

"You make me feel romantic."

"You'll be busy for a while with the EMTs, and then the police. I already gave a statement."

"I'll come find you when I'm done."

"You better," she said, backing up, a relieved smile on her face. "You are truly something else."

Something else, thought Jane as she stepped up into the paramedic van. She could work with that.

301

40

Okay, so I was wrong," said Sergeant Kevante Taylor. "I shouldn't have brushed you off the way I did."

Jane and Taylor stood in a rear hallway at the Ramsey County jail, waiting for one of the guards to come and usher Jane into a meeting room. After spending most of the afternoon talking to officers from various local police departments, Jane was exhausted.

The EMTs had examined her wound as they drove her to an emergency room, where she'd been treated by a young doctor who had cleaned and bandaged it. He'd called it a "through-and-through"—the bullet had entered and exited without making contact with anything important. She'd lost some blood, but not enough to cause a problem. While the wound would hurt for a while, the doctor said, her arm would heal and be as good as new. He prescribed antibiotics and painkillers. A nurse gave her a couple of shots, showed her how to use the shoulder sling they suggested she wear for the next couple of days, and eventually sent her on her way.

Taylor continued, "You have to understand, Ms. Lawless. Police don't usually develop close relationships with PI's. We did appreciate your tips. Also, you should know that you made the right decision, turning that netbook over to us."

"Gee. Thanks."

"Look, I'm happy to give credit where credit is due. You cracked the case before us. That's rare."

"So a little respect after this might be in order," said Jane.

"Point taken." Taylor checked his watch. "Sabrina's been processed by now. She did the smart thing—listened to her court-appointed lawyer."

"You going to offer her a plea bargain?"

"That's not my call. Bottom line, she'll go to jail for the rest of her life if she stays in Minnesota. If Missouri gets their hands on her, she could be sent to death row. Her lawyer was quick to put a deal on the table. That's why you get to see her before she's arraigned. It was part of what she asked for."

A woman emerged from a door a few feet away and called Jane's name.

"That's me."

Taylor stuck out his hand. "Friends?"

"Take my calls next time." She shook his hand and then followed the woman back through the door and down a long hallway to another door.

"If you'll take a seat inside, I'll bring her in."

Jane thanked the woman.

The room was tiny, with nothing on the walls but peeling paint. The only furniture was an old wooden table and four orange plastic chairs. Was there a camera somewhere, Jane wondered, ready to record anything they said? An expectation of privacy in a situation like this was undoubtedly misplaced.

When the door finally opened, Jane stood up. It was the same Dorsey who stood before her, the one she'd come to know, yet subtly changed. Gone were the glasses, the dark scruff, and the layered clothes. Underneath was an androgynous, terribly thin, desperately sad-looking woman. Jane had to get used to thinking of him as Sabrina. She, not he.

They sat down.

Sabrina spoke first. "I asked to see you. You probably want to know why."

The voice was different, too. Softer. A shade higher.

"I'm sorry for what I did to you. You weren't part of this . . . this vendetta of mine. I didn't want to hurt you. You were so kind to take Gimlet. But you were always in my face. I knew you wouldn't give up until you figured out who I was."

"It was Avi," said Jane. "She put it together."

"Yeah, so I heard, but you were right behind her. I'm sorry you got shot. I'm sorry for so much." Her face flushed and she looked away.

"Can I ask a couple of questions?"

"That's why I'm here."

"Did you lace my drinks at the club with ecstasy?"

"Yeah. That was me."

"And the cocaine in my car?"

"I've already given the police the name of the cop I paid to plant it and then arrest you. Again, I was trying to get you off my back."

"How did you convince him to do it?"

"He was a regular. I'd done him some favors. I also knew that he bought his drugs from Shanice Williams."

"The head chef? Are you kidding me?"

"She's been selling out of the club ever since she arrived. Didn't handle it herself. For a cut, a couple of the waitresses set up the deals. They passed on the product in the upstairs bathrooms right before closing."

"Do the police know about it?"

"They do now."

"Shanice's days as a chef are over. GaudyLights will likely go down, too."

"Not my concern."

Changing gears, Jane said, "About the men you murdered—"

Sabrina's mouth drew together as she spit out the words. "The ones who raped my mother? There was no way on earth those monsters were ever going to be held responsible for what they did. It was up to me. I stood at my mom's grave and swore to her that I'd go after them."

"Was Emmett Washington DeAndre's biological father? He said he was there, but he also insisted he didn't take any part in it."

"He's lying—or living in a dream world. Do the math. Like I said, four white guys and one black guy. I know what I saw. It's not the kind of thing you'd ever forget. I hope he rots in hell." She lowered her head, massaged her temples. "My mom and me, we had to move in with my grandmother—her mom—after my mom lost her job. She couldn't work anymore. She said it was nerves. I was pretty small, but I understood what my mother and grandmother were arguing about the first month we were there. Mom wanted an abortion. Grandma wouldn't hear of it. We were Catholics. Abortions were abominations. Then nine months later when my brother was born and he came out black . . . well, right around that time I heard my grandmother shout that my mom was right. She should have aborted 'that thing.' We moved out a few weeks later and never went back. I don't think my mom ever spoke to her again."

Jane was at a loss. Everything she could say sounded lame and inadequate.

"This is more information than you wanted."

"One last question. Why did Elvio murder your brother?"

Sabrina stared at the center of the table for a few seconds, then broke into sobs.

"I'm sorry. If it's too—"

"No," she said, covering her mouth, fighting back tears. "I need to tell someone. I came close to telling you yesterday when I was in your kitchen." She took a deep breath and scraped a hand across her eyes. "This is hard for me."

Jane took a couple of tissues out of her pocket and handed them over.

Sabrina blew her nose and tried again. "Obviously," she said, sniffing, "I'm not gay. Elvio thought I was. I guess everyone did. I could pass for a man, but not a straight man. He'd come talk to me after his shift was done. He'd amble up to the bar, have a beer or two. Over time, we got friendly. One night, right as I was leaving, he waylaid me in the back hall and told me he loved me. He was so desperate. I understand how it feels to live a lie. I wouldn't let him touch me, but . . . I touched him. I didn't realize DeAndre hadn't left. He came looking for me and found me . . . with Elvio."

"And Elvio freaked."

"Big-time. I had no idea he'd go after my brother like that. He was terrified his family would learn the truth. I talked to Elvio after he went to jail, the morning before I flew out to Utah to take out Ken Crowder."

"He's dead?"

"I already told the cops. It's no secret anymore. Anyway, Elvio told me the whole thing was an impulse, something that came from his need to protect himself—and his family—from the truth. He was at a sink washing a knife. DeAndre ran through the kitchen. Elvio shoved the knife under his apron and followed him outside. You know the rest." Wiping at her eyes, she continued,

"My mom completely failed DeAndre as a mother. I understood why, but I hated her for it. I was gonna be different. I was gonna take care of him. Some sister," she said, her voice going flat. "I deserve to be put away." Rising from her chair, she moved over to the door. Before she knocked on it to let the guard know she was ready to go, she turned back to Jane. "Will you take good care of Gimlet? She's all I've got left."

"Very good care," said Jane, fighting back her own tears.

"If they don't put me on death row, would you send me pictures of her? You know, as she grows up?"

"Count on it."

"And tell her I love her?"

"She already knows that." Jane rose from her chair and stood behind it as the female guard reappeared and escorted Sabrina out.

How did a person get her mind around so much pain? Sabrina was a multiple murderer. She deserved to be punished, and yet, as Jane stood staring the closed door, all she felt was an overwhelming sadness for everything that had been lost. One stupid, drunken act had ruined so many lives. Nothing about any of this was fair. Nobody won. Everybody lost.

Welcome to the world of private investigation, thought Jane, tucking in her emotions and walking out of the room to go meet Avi.